EMPEROR'S THRONE

DESERT CURSED SERIES, BOOK 6

SHANNON MAYER

HiJINKS

Emperor's Throne

Published by Hijinks Ink Publishing
www.shannonmayer.com

.

Original illustrations by Ravven
Mayer, Shannon

❀ Created with Vellum

ACKNOWLEDGMENTS

Hey, so after this many books, most people probably don't even read this bit. And if you DO, you're in for a surprise! Thanks to the IT guys that fixed my laptop! Because typing on a teeny, tiny mini laptop was HARD and it wasn't until I got the REAL laptop back that the words flowed well. So don't forget to thank your IT guys, they are often the ones who help keep authors going ;)

Also some of my family members, thanks for being jerks and giving me so much fodder to work with. You. Are. Terrible. And that's helped to make my career. Cheers!

1

Merlin

On his knees with his forehead pressed to the cool tiles of the Stockyards at the feet of a primal goddess was not Merlin's idea of how to start his day, never mind what he suspected would be the rest of his no doubt very short life.

Merlin counted his breaths in and out, allowing the desert heat to sink into him, the dust filling his nose and mouth, while he waited on Ishtar, primal goddess, one-time lover, and current largest obstacle in his way to speak.

A bug tickled along his cheek, little legs dancing on his skin. He didn't dare move to brush it away.

Then again, he wasn't sure he *could* move even if he wanted. Ishtar's power lay thick on him, pinning him to the ground, keeping him in place, and he didn't fight it.

The last thing he remembered before waking in the Stockyards was looking at Flora, thinking he should tell her how he felt because he wasn't sure he would get another chance to convince her to be with him. He could feel Ishtar's call sweeping over him, and he'd known that all his plans were finally falling into place. He'd opened his mouth to tell Flora to trust him, just one more time, and the world went dark without another sensation or memory between seeing Flora and opening his eyes in this place.

Sweat slid down his sides as he wondered what had happened. What had he done to leave Flora behind? He'd had to let Ishtar take over him, but she was a jealous woman, and she might have used him to hurt Flora. He prayed to every deity that he knew that he hadn't hurt the woman he'd found so fascinating, dare he say even that he loved when he'd been under Ishtar's hold.

Riding as close as they had been to the Stockyards and Ishtar's seat of power, he'd been waiting for her to make her move on him. He'd been ready for it.

Now, he just had to get her to hurt him.

His mouth tightened as he considered how much he disliked pain. But pain was a tool, not unlike emotions. You just had to be ready to employ it and understand the effect.

Of course, he was certain that Ishtar believed herself the one to make the moves from the beginning. He smiled to himself.

How well his father and Ishtar had placed themselves into the world, and back in his life, and he'd let them. He'd let Ishtar use her power on him, let his father manipulate his mind. Hell, he'd barely put up a fight.

If he hadn't been the one they'd been trying to fool, he'd have applauded them for their maneuvering. They were both excellent chess players and looked far into the future with each move they made. And he'd learned well at their knees.

He bit back a groan as a foot pressed into his spine, pushing him flat to the floor in a most uncomfortable way. Yes, indeed, pain *was* a tool, and the emotions that came with it would serve him well.

"Merlin." Ishtar's voice pulled him upward, all the way to his feet as if he were attached to her by strings on a marionette. He looked her over, taking note of the wounds the Jinn had inflicted on her. Blood still dripped in places, bruises littered her fair skin, and there were several bones that looked as though they were still offset by the way they jutted under her skin, pushing forward at odd angles. Not a good look on the goddess. That she was alive at all was impressive, but that she hadn't healed more was disappointing.

If Marsum had been a bit more dedicated to finishing the job he'd started and had not been so concerned about running after Zam, he might have actually killed Ishtar. He and his Jinn might have been strong enough.

That would have made everyone's life a hell of a lot easier, most certainly his own. But the truth of it was Ishtar was already too strong, something he'd hoped to avoid. She had too many of her original powers within the jewels, each of which had strengthened over the years with the anger and hatred that had been drawn into them by those who'd held them in trust.

That little tidbit about the stones, he'd known all those years ago when he'd taken them from her. He'd known they would grow in power, taking on the energy of the supernaturals who'd thought they'd been given a gift. That was part of the plan.

"I see my death in your eyes." Ishtar smiled, slow, her eyes darkening with wicked humor. "You cannot kill me. I would think you would have realized that by now, young Merlin."

"There are others who could do the job," he said, spitting out a few grains of sand.

She waved a hand at him, flashing a series of bite marks that went from her wrist to her shoulder. "She is not coming here. She has other duties to attend, problems to solve. You forget she is more soft-hearted than she lets on. That makes her easy to direct."

She. Meaning Zamira. Which meant he'd been right all along. Zam was special; there was something about her that could stop Ishtar. Something he could use.

Something stronger in her than all the powers that be.

Interesting. He'd been watching Zam from long before he'd found her in the Witch's Reign, and she seemed to be gathering abilities the way she gathered underdogs. Which was . . . interesting. He needed her alive.

Merlin's body shook with pent-up anger and the literal inability to move. "She's stronger than you know. And she's going to surprise you, I think." Hell, Zam had surprised him more than once. From the beginning, she'd been a gamble to bet on when there was literally no other person to bring down the wall that separated the humans from the supernaturals, a necessary step in all his plans.

So many twists to the path they'd all been on, and none of them realized . . . no one had understood what he was trying to do.

Ishtar's magic sunk into him, squeezing as if it were a boa constrictor and he the wee tiny bunny it was about to eat. "She'll kill you," he breathed out. "I can see it in her."

Ishtar had hurt the girl too many times. Her heart was too broken by all that she'd been handed in her life to not make a final strike against the ones who should have loved her most and instead handed her off to the hyenas.

Literally, handed her off to the hyenas.

Ishtar snapped her fingers and an overstuffed chair appeared right behind her. Slowly, she eased her body into the chair, her long limbs still moving with grace despite the wicked injuries she'd sustained. Her face was bruised, her torso wrapped with linens, her broken bones slowly piecing back together as she drew energy off the lions—her chosen creature—around her.

"I cannot be killed, Merlin. You know this. I am a goddess of the desert. A mortal would have died with the wounds the Jinn inflicted on me. As it is, a mortal might die yet."

That was the problem; he did know. While his father, the Emperor, had started out a mage, a wizard some would call him, there was humanity at the base of him. And so he could be killed, as could Merlin. As could Zam.

Ishtar . . . was not human. There was no mortality in her. That being said, he had to believe she could still be banished. There were texts, legends, about removing her from the world, about sealing her away.

"Why haven't you just drawn all you need to heal from your lions?" he asked.

"Because they are mine to protect, still. If I took from them, they would all die. That's wasteful, Merlin, when I have a far better source to refresh myself with."

She leaned forward, drawing his eyes to hers. "I see your face, your thoughts are like an open book. That much has not changed about you." She laughed softly, and then winced. Her eyes darkened to pitch black a second later and her lips turned to a snarl. "Even if I did not have these stones in me," she touched her torso and the stones she carried in her lit up as if she'd eaten a handful of fireflies, "I am immortal. I am a goddess."

"Then why do you need me?" Merlin asked, already knowing the answer, already preparing for the pain that would come his way. "What possible purpose could you have for me to be here if you're so sparkly and special?"

"I have my reasons." She stared hard at him until the sweat trickled down his belly and pooled in his waistband. The way she looked at him, like a lion looking at its next meal, was exactly as he'd expected.

She beckoned him forward and he stepped stiffly in her direction, wishing he could stop her and knowing he had to let this happen no matter what it cost him. Slowly, her magic curled around him, peeling his shirt off, revealing a body he was rather proud of.

Ishtar ran a single finger down his middle, between his pecs, between his abs, to rest on the edge of his waistband.

This was . . . unexpected.

"You've got to be kidding." His eyebrows shot up, new possibilities forming. "I mean, I know I'm good, but not that good."

A fling, it had been a fling all those years ago between them, and mostly to piss off his father and solidify Ishtar's help in putting the Emperor to sleep. They had produced a child that he'd only just learned about and wasn't quite sure how to use yet. Ishtar couldn't possibly want another child, could she?

"Again, your face says it all." She crooked a finger at him and he went to his knees at her feet. She slid her fingers into his hair, tightened her hand, and tipped his head so he was forced to look up at her, forced to stare into her eyes. "I do not want your body, Merlin. Not in the way you are thinking."

She bent over and pressed her lips to his. He didn't dare close his eyes, and neither did she. He groaned as he suddenly, and painfully, realized how she was going to do what he'd suspected all along. Hell, what he'd known needed to happen. The *how* of it had been hidden from him, but this would do the trick.

The exchange of energy was part of the kiss, as

she drank down his power to bolster her own, but the other portion was the exchange of wounds.

And there came the pain he'd known was coming.

He screamed into her mouth as his bones began to break, as his skin split and every injury that had been inflicted on Ishtar was transferred to his own body.

And it was killing him, bit by bit, breaking him apart as the mortal he was, but he'd known that was a possibility when he'd come here, when he'd let her take him.

He just forgot what this kind of pain felt like.

The smell of blood filled his nostrils, and the smell of Ishtar's perfume, a heady jasmine that mingled with his screams.

His mind was more open to Ishtar like this, and he had to give her something . . . something true.

All he could think about was Flora, about never seeing her gorgeous green eyes again, the spark in her smile and the sharp bite of her words, about never having the chance to hold her close and tell her that he was sorry for the mistakes he'd made and for not telling her sooner how much she meant to him, that he wanted her by his side always.

That he'd secretly loved her for years but let her go to have a life without him so long ago.

His eyelids fluttered as he let that truth sink into his bones. He loved Flora. The woman was as fiery as an open flame and twice as hot, and she was everything to him. A sudden spike of pain arched his back, but Ishtar held him there as he screamed against her mouth, as his shrieks slid into whimpers and as even those faded and his eyes finally closed. "You have been a thorn in my side for far too long, and I care not that you love her. Love is not strong enough, Merlin. It never was, and it never will be," she whispered against his mouth. "And so you have given me your final gift before you die."

Her hands released him, and he slid to the floor, his mind still remarkably intact despite the fact that he could feel his body dying all around him. Bleeding on the inside, breaking to pieces. Barely, barely, he hung on.

"Why?" He managed that one word. "Tell me that much. Why would you kill me, of all those you could take?"

She laughed. "Say please, Merlin, if you want to know the truth. Before you die, that is."

He couldn't keep his eyes open and the pain was fading which he knew was a bad sign. "Please."

"See, you can listen, you can learn." Her mouth was suddenly against his ear, as close as if they were once again lovers.

"Really, it's quite simple. I see you, Merlin." Her eyes filled his vision. "And I know exactly what you are up to, which means for me, for the world, and mostly for Zam, you have to die."

2

ZAMIRA

It was the first night after the battle with Ollianna and her stupid fucking Swamp witches, a battle that we'd lost, no less. Not just lost but watched as Ollianna—pregnant with a world-destroying monster—escaped to cause havoc on the world. We'd survived, yes, but we'd not been able to stop her, and that loss would bite us all in the ass in three. Two. One.

I curled up my lip as I stared at the fire that Maks had started. We were not far from the crossroads, and into the edges of the desert where the ground was harder and the rocks, more often than not, were boulders instead of sand.

Maks crouched next to the fire, pushing the coals and chunks of wood around, sending sparks flying into the night sky. His movements were tight, sharp, and full of tension that I felt all the way to the soles of my feet. My brother was curled up in his lion form, sound asleep and doing a strange snoring purr that was far too cute for a fully grown lion shifter. That sound and seeing him so at rest eased the curl of my lip. We'd lost the battle, but not the war. And my brother had come back to us, to me. So we had gained, not only lost.

Maks tipped his head at Bryce. "You think we should wake him? His watch is soon."

I sighed. "No, let him sleep." My brother had been through enough, and the least I could do was let him rest in peace. For one night anyway. "I can't sleep anyway. Too wound up."

Maks scooted over to sit next to me, leaning back on the two saddles I was already propped against. He wrapped an arm around me and pulled me close to him. His smell slid around me the same way his arm did. Hot desert sand and a musky Jinn smell that I would have said before I hated. But on Maks, it was fucking sexy.

"Think we can just run away and pretend like the world doesn't need us?" he whispered in my ear. "Let someone else do the heavy lifting?"

I smiled as I put my head against his shoulder, breathing him in and trying not to think about everything we'd been through. Trying not to think about losing him—again. "You think you could live with yourself? I mean, we are trying to keep up to a legend."

"I'd try to live with myself," he kissed the top of my head, "if it meant you were safe. If it meant we could live a long life together without fearing the next monster we had to face. If we could just be together. And if by legend, you mean this infamous Indiana Jones you keep talking about, I've yet to see any evidence."

I grinned. "You'll see. My father would not lie to me, and Indiana Jones is a real hero."

I looked up at him and he leaned in to kiss me. I sighed as his lips brushed mine, then a tiny set of claws tapped against my thigh. I froze, turned and looked down at Lila who sat at my feet, a wide grin on her lips.

"What?"

"Cubs?" She held up a bottle of țuică, the sweet plum liquor that the undersized dragon had an incredible nose for finding. Like a bee to flowers, she was drawn to the alcohol in a way that even she didn't understand. She found bottles of it hidden around the desert like she was on a continual scavenger hunt.

"No cubs," I said even as I took the țuică and capped it. "Let's save this for another night. Besides, if we're going to talk cubs, how about we talk wee baby dragon hatchlings?"

Lila sighed and looked down, scuffing at the dirt with her tiny claws. "Trick is off scouting ahead. He said he wanted a little bit of time by himself."

Trick was another dragon, but he was always dragon-sized, whereas Lila could shift from six pounds to more than a few zeros added to that six-pound figure. A recent feat, to be fair, but still pretty damn impressive. I frowned. "He didn't want you to go with him?" That sounded strange. Trick had made it clear he was interested in Lila, even when she was small.

She turned her face away a moment. "He said he wanted to go by himself. In case my father was around."

I shared a look with Maks and he shook his head ever so slightly. Dragon relationships were not my forte, but if we could keep Lila busy, Maks and I might actually be alone for the first time in . . . well, I wasn't sure how long it had been. Time to see if dragons reacted the same way that I would. "That normal, for dragons to put their little women at home where the fire is to keep them safe?"

With each word Lila's scales along her spine stiffened until she looked like she was attempting to imitate a porcupine. "Yes. It's how the males treat all the females. Like they are incapable of doing anything!" With each word her voice grew in volume, until Bryce snorted and put a paw over his head, muttering something that sounded like "keep it down."

I reached over and tugged on Lila's tail. "You want

to be that kind of lady dragon? Left at home to tend the fire? Waiting for him to come back?"

"No," she growled the word and shot into the air. "I'll be back later!"

I watched as she rose fast into the night sky, her scales catching the little bit of light from the fire, and grinned when she shifted to her larger form that blotted out the stars. "He is so going to get his ass handed to him."

Maks grabbed me by the hand and pulled me to my feet, his mouth hot against my ear. "This is our chance."

He dragged me away from the camp, past the two horses who gave us sleepy yawns and a low nicker from my gray gelding, Balder. Maks let go of me and shifted to his four-legged shape of a desert caracal. He had a tawny body, short tail, and black-tipped ears. In his cat form, he was long-legged and could run for a long time. Grinning, I followed suit; even if my four-legged form was only that of a black house cat, I had remarkable stamina, and far more power in my smaller leaps.

We raced through the rock piles that made up this edge of the desert. My heart was pounding with anticipation. Maks wasn't doing this for no reason. I'd seen it in his eyes, a need that had been building for almost as long as I'd known him.

All this time together, and barely a single chance to be alone. Like *really* alone.

My heart began to thump harder for more reasons than the fact that we were bolting along at top speed, bounding across rocks, leaping our way farther and farther from camp. Part of me knew it was not the best idea to separate from Bryce and Lila, but the other part that included my lady bits was basically telling me to shut the fuck up. Because when would we get a chance to be alone together again?

Maybe never.

Maybe we'd die tomorrow.

Maks and I had been through enough that I could honestly say we deserved this moment. Hell, we'd earned it, and piss on every asshole we'd dealt with along the way that had tried to keep us apart.

Ahead of me, he slid to a stop in a natural cove of rocks that gave the illusion of privacy from the outside world. He shifted back to two legs, leaned against the solid rock and crooked a finger. Like me, he could shift forms and retain his clothes. Which meant I was going to get to strip him myself.

I wanted to dance on the spot.

Dirty blond hair, blue eyes, muscles in all the right places, smelling like the desert, and he had the nerve to give me the smirk along with the finger crook and a wink. Yeah, so my libido was getting ahead of me in a rapid way because I literally shifted shapes in mid-stride and threw myself at him. I mean, what did he expect? How long had we waited for this moment?

His eyes widened as he was forced to catch me, and he barely managed to steady us as I wrapped my legs around his hips. "Don't crook your finger unless you're going to catch me."

"Got it," he growled as he grabbed my ass with both hands and dug into the flesh, pulling me against all of him as his lips landed on mine. "Too long, it's been too long."

He wasn't kidding.

I grabbed the edges of his shirt and tugged it over his head, baring his chest to my greedy hands. Sliding my fingers across his skin, I tried to memorize the feel of him, of the cut of his muscles and the way his skin flicked under my touch. The way he smelled and tasted.

He slowly lowered me so I stood next to him, his hands on my arms, sliding up and down, sending tingles to every part of me. Maybe it was his magic, but I felt it was more like just him and me.

"Zam." He growled my name, nothing but my name, and I wanted to melt into a puddle. Not Marsum's voice, not Davin's voice. Just Maks. I had to swallow the lump in my throat, or I was going to ruin this moment with tears. Damn my emotions and all they did to me.

He leaned over and kissed one of the traitorous salty droplets off my cheek, then kept on kissing,

21

making his way to my mouth, slowing us a little. His tongue moved in and out, lazily, and I matched his pace, reveling in the taste and feel of him.

Part of me wanted to hurry, the other part wanted this moment to last and stretch as long as we could. I wanted all of him, every inch of his skin on mine until you couldn't tell where one ended and the other began. I peeled out of all my weapons, laying the flail and my knives on the ground, then stripped off my shirt while Maks helped. Our clothes ended in a pile at our feet.

He took a step back and just stared at me, his eyes tracing not only my body, but the scars.

And I had a lot of them.

"They each have a story." He ran a finger over a deep scar that rested across my left hip.

I nodded. "As I suppose yours do too?" He had more than his share of wounds and old injuries that were visible to my excellent night vision.

I bit my lower lip and closed the distance between us. "Lots of stories, but not tonight. Tonight is just us."

He grinned down at me, his eyes picking up on the light above us, making them damn well sparkle. As if we were in some sort of romance novel. "No stories tonight. Tonight is about something far more interesting than old battle wounds."

My heart picked up more than a few beats as the color of his eyes deepened and his pupils dilated as if he were about to go hunting. But it was me he was looking at, and I was pretty sure I was looking back the same way.

As if the cat were about to get the cream. He leaned in, his mouth finding mine, and after that, things got a little blurry.

THE AFTERGLOW WAS NICE, LYING NAKED IN HIS ARMS, feeling his heart come back to a steadier beat, feeling my own beating along happily. Was that even a thing, a happily beating heart? Probably not, but I could fool myself for a few minutes at least and pretend all was well with the world, that we hadn't just lost a major battle and would most likely see our own deaths sooner rather than later.

His hand traced along my hip, down my outer thigh and then slid to my inner, stroking the sensitive skin and sparking my thoughts into a direction I doubted he was ready for this soon after our first time. He was a guy, after all. I knew how things worked. I rolled on top of him. "Unless you want to go for a round two right now, I suggest you contain yourself."

Maks's eyes narrowed even as he quirked an eyebrow. "Is there an assumption that I can't get it up a second time?"

"Well, you aren't exactly a teenager, are you? And I'm not worried about the second time so much as I am about how quick round two would be after the first. Because, you know . . ." I held my hand up and then slowly let my wrist droop until my fingers dangled limply. I couldn't help it, he was too fun to tease, and we'd had too many dark moments in our time together not to take advantage of this one that felt light and sweet and perfect. With the man I'd waited my whole life for—even if we were somewhere in the middle of the desert on the ground for our first time. And maybe second if I got lucky.

With a growl, he flipped me onto my back, his body pressed against mine. In a flash of heat was proof that he could indeed keep up with me. That had me panting in seconds as I clawed at his back and our mouths worked in tandem against each other's lips, his hands working magic on me.

Maybe that was even some of it, some of our combined magic rushing through our blood and setting each other off, because I'd never had sex like this before. Like my skin was on fire and every part of my body could set off a series of climaxes with the barest of touches, with the lightest press of flesh on flesh.

Yes, not a bad way to start the evening at all, if I did say so myself, not a bad way to wash away a rather shitty day.

My body coiled, tightening as yet another climax whispered its way through me, the strength of it growing with each stroke of his body on mine as our hearts beat as one, drumming in my ears—

"Sis, we have a problem!" Bryce hollered, breaking through the lust curling between Maks and me like a bucket of ice water, dousing the flames in an instant, my inner core tightening as I lost that climbing sensation.

Fuck, talk about the worst possible timing.

I rolled to my knees and jerked my clothes on with a speed I wouldn't have thought I had in me. By the time Bryce rounded the corner, I was fully dressed, weapons on, and Maks . . . Maks barely had his pants on and was struggling to get things tucked away. He grimaced at Bryce.

"Shit timing, man," Maks said as he pulled on his shirt and picked up his weapon.

Bryce slid to a stop, his nostrils flaring and then wrinkling, no doubt smelling exactly what we'd been doing. I held up a hand. "The peanut gallery can make his snide comments later. What's going on?"

He motioned for me to follow him. I glanced at Maks as he pulled on the last of his clothes and then we headed after Bryce, just a few steps behind him.

"This had better not be just an asshole brother move," I muttered as Bryce hurried us back toward the camp and the horses.

"Yeah, walking in on my sister getting laid is just what I wanted to do tonight," Bryce shot back. "That's the stuff of nightmares, you know."

"Your brother walking in on you getting laid is the stuff of nightmares . . . you know," I pointed out.

Maks muffled a laugh, but I didn't make another noise. As if we'd crossed some sort of divide that lay in the sand between the rest of the desert and our campsite, the world around us seemed to have changed in that short time we'd been gone. Already, my skin prickled with awareness, of something or someone that was not our friend drawing close.

We reached the camp and the horses stomped their feet, restless and irritated. They had survived long enough to know that when bad shit was going down, it was time to run or fight.

Balder bumped me as I went by, his nose pushing into my hand. "It'll be okay, buddy." I lied to him because I had no idea if it would be okay or not.

The firelight of the camp had been doused to embers—or maybe we'd just been gone that long. That was possible. I checked the shine of the stars above, seeing where they were in relation to where they'd been as Lila left to go after Trick.

We'd been gone fewer than two hours.

I did a slow turn, quietly wishing to myself that I could have one fucking night off.

One. Literal. Fucking. Night. Off.

I drew in breath after breath, trying to scent what was coming our way, but didn't find anything that shouldn't be there. Just desert and sand and the occasional animal that belonged.

Hares.

Horses.

Desert hawks.

Frogs.

Some undistinguishable desert lizard.

All of them native.

Bryce was doing the same as me while he walked slow circles around the camp. He pointed at the pile of saddles and gear where Lila slept. "I tried to wake Lila, to get her to do a sweep, but she's out for the count. I didn't even hear her come back," Bryce said. Which meant he'd heard us leave and not said anything.

Maybe I'd forgive him for interrupting then.

I frowned, and looked down at my small friend curled up on Balder's saddle. She was back already? Did she and Trick get into a fight? That was possible. And the opened bottle of liquor next to her supported that possibility. Damn Trick, if he hurt her!

But even for Lila and her love of liquor, not being able to wake her up was a bit much. I bent and scooped her up, bringing her coiled body close to my face. She was breathing, but it was deep and there was a strange smell to her that I couldn't quite pinpoint, but it was sour and sharp and had a tingle that worked its way up my nose like . . . I shook my head. Well, shit. "She's been drugged."

Someone who knew how much she liked țuică had drugged her.

Someone who knew she had a knack for finding the liquor in the strangest of places, like a bee to honey.

Someone who knew she could be our eyes, who knew that she could get us out of a tight situation. Suddenly I wondered about Trick running off. Had it really been him at all? Ollianna had a connection to lizards and reptiles. Could she have taken the big dragon? It seemed a distinct possibility. More than that, though, was that Ollianna knew about Lila's love for the sweet plum liquor.

I ran a hand through my hair, frustration, anger and more than a little worry rolling through me.

"Saddle the horses," I said as I ran to do just that, cradling Lila in one arm. I grabbed my saddle and pad one-handed and tossed them onto Balder. He stood silent, his head up as he stared into the dark, nostrils flaring as he blew out sharp warning breaths like a mini trumpet. But his feet didn't move, and I quickly had the saddle cinched and Lila tucked into one of the saddlebags. She wasn't going to like it when she woke, but it was the safest place for her no matter if we had to run or fight.

I glanced over Balder's back to see Maks already up on Batman and Bryce pulling himself up onto a third horse we'd acquired earlier that day. A deep chestnut-coated horse with a flaxen mane and tail, and high white socks to his knees. He was about as pretty a horse as I'd seen in a long time. Bryce wasn't as comfortable riding as me and Maks, but he could do it, and the gelding was a quiet type; his temperament not near as flashy as his coloring.

The thing was we needed to conserve our energy, and the best way to do that was to keep a horse under each of us.

Worst case scenario, if things got rough riding, Bryce would shift to his lion form and run on all fours. All these thoughts rushed through my head like a stack of dominos crashing into one another, taking the next and the next down.

"I still got nothing. Nothing that doesn't belong, anyway, but the sensation of danger is stronger." Bryce shook his head and turned his horse to the southeast. That was the sensation I got too—that whatever or whoever it was made their push from that direction.

I swung up onto Balder and settled into the saddle. "Let's go. Not running, but let's move. Maybe whatever it is isn't looking for us. Might just be my black cat shitty luck showing up and it's a desert caravan or something."

Bryce and Maks agreed, but neither laughed. Because they knew as well as I did that if my bad luck was showing up, we were all in for a dance nobody wanted.

The four of us—Lila still snoring away in my saddlebag, I kept checking on her— rode straight north along the western edge of the desert. The night was not heavy, but it was a couple of miles before the sensation of being followed and watched eased. Not completely gone, but better, far less intense. I pulled Lila out of the saddlebag and held her in the crook of one arm on her back. Her tail flipped from side to side; she snorted in her sleep as her belly rose and fell.

"She okay?" Maks reached over and scratched at her belly with one finger. She giggled in her sleep and rolled in my arm, curling herself around my forearm, hugging me.

"She seems to be." I pointed at the saddlebag and he pulled out the bottle of țuică that she'd been drinking from. He gave it a sniff, closed his eyes and then nodded. "Golden marushka. It's a strong seda-tive. She'll be out till morning or longer. Especially since she drank most of it herself."

I'd never heard of the drug before. I quirked an eyebrow at Maks. Was it his memory he was pulling from, or one of the other Jinn masters? I was betting on the latter. He shrugged, no doubt sensing my unspoken query.

"But she'll be okay?" I asked.

He nodded and poured the țuică out, then tossed the bottle. "She'll be fine. Fresh as a daisy. But I don't know how long it will last on a dragon her size. Could be a day or more." He paused. "If we'd all drank from it, I'd say the four of us would be out till morning."

A sigh of relief I hadn't realized I'd been holding slid out of me and I gave her a one-armed squeeze, then tucked her back into the saddlebag. "Good." I paused as I closed the flap and tied it down so she wouldn't fall out. "That wasn't one of your memories, was it? About the sedative?"

Maks shook his head. "One of the other's."

In a fight to keep him with me, I'd managed to purge the souls of the other Jinn that resided in his body, but they'd left much of their knowledge with him. Thousands of years of history. In theory, all that information would help us. But Maks seemed to be unable to just access it. Something had to trigger the info before it would come to the front of his brain.

Then again, it had only been two days, so maybe that would change.

"You think Ishtar knows we're coming?" Bryce rode up beside us, his golden eyes glowing in the light of the moon and stars.

"Yes," I said. "I think it's always come down to facing her and seeing whatever this is between us."

Whatever this is—aka her bond with me as a mentor and surrogate mother. Her choice to keep Bryce immobile in a wheelchair with a spell that she could have removed at any time. Her desire for power overcoming any sense of right and wrong.

The lies.

The betrayals.

And all of it wrapped up in my head and heart with the love I had for her as a child so desperate to be loved, so afraid to be alone, seeing only a woman who'd been the mother I'd needed. Or thought I'd needed. I rubbed a hand over my face, hating the pit that opened in my stomach at the thought of facing Ish. Not because I was scared, but because I was afraid I wouldn't be able to pull the trigger as my father would have said. "She's weak right now, injured by the Jinn. It's my best shot."

"*Our* best shot," Maks said, just loud enough to be heard over the hooves of the horses on the hard-packed earth. "You aren't doing this alone."

I forced a smile and nodded as Bryce gave me a look that said he wasn't backing away from this fight

SHANNON MAYER

either. Of course, he had as much reason as I did to hate her. He despised her more; I was sure of it. She'd kept him crippled for much of his adult life, on purpose. To keep us both on a short leash.

But I couldn't help feeling that when it came to the final moment, it would be me and Ish facing one another.

A final reckoning of all that lay between us.

A gust of wind snapped up from the south along with a rumble of thunder from above. I looked skyward, expecting to see Trick headed our way. The storm dragon was strong, and funny, and he loved Lila from what I'd seen, but he'd hurt her. I was sure of it. There was no way she'd have come back by herself and gone straight for the țuică otherwise.

But his sinewy body didn't slide through the clouds. I'd like to give him more than a piece of my mind. I searched the sky, scanning for movement.

Nothing but rain and a few bolts of lightning. I grimaced and pulled the hood of my cloak over my head as the first sheet of rain fell in a deluge. "Lovely."

The thing about the desert was when the sky truly opened up, the rain did not mess around. We might as well have had buckets dumped on our heads as we rode through the night. Sheet upon sheet of rain, straight down on us with no respite. Twice I checked on Lila to make sure she wasn't drowning inside the saddlebag, but she was toasty and dry.

The only one of us who remained so.

A quick glance at Bryce made me hunch down further in my cloak. He was like a drowned rat—cat, I suppose—with his blond hair plastered to his head, rain dripping off his chin. Maks wore a cloak like me, and he'd pulled the hood up. But all the oiling in the world wasn't keeping rain like this out. The only upside was that the barrage wasn't terribly cold, so we wouldn't freeze to death.

But we could drown if we weren't careful.

We slowed, Balder stepping into a knee-deep puddle as we came to a narrow cut in the desert. In a flash of lightning, we could easily see the valley that dipped down between a series of dunes. I shook my head and pointed to the tops of the rolling hills. In no time, that valley below would be full of filthy brown rushing water that would wipe out everything in its path.

The boys didn't argue. They were desert-born like me and knew the danger of valleys in the desert during a rainstorm like this.

Riding along the tops of the hills, sticking to the high ground, I twisted around to look behind us to see if there was anyone following. To see if we'd left our nice warm camp for nothing.

I paused at the top of one of the hills and turned Balder, waiting on a bolt of lightning to show us what—if anything—was behind us. The minutes ticked by and just before I was going to turn him around once more, the sky lit up with a rapid series of bolts that turned the night into day followed by an ear-crashing boom of thunder right on top of our heads. Balder shivered but didn't move.

I squinted, fighting to see through the driving rain that made the world look hazy, even with the bright lightning. All of which made me second guess what I'd seen. Because it was just damn weird. The ground didn't move like that, not even if there had been water rushing over it. Maybe if there were an earthquake, maybe if it were in the valley, I could say it was water rushing, but this wasn't even moving like water.

No, this was moving like something else. "Bryce, Maks." I called them back to me, shouting to be heard over the pounding rain and a sudden, sharp wind as it shoved at us, pushing us north.

They came back to my side, flanking me, and I pointed at the lower ground as the sky lit up again.

"What is that?" Bryce yelled. "Water?"

"Maks, what do you think? Anything in the archives?" I grinned at him as I hollered to be heard.

He pulled a face and then slowly shook his head. "It's some sort of hatch, I think. A massive number of small critters hatching all at once and making a migration of some sort due to the large amounts of rain. That's the best I've got."

Well, shit, that was better than I thought it was going to be. "You mean like a frog hatch?"

I'd smelled frogs earlier but had dismissed the scent. Frogs were part of this section of the desert.

I squinted through the rain and could now see some of the little hopping critters individually—yup, my deduction of frogs was spot on—as they drew closer. Which meant I could see the red lines on them. I could see exactly what kind of frog hatch we were looking at.

"Fuck, they're poison!" I spun Balder and urged him into a lope across the dunes, away from the oncoming hatch. Only . . . they weren't just behind us now. Bryce grabbed my arm and pointed to the east. The ground moved there too.

Maks pointed to the west. And there too.

The scene unfolded in a weird sort of clarity. With something as simple as a frog, we were going to be forced to use the valley below, the one I'd already deemed deadly.

Ollianna had put us in checkmate.

We had to move our asses if we were going to have a chance of getting ahead of them.

"Come on, we don't have a lot of time." I urged Balder down the slope toward the flat and currently dry riverbed. It wouldn't be long before that was no longer the case. But maybe we could outrun the horde if we used the flat ground.

Of course, if we'd had Trick and Lila with us, in their full size, we'd be safe.

Which was exactly the point of removing the two

dragons from our group. Son of a motherfucking bitch.

Check-fucking-mate indeed, Ollianna. I wanted to tip my hat to her. Smart, that witch was damn smart.

Maks and Bryce followed, tight on our heels as Balder slid all the way down the steep descent. The wet ground made for an easy slide, and the water coursing down the edges of what would be the river-bank picked up speed even as we rode it down.

As soon as we hit the bottom, I put my heels to Balder's sides, and he shot forward. Batman with Maks, and Bryce and his new horse, stayed close to me. Batman could keep up with us now, but I didn't think Bryce's horse could. I shouted over my shoulder. "Our best bet is to try and get ahead of them and pray to any gods who might listen that we can do it before the water slams into us."

Bryce looked behind us and I pointed ahead.

"If only we were that lucky that it would come from behind," I yelled. "We're riding upstream. We'll find the water far quicker than we want to at this speed."

Which meant we just had to go as fast as we could and put the distance between us and the frogs. I leaned forward over Balder's neck, letting him set the pace. Not his top speed, because few horses could keep up with that, but close.

I kept my eyes peeled to the edges of the dry

riverbed for any sign of the poisonous little froggy fuckers that had been set on us. I had no doubt it was Ollianna making her first move on the final chessboard we were playing. Clever move too. We'd been fighting off her sand snakes for enough time that we were getting good at dealing with them. But frogs? They could have overrun us at camp if we'd gone to sleep.

If we'd all been drugged, if we'd all taken a drink, just like Lila. Maks had said we'd have been out till morning, and the horror of it hit me right between the eyes.

"Sweet terrible goddess, you really are a clever bitch, aren't you?" I muttered to myself, impressed with the move. Which meant I had to be just as clever if we were going to find a way to stop her.

If she could eliminate us, she'd remove a threat *and* someone who could potentially help her father escape his prison, her father who could take Ollie and the falak down.

Not that I was about to let the Emperor loose. I wasn't that fucking crazy.

Around each slight bend in the riverbed, I held my breath, listening for the sound of the water rushing toward us that would take us out.

Balder's ears suddenly flicked first to the left, then to the right. I looked up the side walls of the valley.

I watched with horror as it moved and shivered with the poison frogs as they followed. "Faster!" I yelled. I held Balder back, letting Maks and Bryce ride ahead of me and then I drove their horses. Balder nipped at their rumps and I let out a low growling hiss that would normally send Balder into a flat-out race, but he seemed to understand that it wasn't for him, not today. We couldn't leave anyone behind. The two horses in front dug in and picked up just enough speed that we stayed ahead of the deadly hatch.

Barely, and as I looked over my shoulder, the valley floor behind us moved with the hopping poison froggers.

I turned back in the direction we were going. A bright flash of light lit up the sky and the stretch of the dry river ahead of us looked as though it were midday. Which meant it gave us an excellent, heart-stopping view of the wall of dark water rolling down the river. It was no small river, but a wave easily topping fifteen feet and approaching too fast. We had to get out of the valley.

Now.

"Fuck!" Maks yelled, peeling off to the left, and Bryce to the right.

I didn't have time to think it through. I went to the left, following Maks. "Go, go!" I yelled. We still had to come out at the top ahead of the frogs.

We still had to avoid the wall of death headed straight for us, rumbling and roaring, the sound picking up volume as the water gained speed. The flood would easily burst the banks, and it would be full of all sort of shit and debris. One blow to the head and you'd sink below the dark waves, never to come up for breath.

"GO!" I screamed the word, both for Balder and the other two.

Balder scrambled hard, not straight up the incline but on an angle that still took us forward. There was nothing I could do now but hang on and pray he didn't slip, that he didn't take a misstep. That none of the horses slipped.

The rain slashed at my face, colder now and stinging as my hood swept back and we crested the top of the embankment. As far as I could see, the ground heaved and humped with frogs, the lines of red across their backs almost neon in the dark.

To drive fear into us in the moments before we died.

Maks looked at me as he and Batman took off at a flat-out gallop. The thing was his eyes said it all. We couldn't fight this; the battle against Ollianna had drained us and we had nothing left.

And that bitch of a witch knew it.

We had no choice except to run.

I knew he was right. Because it would only take one little frog to get through and one of us, or the horses, or both would be dead and dying.

Balder didn't wait on me. He dove into a gallop

and we were beside Maks and Batman in just a few strides, riding on their inside next to the river.

I looked up as the wall of water hit the sides of the embankment like a fist hitting flesh and tore it away from under our feet. Balder grunted and scrambled, and I gave him all the rein I could. "Come on, buddy!"

He gave a last heave and we were out, but the wave wiped out a huge section of the edge above the river. And that pushed us farther west, closer to more of the hopping little fuckers that were now croaking loudly, singing a song of death to us that could be heard over the river and the rain.

Faster, we had to go faster. I tried to see where Bryce was across the river, but there was no sign of him.

Magic, this would be a good time for magic. I looked at Maks. "You got any juice left?"

"I don't know. I can try!" he hollered back.

Fuckity shit damn it, I didn't know what to do. I was too new to the idea of magic to make anything happen unless I was in total crisis. Which this was, but also, it was *frogs*. How bad could they be, right? At least that's what one stupid part of my brain was saying. Frogs. We ate them when there was nothing else at an oasis.

If only the river had swept all the frogs away instead of just those in the valley. They could swim, they could hop, but even they couldn't escape the power of the deluge.

The lightbulb went on inside my head. "Maks! Can you divert some water? To clear our way?"

He didn't speak an answer, just lifted his right hand. A blue-black mist curled out from his fingers and with a flick, sent it into the water on our right, pulling it toward us. A thin curl of liquid flowed out along the smoke and followed us along.

With Maks leading the way, he used his new water whip to snap at the frogs around us. They flew up into the air and came down . . . almost on my head.

"SHIT!" I leaned to the left, dodging grasping sticky fingers as they reached for me, a flash of red lines as I pushed Balder out of the way with my heel. "Not in the air!"

"Sorry, getting the hang of this!" Maks yelled back, the fatigue in his voice thick as he flipped the water at the frogs again and again. It drove them back, but there were so many of them.

Time slipped by, and despite Maks's best efforts, the frogs were getting closer. There still was no sight of Bryce, and for all that I wished Lila would wake up and save us, she remained sound asleep and oblivious.

I closed my eyes, thinking that if I could just get rid of the frogs, we'd be good. That's all we needed.

"I'm running low!" Maks hollered. "We're going to have to . . ." he trailed off as he looked at me, understanding flowing between us. Because there was no *going to have to anything.* The river wouldn't save us. It tumbled and roared along beside us, as certain as a death as the frogs were. Even if we managed to get across, there were still a billion little assholes waiting for us on the other side, and being swept downstream wouldn't help us either, there were frogs in the river back there too.

I held four of Ishtar's stones. Each of them would draw on my energy like nothing else, which meant I had one shot.

Blue would freeze them, but I might miss some of them.

White with black lines would allow us to jump away if I got it right, but that would leave Bryce out there on his own.

Amber was a desert stone, meant to amplify power in a Jinn.

Red . . . red was a stone meant for nothing but destruction, nothing but death.

Red for the win, then.

I fumbled for the pouch on my side, fingers numb from the wet and gripping slippery reins. "I'm going to try something!"

"Don't take this the wrong way, but hurry up!" Maks yelled.

My fingers closed around the red stone, the blood-red rock that the Wyvern had given me. Meant for only one thing: it was one of the three that Ishtar didn't know about, and I was terrified to use it. But when death was coming at you, there was no time to be scared anymore.

I pulled it from my pouch and gripped it so hard, the edges of the rough-cut gem bit into my hand. Destruction was all this could do, and I needed its power to save us.

Seeing as I wanted to destroy a hatch of frogs, it was going to have to do the trick.

I breathed out a shaky breath and with it reached for my magic that that was so new to me. Connecting with my magic was like opening a door inside my head and letting it in. Or out, depending which way you think the door swung.

"Hurry!" Maks yelled, panic lacing his voice.

"Not helping!" I yelled back and the magic flared in me, circled around the stone and seemed to drive into it.

I just wanted the frogs around us gone. Dead. They needed to be dead.

How?

I gasped. That was not my thought, that was not my voice inside my head. But I answered it, knowing there was not a single damn second to waste. "Stop their hearts!"

A flare of red shot through me and my head snapped back, my fingers flexed, and I almost dropped the stone. Almost.

Heat prickled along my spine, and I could see it behind my closed eyes. Rays of red light slashing outward, a million, million, million miniscule red lines driving out and into all the frogs.

The world circled around me and I slumped in the saddle as the power fled back to the stone. It took the last of my efforts to shove it back into my pouch where I held the few stones we'd gathered.

"Did it work?" I managed to get the words out as Maks rode back to me. "Are the frogs stopped?"

Maks grabbed my shoulder and helped me sit up. "Was that what I think it was?"

I nodded, and then I closed my eyes and the world slipped away.

4

I woke with a start, thinking I was going to be covered in poisonous, sticky, grasping little frogs as they croaked and hopped all over my face. Flailing, I flicked my hands over my body as if it wouldn't be too late already had one actually touched me.

"You're okay. You're okay!" Maks had a hand on my shoulder and the night around us was still dark, the river rumbling in a roar off to our right. A quick glance up at the stars and the moon said it all. I hadn't been out cold all that long. Just long enough to freak me out.

I blinked a few times, a yawning chasm of hunger and fatigue hitting me at the same time. Maks shoved a hunk of dried meat into my hands. I touched my belly and found I could count my ribs far easier than just the day before. The magic had literally taken the stuffing out of me.

"Eat. That was a lot of energy you used up."

I barely tasted the meat, and all but swallowed it whole. There wasn't a lot of food left, though, and I didn't know when we'd have time to hunt again, so I filled the rest of my empty belly with water, drinking most of my flask down and distantly wishing it were țuică.

Anything to numb the bone-deep fatigue and gnawing sensation that this night was not over yet.

"Are they really all gone?" I looked around, waiting for the ground to move.

"Well, dead, but not gone. We're going to have to ride careful, slowly now." Maks pointed at the ground. Still covered with frogs, only now they were not moving, not even a flinch of the tiny bodies. I grimaced.

"That's going to stink like rotting frogs by the end of tomorrow," I mumbled around the last bit of dried biscuit.

He laughed. "But not like rotting you and me and two horses. That would be worse."

Black humor, no time like escaping death to put it into play. I grinned, and then twisted in my saddle to look at the far side of the river. I reached out to Bryce through our connection to the pride and found him. He was worried, but not hurt. A sigh of relief spilled through me.

"Bryce is okay. He's ahead of us," I said.

"We'd better hurry or he might not realize that he's riding on frogs," Maks said, and my stomach lurched. The rain was still coming down, and it was still dark out. Maks was right. Bryce might not even see the frogs now that they were still, their red lines no longer glowing with imminent death. Damn it, there was always something.

We kept the horses moving at a brisk trot, weaving around patches of frogs, moving them with Maks's water whip only if we had to. His face was drawn. This day had taken us to the end of our reserves and then some.

The bodies of the frogs were endless, heaped on top of one another as they'd seethed toward us, a river of death on both sides.

Seeing how close we'd come left me in a cold sweat.

"They were pushing us north, toward Ish," I said. "Is that what Ollianna wants for us?"

"Maybe to have Ish finish you off." Maks nodded. "It makes sense to pit us against other enemies first, to weaken and then kill us. It's a move you use in battle if you have to fight on more than one side."

I didn't like that his thoughts lined up with my own. "She's going to harry us until we face her, isn't she?"

His blue eyes looked into mine, worry etching the skin around them. "Yeah, that's what I'm thinking.

Assuming she doesn't manage to force us to our deaths first. It's a smart tactic, having others do her dirty work. Best case, we all kill each other and she's free to rule on her own with no one to face her."

I agreed with him, just a nod because it made me sick to my stomach to move my head. He was right. But that didn't mean it wasn't going right into the shit hole for us. We still had to face the others. Ishtar. The Emperor. And then Ollianna and the falak child she was going to produce. A child with a bloodline to the Emperor. Fuck, what would that do to the falak? Make it stronger, no doubt.

As we rode, an idea came to me, a possible solution. One that no one was going to like. Which was why as soon as it came to me, and I saw the merit in it, I held it close to my chest as far away from Maks and Bryce as I could. Either of them would take one look at me and be asking what I'd thought of—curses of not being able to control my face.

Five minutes later, Bryce and his horse came into view. Moving quickly, avoiding the frogs as we were. "Sweet oasis water, I thought we were all dead." Bryce shook his head, flinging water in every direction. The rain was easing off, still coming down, but not in heavy sheets. The worst of the storm was blowing over. But that wasn't what had my attention.

I glanced at his horse, saw the sweating, foaming mouth, the wide rolling eyes. "Get off your horse."

Bryce looked down, not understanding. Not knowing horses like I did. "He needs a break?"

The horse collapsed before I could do anything, forcing Bryce off. He stumbled and had to hop to avoid stepping on the frogs around him. The poison took the horse so fast that even if I'd had my hands on him, I wasn't sure I could have saved him—especially as drained as I was from stopping the frogs in the first place.

Worse even than watching the horse die was the reality that if I hadn't used the stone, that what I was looking at would have been our deaths. We all would have ended like that poor boy, heaving and struggling for breath as the poison ramped up through him. This would have been Lila too, if she'd survived the initial onslaught and crawled out of the saddlebags, still sleepy and stumbling on the frogs.

The horse heaved for breath, a wet, horrible breath. I pulled the shotgun out from under my leg where it rested, aimed and pulled the trigger before his suffering stretched on. The boom rattled the air, but neither of the other two horses so much as flinched. They'd been around weapons of all sorts for years. Balder reached back with his nose and bumped my leg, gently, warmth from his muzzle and breath seeping into me.

Somehow, he understood. I'd given that poor horse a merciful death. Poison could take a long time to kill. I tucked the shotgun away into its sheath under my leg, then rubbed a hand over Balder's neck. "I know, buddy. I know." He'd nearly died only a few weeks before, but we'd been able to bring him back. I didn't know how much he understood or remembered, but he seemed to grasp that this could have been him.

The horse with no name stretched out, its limbs slowly going limp, and the light in its eyes fading, going dull. I made myself watch, not out of any morbid sense but because I had to remember it could happen. I could lose someone I loved, or I could be the one to die. We'd been lucky. Bringing Bryce back from the dead—or whatever kind of limbo he'd been in—was not something I thought we'd be able to do again.

Which meant I would do what I had to do to keep those I loved safe. No matter what the cost to me.

I shook my head and snapped fingers at Bryce when he bent to the horse. "Leave the gear, it's smeared with frog goo. We don't need a repeat of that demonstration."

Bryce straightened, opened his mouth to argue and then quickly gave me a nod. Letting me lead. "At least I have boots on."

"They're my boots, so try not to ruin them," Maks said.

For just a second, I thought Bryce was going to deliberately step on a frog—*because boys*.

"Don't," I said.

"I wasn't."

"Bullshit." I pointed at him. "So don't."

Maks looked between us. "What did I miss?"

"Nothing," Bryce and I said in tandem, and in that moment, I was ten years old again, standing in front of my father with Bryce at my side, trying to get out of trouble for one thing or another. That memory was bittersweet, and I held onto it. Grateful for the flash of the past coming back to me. There weren't many of my memories that were good and sweet, and not painful to recall.

So much death, so many lies from those who were supposed to love me, so much shit in every sense of the word.

It was a wonder I wasn't more broken. Or maybe I just didn't see it anymore.

But that sweet memory, the two men at my side, Lila tucked away sleeping, they were the reasons to keep on fighting, a reason to take whatever bit of hope I had that I could keep them all safe.

"The frogs thin out in the next few minutes. At least there weren't that many when I rode toward you." Bryce took one last look at his mount, then continued on, leading the way through the green and red valley of dead frogs, more visible with each second as the clouds above us cleared and the moon came out, lighting our way.

The dying horse, the dead frogs . . . it was all the

way of the desert. Those around you died, sometimes friends, sometimes family, and you had to keep going. You had to learn to grieve when it was safe, not when your heart wanted to, and you had to know when to retreat, when to fight, and when to give in . . . No, I wasn't going to think about that.

A part of me worried that if I thought about my plan, Bryce or Maks would somehow know. Stupid, maybe, but they both knew me so well and in different ways, I wasn't sure I could keep my plan from them if I thought about it.

When the time came, I just had to do it. I would give Ishtar what she wanted if she stopped Ollianna and the falak. My guts twisted just thinking about Ishtar, of putting myself back into her hold. But what choice did I have? She was more powerful than anyone save maybe the Emperor.

I had to be ready to bargain.

"What do you think that was all about, the frogs, I mean?" Bryce asked. "Other than trying to kill us. Because I feel like there are better ways."

I blew out a breath. "Ollianna. She's going to harry us until either she's dead, or we are. If the frogs cut our numbers, or killed us all, it would have been a bonus."

Bryce shook his head. "Not us. You. The frogs ignored me on the other side of the river."

Maks let out a low growl that he blended quite

nicely with a curse. "Then we have to go after her first. We can't deal with Ishtar while Ollianna is on our heels."

I didn't think that was the answer. I wanted to go after Ishtar. Ollianna wanted me to go after Ishtar.

Doing what Ollianna wanted wasn't going to be good for us, even if I did manage to convince Ishtar not to kill us.

The line of the wooden handle on the flail that had become such a part of me gave a not-so-subtle tingle across my back. The flail was my weapon through and through, but to bring my brother back from the limbo he'd been stuck in, and to save myself and Maks, I'd traded it to the Emperor. I'd not put a time limit in when he could have it.

I was kind of thinking once I was dead and long gone. I grinned and the wooden handle gave a sharp zing across my back, far more than a simple tingle. I yelped and put a hand to it, heat cutting into my palm like a hot brand. "What the fuck?"

Another sharp snap that arched my back and made the breath whoosh out of me. "I'm sorry you didn't get to eat any frogs!"

You traded the flail. You must give it to the Emperor.

There was that voice again. "Not yet." I bit the two words out.

Yes. Now. The deal must be done.

I groaned and turned Balder toward the west, and the pain across my back immediately subsided. My chin dropped to my chest as I thought about resisting the summons. As I thought about my plan going to shit right in front of me. "Fucking hell."

I grimaced and urged Balder forward in the new direction. Yeah, the pain was gone now. "Are you sure?" I whispered the words, already knowing I was probably losing my mind.

Yes. You need to trust me now. You did once. Your plan is good. Use it on the Emperor.

I swallowed hard, finally recognizing the voice. "Marsum."

There was a sensation that rippled outward from the flail along my spine wherever it touched that could only be described as laughter. Marsum's soul had been taken in by the flail, and now he was directing me. And laughing at me.

Son of a bitch, I thought we were done with him and his interference. Even if he'd turned out not to be the right asshole we'd always thought.

"Did you say Marsum?" Maks was at my side in a flash, his eyebrows creased with worry.

I touched the flail. "He's in here, right? I can hear him in my head."

The dip of Maks's brows went deeper yet. "Are you sure?"

"Yes." I rubbed my hand over my face, my plans for Ishtar going right out the window. I wished Lila was awake. I wished she were on my shoulder being a sassy little bitch who helped keep me grounded.

"We are changing directions," I said. "Ishtar will have to wait."

"What? Where are we going?" Bryce hurried to catch up as I dismounted.

"Get on Balder. I'll ride with Maks. We need to cover ground. No doubt Ollianna knows we killed her frogs. And if I were her, I'd try again to kill us right away." I took a breath and stepped through the doorway that was the space in my head between me on two legs and me on four. In that breath, I became a six-pound house cat, black as the night around me, but the flail was still attached, absorbed into me as my clothes did and was still striking sharp pains into my back. As if I were going too slow.

"I hear you. Knock it the fuck off," I grumbled. I took a teeth-grinding, running leap and ended up clinging to Maks's belt, my dagger-like claws nearly cutting it in half. He scooped me up and tucked me under his cloak away from the rain. Gods, he smelled good, and the pain eased, leaving me with a strange sense of euphoria.

"Keep going west," I said.

"West is going to take us toward the wall, or what's left of it," Maks pointed out.

"I know, but I made a deal and the flail is holding me to it. I have to take it to the Emperor. And I have to take it now." I didn't want to, but if I was being forced to go, I would try to find a way to kill him. Letting him out of his prison was a terrible idea. Just fucking awful. And that's what he wanted the flail for —to free himself. Besides, my plan I'd had for Ishtar wouldn't work on the Emperor.

You sure about that?

I wasn't sure how I felt about Marsum in my head. He'd been the bane of my existence for most of my life, but in the end, I'd found out it hadn't been him at all, but an older, more powerful Jinn that had been trying to kill me. Marsum had helped to save me and Maks, his son, and for that I would be grateful for the rest of my life. But that didn't mean I would put up with his shit.

"Freeing the Emperor dooms us," I said softly. Maks agreed with a grunt, not realizing that I was talking to Marsum.

If the Emperor got loose, well, to say both human and supernatural worlds would be in trouble was an understatement; that's what Merlin had said. The Emperor wanted to rule, and that was why he'd been stuffed into his prison in the first place. Because his idea of ruling was making the humans subjects and food, and the supernaturals over them. All the while that he—the Emperor—did whatever the hell he wanted. Tyranny on a large scale was not something I would willingly sign up for even on a bad day.

My thoughts circled and the warmth of Maks's

body sunk into me, making me curl tighter against him.

"Did it ever occur to you that the Emperor was lying about the falak?" Bryce said, right around the time I was dozing off.

I blinked awake. "What?"

"Let's be honest. The man that is your grandfather hasn't been really honest with you up till now. He's lied or given half-truths every time you've spoken with him. So maybe he was lying about the falak. Maybe if you kill the Emperor, the falak won't be the terror he says. Maybe that's just a way for him to keep anyone from killing him."

Bryce wasn't wrong. The Emperor had been the biggest liar of them all, and that was saying a lot considering I'd been dealing with Ishtar for years and the lies she'd spun to keep us close and complacent. If Bryce was right, that changed things.

"I have no way of knowing. None of us do. And do you want to gamble the world on a hunch?" I stretched and leaned out the front of Maks's shirt, hanging there and staring at my brother. The words of Titiana, the queen of the fairies, were still humming along in my head. And I didn't like them. I didn't like them one bit. Because the more I saw of what Ollianna was willing to do, the more I was beginning to feel like the Emperor might not be the biggest threat of all. And for the moment, he was still in a prison that he couldn't fully escape no matter how hard he tried.

I grimaced. I did not like that idea that was curling through me. Or where it could lead. Death waited, it was just a matter of who that creepy bastard got first. I let out a long sigh. "Can we all just agree on one thing? No matter what happens, no matter if I live or die, *one of us* has to kill Steve."

Bryce gave a snarling growl. "Gladly. He's turned the pride against you. Hell, he turned Darcy against you!"

I grimaced but was also glad for the change of direction in the conversation. "She was only friends with me because there was no one else. Kiara was too young, and there were no other female shifters. It was a pity friendship. At best. She'd rather see me dead now too."

I'd seen her and Steve in a vision of sorts, and she'd . . . been clear in her distaste for me as a shifter, as a person.

Maks wrapped a hand around me and I leaned into his touch, buried my face in the palm of his hand. Darcy had been my only friend for a long time, and I'd thought we were best friends. The kind that would end up old and gray together, laughing about the shit we got into when we were young.

I'd forgiven her when she'd slept with Steve while he and I were still married, because I blamed him, and she let me believe it was all him, that she tried to resist, but couldn't because he was an alpha. But now that he had his own pride, her true colors were showing. She was a user of people, and that had included me when she'd needed me. Now that she didn't think she needed me, I was out. I wasn't about to have that kind of toxic shit in my life.

Life was hard enough without adding those who'd use you up and treat you like you were nothing.

I lifted my head.

"Death to Steve." Maks curled his free hand into a fist. Bryce returned the gesture and fist-bumped him. "Death to Steve."

I grinned. "Death to motherfucking sheep-fucking Steve."

Bryce burst out laughing. "Shit, I always forget about that."

"I don't." I gave a toothy, feline grin. Death to Steve was a good distraction for the reality that we'd turned away from Ishtar and were headed straight toward the Emperor's Throne. Straight into a place that would—not could—spell death for us. Yes, I had a plan. I tweaked what I was going to use on Ishtar to the Emperor. But that didn't mean it would work. My plans often went sideways.

And the Emperor was batshit crazy, a split personality that could not be trusted even if he did give his word.

Part of me thought the going would get easier, our path less littered by things trying to kill us. That if we headed toward the Emperor we'd be doing what he wanted and so we'd be okay.

But the thing was, I forgot to take into account where Ollianna wanted us to go.

And it was not toward the Emperor.

5

The night tightened around us as we continued to the west, toward the Emperor's Throne. The darkness felt as though it deepened its hold on the world as it went on rather than easing with the sun that wasn't all that far from rising. I glanced up, no longer sleepy despite my place in Maks's arms. Perks of being a house cat, I often got the best seat in the house. I forced myself to leave the shelter of his body and pulled myself up onto his shoulder.

"Does it seem darker to you two? We are almost at dawn. It shouldn't be darker." I swiveled my ears and my head, searching for . . . something. Anything that would give me a clue as to what was going on now. Because there was no doubt in my mind we weren't finished for the night. A shiver rolled down my feline spine and made the tip of my tail twitch with irritation and anticipation.

"It is nearly dawn," Maks said. He pointed above us at where the moon sat low in the sky, touching the edge of the horizon. "And you're right. It should be lighter out by now."

Bryce grumbled a string of rather creative curses that at another time would have made me smile. As it was, I didn't disagree with a single one of them. Basically, we were at a "what the fuck now?" moment.

"Hurry the horses up. And go south," I said softly.

"Could be a trap," Bryce said.

I couldn't help the laugh. "Of course it's a trap. A trap that will come from the west to block us and send us back toward Ishtar. I have no choice. I have to go west. I have to get the flail to the Emperor."

The flail, in response to my words, gave a shiver as it did so often, only this time I could feel it under my skin, like a sliver that had been embedded in my body.

"Shit." Maks growled the single word, spun Batman and we were off, racing through the strange dark that shouldn't have been dark at all. I dug my claws into the shoulder of his cloak, careful not to nick him with my razor-sharp tiny talons. The wind whipped through my fur and I leaned into it, eyes closed and breathing deeply. I scented it as best I could, but there was nothing . . . wait . . .

"I've got something." I frowned and tasted the air

with my mouth open, trapping the smell against the back of my tongue for a better "look" at what I'd picked up on. I curled it around my mouth as I attempted to work it out.

"What is it?" Bryce asked. I looked at him, riding easily on Balder right beside us.

"Reptilian, I think. But I've never scented anything like this before, and the more I smell it," I licked my lips and drew a breath again, "the closer it is, which means whatever it is, it's quick."

"Okay, moving fast, reptilian. What else?" Maks asked.

"Some sort of elemental creature, I think," I said. "There's magic mixed in with the reptile. I'm not sure if it's Ollianna or the creature itself." I paused. "Bryce, see if Lila is awake yet."

She'd been out cold all night now, she had to wake soon. And now would be an amazing moment to pop out of the saddlebag and sweep all of us to safety.

"She's asleep. Breathing but asleep," he said a moment later.

That was good and bad. My chest constricted as I looked across to the saddlebag that Lila was curled up in. Except for the bulge of where she was balled up, there was no way to tell she was in there. Damn, we were lucky that she'd been small when she'd drunk the loaded țuică. If she'd been in her larger size, we would've had to leave her behind.

The frogs would have had her.

That realization hit me in the center of my chest, and I chased the fear with a spurt of anger that I directed straight at Ollianna. I should have known not to trust a witch, even if she was related to me. When she'd come with us out of the Swamp, I only saw a kindred spirit who wanted to escape a situation that was so like my own. Not fitting in, knowing the others thought less of you and might kill you for being different if they got the chance.

She'd played on my sympathies, and I'd fallen for it, hook, line and sinker.

The wind shifted around us again, swirling in from the south, and whatever spit was in my mouth dried up along with thoughts of Ollianna.

It changed again, coming in from the east, then the north.

"There is nothing natural about that wind," Bryce said.

"No, there's not," I said softly. "It feels like the Swamp."

Maks grunted. "Smells like it too."

Bryce wrinkled up his nose. "Like something is rotting."

I did my best not to breathe deeply; at the same time, the scent of the wind told me a great deal. Ollianna's witches were still with her. They were still helping her.

Awesome.

I unhooked my claws from Maks's cloak and leapt

off. I landed on all fours, and just crouched there, feeling the earth around us, feeling the pulses of energy that made up this place I called home. The two men and the horses slid to a stop next to me, dust curling around their legs.

I closed my eyes, sifting through all the energy, letting it flow through me and then feeling it lock into me like a fishing hook attached to a thousand lines of everything around me.

"Dad used to do that," Bryce said, from what sounded like far, far away.

Extending my claws into the dirt, I dug into the desert. Our father had done something similar to this, only it had been to the pride he was tied to. I wasn't sure if he'd ever been able to sense all the world around him.

I know why you can do what you do, but I think I'll let you figure it out.

I ignored Marsum and continued to reach for whatever it was coming toward us—a creature for sure, reptile, but otherwise I couldn't pinpoint it. A sharp snap of power, like the crack of a whip, smacked at me, and I gritted my teeth, feeling the power of the witch behind the blow. It felt like the one they called Mother.

She was old, and strong, and frankly, I was surprised she was helping Ollianna.

I got the impression she hadn't much liked her young daughter.

I let go of the energy, knowing that it was not worth the fight to see what was coming. It—or they—would be on us in minutes.

"Ollianna doesn't want me to see what's coming," I said. I looked around us, the darkness still weird, but duskier now, and it was accompanied by something else that made my heart sink and pick up speed at the same time.

This was a game changer. The heat of the desert was sinking back in and the cold-soaked ground was giving us more challenges.

"Is that fog?" Maks asked.

"Yeah, but I'd bet you all the jewels I have that it isn't natural, and that whatever reptile she's hiding from us is in it," I said. Dirty white billows of fog rolled forward, and all around us. Though it wasn't that high, maybe as tall as Balder's back, I couldn't see any place that it hadn't covered from any direction, giving the impression that we stood in a sea of white. The night faded finally, the light shifted, but it didn't help us much.

We were surrounded. So much for driving us toward Ishtar. Apparently, we were going to be straight up attacked.

I walked through the doorway in my mind that took me back to two legs. "We can't outrun this."

Maks motioned at Bryce. "Let your sister ride. She can do more damage from Balder's back, and you can do more damage as a lion."

Bryce gave him a look, just a narrowing of eyes, and I held up a hand. "He's not being your alpha, Bryce. He's just making good sense as someone who has years of battles trapped in his head."

Bryce rolled his shoulders and slid off Balder's back. "Sorry. It's an old habit from dealing with the sheep fucker. I'm working on it."

Maks gave a dry laugh. "Yeah, I imagine that would stay with you." He pulled his weapon from his waist. It looked like a foot-long stick, but as he held it, the weapon extended into a six-foot-long pike with a curved blade on the end. A weapon of magic that he'd stolen from the Blackened Market.

He took a few swings with it from Batman's back and the horse stood like a statue without a single flinch. Both horses were trained for battle by yours truly, and despite what we were about to face, I was proud of them. They had carried us so far in this journey.

"A little further, boys." I leaned forward and gave Balder a scrub on the neck, then reached over and did the same for Batman. A good horse is a hard thing to find, and I'd managed to find two that made every other horse look untrained, making Balder and Batman look like freaking unicorns with their brains, speed, and loyalty.

Balder snorted and pawed at the ground with one front foot, then the other. If I didn't know better, I'd think he liked going into a fight.

I sat up and stared out at the oncoming fog. I didn't pull the flail from my back. I knew I would have to, but not yet. Instead I reached under my leg and pulled out the shotgun with the grenade launcher under the barrel. Even though my skin prickled with the imminent fight that was coming, and my adrenaline coursed hot through my veins, I kept my movements smooth. Kept my breathing even and steady.

Balder started to jig under me, snorting and tossing his head, then plunging forward as he quite literally chomped at the bit, picking up on my energy despite my attempt to keep things calm. "Easy, you'll get your chance." I leaned forward and patted his neck again.

The fog crept closer and with it came a sound that crawled its way toward us. A weird clicking, like the chatter of teeth, followed by a series of guttural growls. Not just one though, there wasn't a single reptile making the two sounds. It came from all sides, and many throats.

I grimaced and backed Balder so we were next to Maks and Batman, but facing the opposite directions, protecting one another's flanks. Bryce sat beside me, having shifted to his lion form, his golden coat dull in the weird foggy light.

"You want to try and talk to them first?" Maks asked.

I frowned. "It won't get us out of a fight. Let's just kill them and be done with it."

He nodded and his forearms glowed with magic as he gripped the pike, but I could see the pull on him.

"You want the amber stone?" I asked him.

He shook his head. "If I use it now, it'll drain me completely. I don't have the strength to control it. Same for you and the other stones. Don't use them."

I ground my teeth. "Exactly what Ollianna wanted."

Maks nodded. "My thoughts too."

The fog spilled closer and closer until it was near enough I could reach out and touch it.

Before I lost sight completely, I lifted the shotgun, took a breath, aimed and squeezed the trigger, shooting into the fog, hoping to hit something, or maybe make whoever it was more cautious at the very least. The boom rattled the air, but was absorbed by the fog around us, dampening the sound.

"It didn't hit anything," Maks said. "I'm going to stir up the desert with what strength I've got left. See if I can blow this fog off."

Bryce let out a growl as the swell swallowed us whole. "Stay close!" I yelled.

I pushed Balder sideways, toward Maks and Batman, but they were already gone, somehow swept away in this strange sea of clouds.

"Bryce?" I yelled for my brother.

Someone answered but it wasn't him. A figure stepped toward me, nothing more than a silhouette really, but the solidity of him (pretty sure it was a him by the breadth of the shoulders) was very real.

"My queen has a message," the figure said. Not in a hissing voice as I'd expected. No, it was deep and rather gravelly as though he held rocks inside his cheeks as he spoke.

"She can fuck right off and keep fucking off until I tell her to stop her lily-white ass. She's a coward. Why isn't she here?" I snorted, knowing damn well that Ollianna would be watching this somehow, maybe seeing it through her creature's eyes even.

"She gave you your life at the last battle. She could have killed you. She showed you mercy. She tried to direct you to where she wishes you to be, and you are defying her. Turn to the north, ride to Ishtar and she will spare your life." He stopped about ten feet from me, but I still couldn't see any features. He wore dark armor that covered him from head to foot with a glint of weapons here and there, the barest flicker of metal.

"She was knocked up and protecting her demon spawn, and if she could have killed me then she would have." I slowly raised the gun, aiming it at him. "So unless your message is she's chosen to kill the falak and stop this madness, I think we're done."

I didn't wait for an answer, an answer that would never satisfy me.

I pulled the trigger and the gun bucked in my hand, jamming me in the shoulder.

He roared as he flailed backward, the slug hitting him right in the chest. The fog thickened and the sound of scales slithering across the hard-packed earth filled the air around us. I looked down, waiting for the ophidians to appear. The snake-like creatures slid under the sands and would suck you down in an instant, their venom as deadly as their crushing coils. Only they didn't like hard ground and we were on hard, hard ground.

What the fuck were we up against?

Jaw clenched, I kept Balder as still as I could, looking to where the reptile man had stood in front of me. He was gone, swallowed up by the fog. Hell, I didn't even know if I'd killed him or not.

A bellow of rage to my right was just enough warning for me to swing around and raise the gun a second time. The face that appeared out of the fog sent a bolt of fear straight through me, and I hesitated on the trigger. Not because I didn't want the thing to die, but because I was frozen with pure shock in a way that I hadn't been in a very long time.

As big and tall as a man, the creature was reptilian from its barely-there nostrils and slanted huge yellow eyes with horizontal slits, to the dark green, sometimes black scales that covered its body from protruding snout filled with rows of teeth, over the top of its head, down its neck and over its limbs. His limbs. Clawed hands dug into my arms and I snapped out of my shock, barely leaning back and avoiding the teeth that came snapping at me.

"Balder, go!" I yelled, unable to use my one leg with the creature pulling on me. Shit, he was pulling me out of the saddle!

Balder lurched forward a step as I wrestled with the reptile man thing, and then stopped as he felt me slide. Snarling, I regained my balance and bared my own sharp canines at the creature, letting out a growl.

He started to laugh.

His hands loosened and I jerked one arm straight up, breaking his hold on me. "Go suck a rotten egg!" I yelled as I pulled the flail from my back and drove the spiked end of the handle down into the creature's shoulder, right at that sweet spot between neck and torso.

The flail pulsed and jigged against my palm as it drank down the life of the creature, gone so fast that the body shrunk before my eyes at high speed, skin folding in and crinkling like dry paper. With a whisper of detaching from the wound, the flail released the creature and its body slid away from me. I did a slow spin with Balder, looking, waiting for another one, not daring to shout out for Bryce or Maks.

I reached back into the saddlebag, feeling for Lila. She was there, her scales a perfect temperature and her chest rising and falling. I tried my connection to her to wake her, but that golden marushka in her system was keeping her fully under.

I swallowed hard, suddenly more worried about her than I was the creatures we were facing. Part of me had thought she was just sleeping heavily, like one does after being drugged. I'd thought she'd be awake by now.

I'd been distracted by the frogs.

And now these creatures.

My heart clenched as the possibilities started to spin through my head. What if this wasn't just a sleeping draught that she'd downed, but something else that we'd missed? Something more sinister? Damn it, I should have thought of it before, but between everything—

A scaled body lurched at us out of the vapor, fast like a striking snake, dark armored scales dripping with moisture from the fog. Balder spun and double barreled the creature, kicking out with both back feet and nailing it right in the chest before I could react. The crack of bone and a grunt of the creature was all I heard and then it was gone again, disappeared back into the fog.

"Come on, Maks," I whispered to myself. He had magic, Jinn magic, and with his connection to the desert, he should have been able to do something, even if it was to make the fog dissipate as he'd said. But he was also exhausted; we all were.

And fucking Ollianna knew it.

I put my heels to Balder, not to go quickly, just to move. Staying right with two dead bodies of the creatures I'd killed was not a smart move. I could smell them, even through the thick moisture, which meant the reptiles could find them too just as surely.

I didn't know how the creatures were finding us, if it was smell or hearing, or some other sense I didn't know about, which meant I had to assume it was all of those senses. Moving through the fog was surreal, like stepping through a dreamscape, only the dreamscape I'd been in had some solidity to it. I kept breathing deeply in an attempt to pinpoint the next reptile, but the moisture was making it difficult. Like scenting in the rain.

The ground rumbled and the air around me shivered . . . and the fog began to move and swirl around us. A grin slid over my face as the mist was forcibly pushed away until there were only patches here and there.

But the smile didn't last, not when I saw for the first time what we were facing in its entirety.

"Balder," I whispered, my heart plunging to the soles of my feet, my hand tightening on the flail, "my old friend, we're going to die."

6

MERLIN

Strange to find that after all Ishtar took from
him, he could still think, and feel pain, and
wonder just what was happening around
him. Mind you, he was supposed to be dead.

There had been a moment after Ishtar had let him
go that another set of hands had touched him, and
he'd had just enough strength left to weave a little
magic through her.

A desire to help him.

It looked as though that last spell had worked.

"Hold still," a low whisper curled through his ears.
A woman's voice. Not Flora's, though. Someone else,
someone young and a little familiar.

Hands brushed over his body which sent shooting
pains flying along his nerve endings, drawing a gasp
from his parched lips. Parched. Again, not something
that should be happening if he were dead, which

77

meant he really had survived Ishtar. Pain, thirst, those were concerns of the living, not of the deceased.

"I said hold still. You'll pull out the stitches. As it is, you're going to have some serious scars."

Merlin forced one eye open, the other he wasn't sure . . . was it gone maybe? He wanted to lift a hand and touch his own face, but there was no energy within him to even do that. Damn Ishtar and her pettiness.

Talk about an eye for an eye.

One slow blink revealed a gray ceiling above painted with a bright sunburst in brilliant gold, red, and yellow flames, lions circling it, running between stands of trees and water that spilled out in tendrils of multiple rivers. Golden Bright Lions with their mouths open in a silent roar. The fresco was stunning, and Merlin's heart beat a little faster.

This was better than he could have hoped for.

A face leaned over him, blocking the view. Long golden hair that curled at the ends, bright golden eyes, full lips. An angel for sure. Or a devil for keeping him alive and making him suffer, he wasn't sure yet.

"I don't know if you remember me," she whispered. She brought a cloth to his face and wiped it across his brow. "The fever finally broke, but you'll be weak for some time. You have to stay quiet. You can't make a sound or she'll kill us both."

She turned; there was the sound of water dripping, and then a metal ladle was against his lips and the cool liquid pooled into his mouth. It hurt to swallow, the first few gulps were like sandpaper in his throat, but it eased, and he drank down two more full offerings.

"That's enough, more later," the girl said. Girl, woman. She was a Bright Lion, one tied to Ishtar and she was helping him, just as he'd hoped.

His curiosity got the better of him. His spell would have only worked if there had been a desire to help to start with, even if it was just a seed. "Why?" He managed the single word and she went still in her movements, just pausing for the briefest of seconds before continuing to move through the motions of cleaning up.

"You would help Zam. And she is my alpha. I won't abandon her like the others have. Even Ford has turned from her because he wants her and she loves Maks." She rotated her head toward him and her eyes narrowed into slits that made her look even more catlike as they glowed gold with her emotions. "You *will* help her."

His lips twitched, working toward a smile. "Yes."

She smiled for both of them. "Then we stay quiet, you heal, and when we can, we escape."

"Name?" He whispered the word as sleep began to tug at his eyes.

"Kiara."

SHANNON MAYER

* * *

SHE WATCHED HIM SLIDE UNDER THE SLEEP THAT ONLY came to those who'd been injured badly or were coming back from a deep sickness. Fatigue nipped at her heels, but she still had much to do. Telling the others that she was not well had kept her confined to her room for the time it had taken to bring Merlin back from the brink.

That Ishtar had asked her to remove his seemingly lifeless body from the throne room on that night had been a slap in the face. That was a task normally given to a human or a slave. But from the minute she'd put her hands on him, she'd known she had to help him.

She hadn't cared what Ishtar would do to her if she was caught. Her lips tightened as she thought about how they'd all been fooled by Ishtar, how they'd thought she'd loved and looked out for them. Just like she, herself, had been fooled by Steve. But Zam was not like that, and she'd always watched out for her, like the family she was, no matter that they were different kinds of shifters. It still churned in her guts that she'd believed the lies Steve had told her about Zam. About her being weak and jealous. When that wasn't the case, not at all.

Kiara would not make that mistake again.

The low snarl that trickled past her lips was out before she could catch it. But then again, there was no one to hear her. No one to stop her from expressing herself.

With everything in the room tidied, she stood and glanced at Merlin. She'd sewn his one eye shut; the orb had been totally destroyed. The rest of the multitude of wounds that covered his body were either bandaged or stitched closed by her hand, so in theory he'd survive. But he was so weak, and she wasn't sure how long they had before they would need to slip away. She stepped out of the room, closing the wooden door tightly behind her. She needed food for herself and for Merlin if they were going to get through this.

No, they would get through this, and then they would help Zam.

Darcy had come to the door a few times while Kiara had been "sick," but she'd kept it shut, and kept the incense burning heavily to mask the smell of the wizard. Even now, the incense bowl was burning away, keeping the room full of the smell of sage and saffron.

In bare feet, she padded silently down the hallway, the cold, smooth rock below her feet that had once been such a comfort, a feeling of home, now chilling her. This place was full of dangers she'd never realized, and she had to find a way to navigate them on her own.

The main hall opened ahead of her, and dinner was underway.

Everyone was there. Ford, Shem, Steve, Darcy, Ben, and Frankie the half-Jinn, half-lion shifters, and Asuga. They were all eating, and the only one who was talking was—no surprise—Steve. Asuga was curled up to him on one side, Darcy sat on his other shooting daggers from her eyes at the younger cheetah shifter.

"I can't believe she's sending us out. And for what? A loser." He slapped a hand on the table.

Darcy shook her head. "She must have reasons. I trust her. Even if it seems . . . strange."

Kiara slowed her steps, in part to not alert them to her presence, in part because she wanted to hear more of what was happening.

But Steve lifted his head in her direction right away and had the nerve, the damn *nerve*, to wink at her.

Her spine bristled and if she'd been in her four-legged form, all the hair would have stood on her back right down to the tip of her tufted tail. She walked slowly to the side table where the food was laid out. She spooned up the soup, and put together a large plate of food, mixed meats and a few slices of flatbread. Balancing it all carefully, she turned and walked back out of the room.

Footsteps behind her, quick, hurried and heavy, sent her pulse hammering in her throat. She'd face

Steve one day. She was sure of it, but not now, not here. The timing was terrible and she couldn't risk it, not for Merlin's sake.

"Hey."

A breath of air whooshed out of her and she turned her head to the older, crazier lion that she was less than sure of even if he was Zam's uncle. "Shem, what are you doing? I'm still not feeling well." She didn't take another step, though, because what if he figured out that she wasn't sick? It would blow her cover and Merlin's.

"Are you with child?" His question was blunt and hurt her in a way she was trying not to think about.

An answer didn't want to form on her lips as she struggled to find the words. So she just shook her head.

Shem leaned down until his mouth was barely off her ear. "You need to tell them you are, or they will want to know why you are really sick, and then the real secret you hide will be found out. I think you don't want that."

Her eyes went wide and the plate rattled in her hand as a tremor ran through her. Shem smiled. "Here, let me help you, you must be awfully tired."

Suddenly Steve's wink made more sense. He thought she was still with child? But he knew, she'd told him that she'd lost the baby when they'd been trapped by the Jinn. The stress had been too much, and the animal side of her aborted so she could escape easier. Shem took both bowl and plate from her and followed her to her room.

She moved on autopilot, opening the door and letting him in, then shutting the door behind them both. "How did you know?"

Shem lowered the bowl and plate to a side table, then crouched next to Merlin. He waved a palm in front of Merlin's face before he answered. "I saw you take him out."

"I took him out the back, toward the cemetery," she said.

"But you were gone a long time." Shem kept a hand floating above Merlin's body. "Long enough that I noticed. Far longer than needed to dig a shallow hole and bury him. So I followed his smell, and it led all the way to your window." He lifted both bushy eyebrows at her and she frowned.

"I used a scent diffuser."

"But I was looking for him. I thought the same thing as you, that if he wasn't dead, we need him." Shem sat back and gave a heavy sigh. "You did good with him. But you need to sleep. I will watch over him."

Kiara's jaw twitched and she reached out with one hand, placing it against Shem's face, then slowly curled her fingers into his skin. "If you try to fuck me over, Shem, I will tear your goddam throat out if it's the last thing I do."

He raised a hand and placed it over hers, slowly

loosening her fingers. "I would expect nothing less from someone who has learned from Zam."

A flush of warmth, maybe a little pride, slid through Kiara as she lowered herself to the pallet bed she'd made on the floor. "Wake me if something happens."

Shem nodded, blew out the candles in the room and then sat next to her. "You got it, Alpha."

KIARA WOKE HOURS LATER. THE DOOR WAS CLOSED still, and the smell of two men filled her nostrils, reminding her that she was not alone in trying to get help to Zam. She sat up, wondering what had pulled her from her sleep. The clatter out her window drew her to her feet, and she was at the shutters in seconds, peering out. All she could see was the hind ends of two horses, the riders indistinguishable under the cover of darkness.

A tap on the door spun her around, and a whiff of male lion made her hurry to the door. "What do you want, Ford?"

"She sent them after Zam, Kiara." The sorrow in his voice was thick enough to cut through every defense she'd been putting up. "Zam is in trouble, and Ishtar sent Steve and Darcy in to finish the job."

Kiara flung the door open, already knowing what she had to do. "Then why are you standing there looking sad? We have to stop them." She looked back at Shem who was awake, barely. "Get him," she pointed at Merlin. "We leave now."

Though how she was going to get them past Ishtar, she wasn't fully sure, but she had to try. Damn it, she had to try.

7

ZAMIRA

The fog around us cleared away with Maks's magic pushing it along, and the sun was suddenly there on the eastern horizon, lighting up every horrible thing we faced. Like . . . the entire army of reptilian creatures that encircled us, too many deep to ever survive. Hundreds, we faced hundreds of armed creatures that stood on two feet, then dropped to their bellies to run across the hard ground like big-ass geckos easily over twelve feet long when taking their tails into account. Their ranks formed and reformed as they shifted around us, waiting for some signal to attack.

Maks and Bryce were to the left of me. "Can you call any gorcs?" I whisper-shouted at Maks, trying to think of just how we were going to do this. How the fuck would we survive?

He shook his head. "Nothing close enough." His

eyes met mine, speaking volumes. He was exhausted, all his power used up between battle after battle.

So there it was. My answer was simple—we wouldn't be seeing the end of the day.

My eyes found Bryce's and I saw there what I already knew. There would be no getting out of this. I backed Balder up until we were side by side again with Maks and Batman. I looked down at Bryce who was on my other side, bright red blood on his muzzle.

"They taste like desert lizards," he said. "I think she's made them bigger, stronger, just for this."

I didn't know how that was possible, not when she didn't have the stone of creation. I reached for the red stone that had belonged to the Wyvern. But the thing was, I had nothing left in me as far as the magic went either. I was tapped out.

"She drained us," Maks said softly, "knowing we'd throw everything at the frogs, taking Lila and Trick out of the picture, then sending this army against us."

Checkmate indeed.

I swallowed hard. "Then we go down swinging." I looked to Bryce. "Sorry to bring you back to this side of living, only to get you killed again."

He snorted. "At least we go down together, as family."

"Give us the stones." The voice rippled not from one throat but all of them at once.

I shrugged, feeling that strange sense of knowing

how this would end, and embracing it. To Balder, I whispered, "If I fall, you run. Run fast and hard, find Merlin if you can, get you and Lila out of here."

He looked up and back at me and gave me a slow nod. I took my pouch with the stones from my waist and tucked them into the saddlebag with Lila.

To the reptiles, I smiled. "Make me."

There was one more moment of pause, like either they were shocked, or Ollianna wasn't sure she'd heard me correctly—because again, I was certain she'd be watching this.

The reptile men rushed us, and the fight was on like Donkey Kong, as my father had said more than once, even if I didn't have a clue what he meant. It sounded good.

I swung the flail, slammed it into the head of one reptile as I spun Balder to the side, pulled the spiked ball free, and swung it across my body to the other side of us. The weapon didn't stick as hard as it could, and even as I thought it, the spiked balls smoothed out, the metal becoming as slick as if they'd only been made that way, and they bounced off heads and bodies even better, making for faster wounds. Better injuries that didn't slow me down.

Thank you, magic weapon. The handle warmed against my palm.

All around me, bones broke and snapped as Maks and Bryce hammered at the reptiles, the roar of Bryce as he challenged them, the boom of my shotgun as I pulled it loose and used it until the shells were spent, the grenades gone.

I dropped the gun as the sun rose in the sky, brightening the clouds. Maks bled from multiple cuts and bites on his arms, Batman had a chunk of flesh missing from his hip, Balder had bites all down his side.

It won't be enough. You need to dig deep and pull on the magic. You have to kill them the way you did the frogs. Marsum's voice was loud inside my head, distracting me. A reptile grabbed me and pulled me out of the saddle, its clawed hands digging into me hard, squeezing me tightly. I twisted in its hold as I fell, shifting out of instinct back to four legs.

I landed lightly, knowing there was a chance to save my brother and Maks. "I have the stones!" I yelled and then bolted, using my small size to my advantage, running for all I was worth, dodging between the reptile men's legs, over their bodies as they dropped to all fours. I bounded and spun, just small enough to be hard to catch, big enough to be too fast.

I was at the edge of the reptiles now and I could see the open desert. I would take them west, I knew it was a chance that wasn't great, that maybe I wouldn't get far but . . . everyone else would be alive. Lila, Maks, Bryce, Balder and Batman would be able to go on.

Balder would run, the way I'd told him to.

Idiot, they won't go on, not without you. You are the driving force here.

"Well, help me then!" I snapped as I passed by the last of the reptile creatures. I dared a glance back and they were following me, the seething mass of scale-armored bodies and flashing teeth as they scooted across the ground. Dust flew up around them. I bolted, running as fast as I could, stretching out and for just a moment wishing I had Lila's ability to shift size.

I'd been that jungle cat I was meant to be just once, and to own that shape again would give me the chance I needed . . . I didn't close my eyes but wished with all the hope and energy I had in me that my luck would turn for once and I would be able to at least die with my real four-legged form.

That I wouldn't die hissing and spitting, crushed in a set of hands that could easily wrap around my entire body.

The tang of metal bouncing off a rock next to me scooted me sideways. More thwaps around me said it all. The reptile boys had found something to shoot at me.

Over and over, the metallic bolts hit the ground around me to either side as I zigzagged, running flat out for a section of high rocks that I could use for cover.

Belly low to the ground, I gave it all I had, turning on what was left of my speed, panting for breath.

I wasn't thinking about surviving, just thinking about giving the others a way to escape. Giving those I loved a chance to get away, to find a life outside of all these fights, away from the struggle to survive. That was all I could think as I raced away, drawing the creatures to me and away from Maks, Bryce, Balder, Lila and Batman.

A tear caught at the corner of my eye, blurring my vision. Something slammed into me, an armored head crashed into my right side and flung me up so high that my legs splayed out. The moment slowed as I spun high through the air. The reptilian creatures had followed me, and Maks and Bryce were harrying the rear, but for the most part they were being ignored.

If you're going to make a go at surviving, whatever it is you plan, you must do it now.

Marsum's words unlocked something in me, a fatality that meant there was nothing I wouldn't do. Nothing I wouldn't see through to have another look at one more sunrise, one more sunset, one more touch from Maks, one more laugh with my brother, one more fight of who knew Shakespeare best with Lila.

The moment picked up speed as I fell, landing on the back of one of the reptiles. I dug my flail-strengthened claws into his back, dragging them through his flesh and letting the magic of the weapon drain his energy straight into me. They came at me over and over and I bounced from one to the other, taking hits, but mostly able to dodge them as I took in their life-force. The blows I felt were glancing, and they healed quicker than ever, the power of the flail doing its job.

I was too small, too quick, and the energy I was gaining from them through the flail made me faster until the world around me was a blur.

The air around me shimmered as I bit into the scaled hand of a reptile creature. He let out a booming bellow as I crunched through flesh and tore the muscle away from the bone. I bounced away from him and landed hard, heavier than before. The air continued to shimmer around me, heating under my fur as though I were bathing in the sun and not fighting for my life.

I didn't have time to question what was happening, though I could feel the shift sliding through my bones, could feel the power of the jungle cat sweeping over me. A power I'd felt before and it was not my own.

Ollianna . . . she could see through the eyes of her creatures and she could see they couldn't catch me as a small house cat.

But the jungle cat I was meant to be was bigger, and while not slower, there would be more of me to grab. She'd done this before, given me a moment I thought was a gift. Now I understood it for what it was.

A tie to me, a tie to this side of me that she had her proverbial claws in.

Shit. Fuck. Bitch!

I let out a hiss and it wasn't a house cat's vocal cords, but the snarling growl of that jungle cat that I wanted to be so badly. She'd done it to make me fail.

Not today, lizard queen. Not today.

"Even like this, I'm going to kick your ass, Ollianna!" I roared the words as my seemingly oversized paws flew at the reptile creatures, sending them flying with the blows. I grabbed them around their legs, snapped bones with a single bite, and generally caused far more destruction now that I was bigger. Stronger.

Maks and Bryce were yelling at me to hang on. They were coming.

Claws slashed through my side even though I tried to dodge, sending a searing pain across my ribs. I drew on the energy the flail had been absorbing and the wound healed, but how long could I keep this up? There was too much of me. I couldn't avoid the blows.

The flail will give you the energy you need to stop the reptiles, use the stones!

Sucking hard for air, I kept on fighting, barely able to think about magic, never mind actually use it as Marsum was suggesting.

Because I couldn't use the stones. I'd left them with Balder.

Either I was an idiot, or I was a genius. Because the stones were what Ollianna wanted, what Ishtar wanted and probably what the Emperor wanted. At least if I died here, the stones wouldn't end up in Ollianna's hands. At least, not right away.

Time slid by, ticking along; the sun moved through the sky and I moved with it, unable to see anything but the bodies piling up around me, feel the bite wounds on my flanks that weren't healing, the fatigue in my muscles as new, fresh reptiles came at me. Over and over.

I stumbled over a body and flung myself out of the way of long snapping jaw, the tips of the teeth catching at the skin under my neck and tearing at it. I kept rolling and realized that there was a change.

I had my back to the rocks I'd been running toward, and there were only a half-dozen lizard men left. Maks and Bryce and the two horses were behind them, and I was in front. We'd fucking done it.

Holy hand grenades, we'd done it.

My body trembled, and my lungs heaved for air as I panted hard, parched and exhausted in a way I'd never been, not in all the battles I'd faced. "Come on then, fuckers." I growled the words. "Let's finish this."

The lizard men looked to one another, dropped to the ground and . . . they shrunk. They reduced to the size of desert lizards and scooted away, heading south. All around us, the bodies of the reptile creatures we'd been fighting did the same, their large bodies turning into the creatures they'd been pulled from. Hundreds of tiny little desert lizards, dead.

My legs were shaking so badly, I could barely stand. I gave up and let myself fall flat on my belly, legs splayed out. If something came at us now, we were done. There was no fight left in me.

Which is why the sound of horse hooves coming from the east barely drew my head off the dusty ground. I blew out a breath, recognizing the horses before I saw the two people on them.

They slowed as they approached, blond hair glistening in the midday sun. Midday, maybe later.

We'd been fighting for hours and now mother-fucking, sheep-fucking Steve and Darcy showed up.

How was I not surprised?

8

M aks and Bryce moved as a unit, flanking one another as they inter-cepted Steve and Darcy riding into what should have looked like a massacre of ridicu-lous proportions. A bunch of tiny lizards blanketed the desert, I mean, how hard could it be to kill tiny lizards, right?

Steve's eyes swept the scene, and he looked at me. "Who is that?"

Oh, this was going to be rich. One of the things Steve had always enjoyed pointing out when we were together was that I was lucky to be with such a big strong lion, seeing as my own form was so useless.

How's this for useless, shithead?

I forced myself to my feet, stretching out and lashing my tail, feeling every inch the jungle cat. But even as I did, the magic Ollianna had put on me, stripping me of whatever curse I still had, faded. My body shimmered around me and my body slipped back to the six-pound house cat.

"It's me, asshole." I didn't want to shift back to two legs this exhausted, but I couldn't stand the condescension in his eyes. Even now, a small part of me wanted to shrink away from that look. A small part of me still hurt when those around me thought less of me.

I opened the doorway in my mind between four and two legs, and took a horrible, gut-wrenching step through. There was a moment where I thought maybe I wouldn't be able to do it, where every muscle in me seemed to get stuck.

That could not happen. I was not getting stuck between an animal and a human shape. I'd heard rumors of that happening, we all had. Of those who weren't strong enough getting jammed in between, part animal, part human, and stuck there the rest of their miserable lives.

Nope, not today.

With the last of my energy, drawing all I had from the flail and my own reserves, I pushed through.

A step stumbling forward, and Maks was there, catching me. I leaned into him, using the moment to whisper a warning. "He still belongs to Ish."

Maks nodded and helped me stand.

"How sweet. You like fucking the Jinn now?" Steve shook his head. "Talk about lowering your standards. Then again, it's not like you were going to get another shot at me." Steve's golden eyes glittered and danced, and it was in that moment I realized something.

He wanted me.

Maybe not because I was the best in bed, or because I was the most beautiful, but because I defied him. He wanted to win, and with me, he'd lost.

Bryce cut between us, a bigger lion than Steve ever was, blood coating a good part of his head. Darcy's eyes went straight to him, and I could all but see her calculating which male lion was stronger. I grabbed my brother by the tail, tugging him back. "Wait. Before we kill them, I want to know why they're here."

Bryce shot me a look over his shoulder, and gave me a nod, not unlike Maks. They were letting me speak, letting me be the alpha of our pride.

I drew a breath and let go of Maks to stand on my own two feet, even if it was hard to stay upright. I looked from Steve to Darcy and back again. "What do you want? Or maybe I should ask you what the bitch you work for wants?"

Darcy startled and then relaxed. I wanted to roll my eyes but managed to keep from doing so. I didn't really want to antagonize them. They were fresh. We were not. The fight would be brutal, and I didn't want to chance that they would hurt us worse than we already were.

"Ishtar," Steve said, and then curled his lips. Oh, good, whatever he'd been sent to do or say was not something he wanted. Which meant he probably wasn't here to kill us. Interesting.

"Did you escape her?" Maks asked. "Is that why you're here?"

Darcy shook her head. "No, she sent us. To *help* you."

My eyebrows could not have shot higher into my hairline if I'd painted them there. "What?"

I had to have heard wrong. There was no way Ishtar would have sent them to help us. Spy on us, hurt us, harry us the way that Ollianna was, but help us, never.

Darcy gave a delicate shrug. "She did not tell us why, only that we were to ride here as fast as we could and help you against a great battle you were facing from some other witch . . . Olivier or something like that."

I frowned, calculating the distance between the Stockyards and where we were. Four hours at a hard ride at best. "When did you leave?"

Steve smiled. "Midnight."

Nearly twelve hours before. I snorted. "We don't need your kind of help, so, off you fuck, and tell Ishtar to do the same."

I went to Balder and ran my hands over his face, neck and body, checking him for wounds. I found a number of scrapes and cuts, then checked Lila again and found her curled tightly around the bag of stones. I pulled them from her tiny grasp and attached them to my own belt. "Maks, you want to check Batman?"

"Already on it. I've got the hacka paste if you want some."

"Bryce, let me put some on you too," I said as my brother shifted back to two legs. Buck naked and covered in wounds. Again, nothing was major. Because the creatures hadn't been after him. Ollianna thought she could just overwhelm us with numbers, kill me and be done with it.

Joke was on that dumb-as-a-rock toad.

The thing with Steve was he hated to be ignored, and Maks and Bryce, goddess love them, followed my lead. A glutton for being the center of attention, it wouldn't take long for Steve to . . .

"Don't you fucking ignore me!" he roared. "I'm here to protect your useless ass, for reasons I don't understand. She should let you die as far as I'm concerned!"

I kept my back to him, treating my horse's wounds, and then Bryce's after he'd slipped on some pants. "Steve, you can go right back to Ishtar and tell her I said she can fuck off too. I don't want you here. No one wants you here."

I smoothed Balder's mane to one side, loosened his girth and started walking him away from the scene of all the little lizards. My stomach rumbled and I made a quick, brutal decision and scooped up a half-dozen of the small reptiles. They were good eating, and I was starving.

I wasn't sure when we'd get a chance to hunt, or even stop, and we needed to take advantage of the unintentional bounty. I motioned for Bryce and Maks to do the same.

"We can't go back," Darcy said. "We were sent to protect you, all the way to the Emperor. If we return, she'll kill us."

I snorted. "Sounds like a great person to follow if you ask me. Really, a brilliant move on your part to throw your lot in with her."

"We had no choice," Darcy said, softening. Another time I would have believed her voice, the tone in it. I spun and pointed one of the flopping dead lizards at her.

"There is always a choice, Darcy. Just like you had a choice." I gave her a wink as if it were a big secret between us that she'd slept with Steve the first time in an effort to steal him from me. I mean, what's a little husband fucking between friends, right?

Gods, I'd been a fool to believe her then.

I looked at Steve. "You know what, she told me that you made her fuck you the first time. That she had no choice. And I believed her. So if she can make me believe her lies, Steve, you'd best watch yourself. Because she's eyeing up Bryce like he's the next hot meal on the plate."

Chew on that, you snaggy shithole of a friend.

Bryce jerked like I'd slapped him on the ass; Darcy paled, her jaw ticked, and for the first time, I think I saw a bit of the real her. Angry, jealous, and willing to do anything to claw her way up the ranks. Including pretending to be the friend of the girl who was married to the strongest lion of the pride.

I kept on walking, Balder next to me, Maks and Bryce beside me in a matter of seconds. Steve and Darcy were behind us as if they weren't sure if they should follow or not. I didn't give a shit either way. Bryce had the slightest limp to his stride. He pulled on a shirt as we walked. "That was . . . unreal back there."

"Oh, she's always been a bitch. She just hid it well." I waved him off.

"No, not them." He glanced back, and I did the same. The pair of them were following. "You fighting, Zam. I've never seen anything like it. It was like you were a whirlwind. They couldn't catch you." He slung an arm across my shoulders and pulled me into the one-armed hug that he was so good at. "Remind me not to fight you. Ever."

I looked up at him. "I was a six-pound house cat for half of it."

"I know. And that was the most terrifying part." He wasn't laughing at me, not in the least. "You moved like you were riding lightning and every-where you touched they went down. They didn't want to fight you. They started balking partway through, holding back, which gave you more time. We were killing them from the back and they barely looked at us. It wasn't until you turned into the jungle cat that they got bold again."

Maks grunted. "That didn't slow you down much, though I suspect that was the goal. You hit as hard, as fast. Your brother is right. You were amazing to watch. I don't think Ollianna knew what she was going up against."

Bryce chuckled. "I felt rather useless myself."

"Never," I leaned into him, holding him tightly, "I was fighting for you and Maks. For Balder and Lila." I wasn't sure how to feel about what they were saying. I'd just been fighting. Doing what I'd been doing my whole life. "However, I do need to rest. And eat."

We were between the large rocks, now, weaving our way through. I knew the area better than most, being so close to the Stockyards as it was. "There's a good spot with a small spring where we can take a break for the rest of the day."

Steve brushed past us. "I'll lead."

Darcy followed him, her back stiff.

"You want to argue with them?" Maks asked. I shook my head.

"Not today." I paused and went to the saddlebags, pulling Lila out. I cradled her to my chest. "I don't want them to know she can shift size. But that means I need to find a way to wake her now."

Maks put his palm over her. "What if you go to sleep, go into the dreamscape and find her that way?"

I blinked up at him. "See, that's why I love you. You're a smart guy."

"I thought it was my good looks and charming magic." He laughed at me and Bryce mumbled something that sounded like *gross, get a room.*

With Lila's small, warm body close to me, and a plan to wake her in hand, anxiety that had been holding onto me slid away and I nearly went to my knees. Maks caught me with one arm around the waist. "Bryce, you want to get a bedroll ready for her."

"On it."

The two of them worked around me and the exhaustion took me, step by step. I barely made it to the blankets that Bryce laid out near the spring.

"What the hell? It's not nap time," Steve snapped. "We want to get going, get this show on the road and get you out of our hair."

Bryce let out a low rumbling growl and that was about the last of what I heard. Personally, I was fine with Bryce laying Steve low, but then Darcy would want Bryce. And there was no way in hell she was getting her claws into my brother.

No, he was far too good for her.

Sleep washed over me in a wave, but I fought the darkness that would be restful and forced myself into the dreamscape that the Emperor had built long before I'd been born. He'd done it so he could keep a hand on the world, watch what was happening and prepare for his eventual return. That had been his plan.

All along, I'd been trying to stop him, and now here I was, riding straight to him with a weapon that could release him from his prison.

The dreamscape mimicked the real world and I found myself lying on a bedroll next to the spring as it burbled and gurgled, Lila still tucked tightly in my arms.

"Lila, wake up." I gave her a little shake and she shivered in my arms, the most movement she'd made since she'd drank down the țuică. What had Trick said to her that sent her back to the camp so fast, and to drink down all that liquor?

What if it was a combination of heartache and alcohol keeping her under?

Seriously, I was going to kill that dragon the next time I saw him.

"No," she mumbled.

I looked around us, trying to think of something that would bring her around, but I doubted a bottle of țuică was a good idea after that last one. "I stumped Maks with a quote from Will."

One eye slid open a crack, then shut.

I smiled to myself. Whatever hold was on her, I was going to crack it. "'The barge she sat in, like a burnish'd throne, burn'd on the water.'"

Lila's body shivered again.

"I was surprised, and I told him that you'd have gotten it right off the bat. Hell, I'd bet money on you knowing." I ran my hand over her head. "Lila, come back to me."

"*Antony and Cleopatra,*" she grumbled. "How in the hell could he have not got that one?" Very slowly she lifted her head, her eyes still more closed than open. "What's wrong with me?"

I held her tight as I stood. "Ollianna drugged the țuică with something called golden marushka. And I'm guessing you and Trick had a fight?"

Lila went very still, and I thought she'd gone back to sleep until she crawled her way up to my shoulder and tucked her head against mine, hiding under my hair. "I should never have wanted to be big. It ruined everything."

I lifted a hand and rested it on her back. "You and me both."

Her tiny claws dug into the edge of my ear as a sob rippled out of her. "He . . . I caught up to him, and went small, thinking to surprise him. He was talking to another dragon."

I frowned. "Okay. Was it your father?"

"No, that would have been better," she whimpered and my stomach fell.

"He fucking didn't."

"Yes. He . . . never really liked me, Zam. He just knows that I'm heir to the throne, and the other dragons sent him after me. To bring me back. He said that he loved her."

I pulled her from my shoulder and held her tightly as she sobbed against my chest. "Men are assholes, they really are," I whispered.

"Even Maks?"

I smiled, though it was hard. "I had to suffer through Steve, Marsum, and Davin before I really got to have Maks in my life. And for that, I wouldn't change a thing. No matter how much heartache there was from those assholes."

I kept walking, climbing through the rocks while Lila sobbed her heart out, waiting for the worst of the storm to pass, and wishing I could kick Trick's ass repeatedly. "Is that why you didn't wake up?"

"I don't think so." She hiccupped down a final sob. "I can feel the magic in my system still."

"So not just sleep?"

She shook her head, jeweled eyes still glittering with tears. "No, I think maybe now that I know that it's the drink, I can push it elsewhere. But it has to wear off."

I didn't quite follow what she meant. "Explain that to me."

She tapped the claws on one foot against my collarbone. "The magic wants to attach to an aspect of me. Being awake is an aspect. Being able to shift sizes is an aspect. I think I can manipulate the magic to go there, so I can be awake. But I won't be able to shift sizes until it wears off."

I blew out a relieved sigh. "I'll take you awake, thank you. You're strong in your small size, Lila. I think this whole time we've been so focused on being what we think we're meant to be that we're missing out on the good of what we are."

I told her about the fight with the lizard men, about what Bryce had said and how I'd felt fighting both as a house cat and then as a jungle cat. There were positives in both, but I understood the smaller version better, knew how to fight in a way that I didn't as a big cat. Not everything translated along with the size. And I told her about Darcy and Steve, and that it was better that they didn't know she could shift sizes.

"Ollianna wants you to face Ishtar for her, then?" She braided my hair off to one side.

I shrugged. We were sitting on the top of the rocks looking out across the desert, toward the Stockyards where I'd started this journey so long ago. I felt like I could almost see . . . I frowned. "Lila, do you see that out there?"

I stood and she flew into the air, her wings flashing in the bright sun. "Yes, it's a body floating along. Weirdly. Very weirdly."

"Who the hell would be sleeping in the middle of the day?" I scrambled down the rocks and began to run toward the body. It wasn't the Emperor, and it wasn't Ishtar or Ollianna. Though all three could walk this realm, I had no doubt they were awake and working their magic on the goals they had set.

They didn't expect me to sleep during the day.

Or anyone else, for that matter.

The desert flew under my feet until I was close enough to the body floating along that I could see who it was.

"MERLIN?" I shouted his name and fell into step beside him, finally understanding how he was being carried. On a travois behind a horse, dragged away from the Stockyards.

I bent and brushed a hand over his face. "Merlin, wake the fuck up, man!"

He groaned and lifted a hand as if to bat me away. Lila landed on the travois next to him. "Yes, wake up!"

One eye opened. Just one, the other was stitched shut, and it was then that I saw just what bad shape he was in. "Hot crap on a camel's ass, what happened to you? And who are you with?"

"Wait for us," he breathed out the words, and his body faded from the dreamscape.

Wait for us. Who was he with? Flora? That seemed the most likely since they'd been traveling together. But that didn't tell me just what in the hell had happened to him.

"He's headed our way," Lila said. "Or where camp is anyway."

I looked at the distance. "They won't be more than a few hours."

Lila flew beside me as I jogged back to the camp—even if it was in the dreamscape, I didn't feel like exploring. The dreamscape was dangerous on a good day, and my day had been pretty shitty so far. Fighting off lizard men and ending with Steve and Darcy as escorts to the Emperor. What a crock of shit that was. The reality was likely far more sinister. If they had a chance, I had little doubt they'd kill us, take the flail and take it to the Emperor themselves.

Even as I thought it, the truth settled in around me. Fucking hell, this was the last thing I needed.

Strike that, the last thing I needed was a wounded Merlin headed my way, but I was about to get that too.

Yippy fucking skippy.

9

KIARA

Getting out of the Stockyards had been far easier than she'd thought. With Shem and Ford helping, she'd managed to load Merlin onto a stretcher and tie it behind Buttercup, the pretty little palomino she'd always enjoyed riding.

"Why did you send the kids into the hills?" Ford asked as they rode out. "You don't think Ishtar . . ."

"Yes, I do," Kiara said. Benji had agreed to go, scooped up Frankie and they'd made a run for it. They could survive there. She was sure of it. Asuga hadn't been interested in leaving.

And Ishtar had been asleep in her chamber.

Asleep.

It made Kiara nervous that they were being set up.

Ford and Shem had each taken a horse, and they'd

SHANNON MAYER

ridden out less than two hours after Steve and Darcy. The problem was, Steve and Darcy had ridden as if they were out for a pleasure cruise down the river Nile.

"Why are they going so slow?" she'd asked Shem. Ford was sullen at best, barely speaking. As much as he wanted to go after Zam, he still had his panties in a twist over the fact that she'd sent him away and chosen someone else. Kiara understood, though, why Zam had done it. Ford was strong, and when he'd arrived at the Stockyards, Ishtar had drawn off his strength instead of the children's. He was being a hard-headed fool to not see that Zam had made the right choice, as hard as it was. That was the cost of being an alpha, making choices no one else wanted to.

"My guess is they don't want to do whatever it is that Ishtar has sent them to do." Shem spoke quietly, they all did. Even though they were a good distance back, there wasn't much to hide them from Darcy or Steve if one of them should look back. It was a testament to their arrogance that neither one so much as glanced over their shoulders.

"But she was sending them after Zam." Kiara frowned. "Wasn't she?"

"That's what we all heard," Ford spoke finally. "If it was to kill her, he'd be hurrying. I agree."

Shem gave a low hum. "Maybe they've not been sent to kill her, but to capture her? Is that possible?"

"But even that, Steve would be ecstatic to do," Kiara said. "He . . . he hated her in a way that can only come from having loved someone once." She worried at her bottom lip, thinking. "I wish Merlin was awake."

Merlin, of course, passed out in the stretcher, was of little use and they couldn't make much headway with him anyway. So, in a strange way, it was good that Darcy and Steve were dawdling their way toward their destination.

The night passed, and by midday they had closed the gap even further on the pair ahead of them. At least she thought they had until Steve spurred his horse forward, and he and Darcy took off.

"Shit," she growled, wanting to go after them. "Ford, stay here with Merlin and Shem."

She cut Buttercup from the stretcher, letting it drop hard to the ground. Merlin groaned, but there was no time. She booted her horse forward before they could argue with her. She wasn't going to let Steve win whatever game Ishtar had set him up to play.

Buttercup raced across the ground and Kiara urged her on, the way Zam had taught her to ride. A whiff of death caught at her nose and she slowed the mare, scenting the air and changing her direction slightly.

What she found confused her more than anything. A thousand or more tiny desert lizards were strewn about. Most of them around an empty spot, as if they had been fighting a single person. Her heart was racing as she visualized the fight happening. Whatever the lizards were, she doubted they'd been as they were now.

The paw prints she could see in the center were not lion, but they were a big cat mixed with that of a small house cat. "Zam?"

Kiara turned and scented the air again, found the trail she was looking for and booted her horse forward. Through the twisting rocks, she raced, the smell of lion and horses growing stronger with each stride.

A straight stretch rose ahead of her, and at the end were Steve and Darcy's horses . . . and Balder and Batman.

Her heart tangled in her throat as she raced down the track, anger flaring in her gut. If Steve had hurt her family, she was going to slaughter him on the spot.

Two men stood up in her way as she drew close. She recognized Maks right away, but it took her a moment to realize Bryce was *standing* in front of her. Her lips parted and she breathed out a sigh of relief, knowing that if Maks and Bryce were here, Zam would be okay.

But she still had to ask. "Zam's okay?"

Bryce grinned up at her. "Sleeping, but okay."

"Who the fuck cares?" Steve commented.

Kiara slid off Buttercup's back and strode over to him, every inch of her bristling. She jammed a finger into his chest, hard enough to shove him backward. "Everyone but you, sheep fucker."

She turned her back on him, and that was her mistake.

Fingers tangled into her hair and yanked her back, exposing her throat. "You are no alpha."

A bellow of a roar shook the rocks around them, Bryce coming at them, and it was the distraction she needed. Steve's fingers loosened a fraction and she spun and drove her elbow into his solar plexus hard enough to feel the bone crack. Or maybe it was her elbow, she didn't know and didn't care. She pulled back and drove it in again, and he let go of her hair completely.

She stood as he bent over, trying to find his breath. "Bryce, would you keep Darcy off me?"

"My pleasure," he growled as he leapt between her and the oncoming Darcy. Both were in lion form, both were snarling. But none of that mattered.

Kiara grabbed Steve by the hair and slammed his face into the rock wall. Just once, that was all she needed to do. He slid to the ground, blood pouring from his nose, still struggling to breathe. She leaned over him and whispered in his ear, "You. Do. Not. Rule. Me."

He lifted his head, enough to look her in the eye, and the contempt was as thick as molasses and just as dark. His blood trickled down to his mouth, and it coated his lips and teeth. "Finish it, then. If you're so tough."

She smiled then, and let him see all the anger, all the hurt and pain he'd caused. "What you did to me was bad enough, but what you did to Zam was worse. I'll let her kill you. I just wanted to get my blows in before you were dead."

Deliberately, very deliberately, she turned her back on him and walked the distance to where Maks stood, watching.

"I've been waiting to do that," she said, a little embarrassed. Maks gave her a smile and nodded.

"I think we'd all like our turn to beat his ass."

That drew a laugh from her until she saw Zam sleeping on the bedroll behind him. She hadn't moved through all the commotion. "Is she really okay?"

"She'll be fine. She just needs rest." Maks sighed and Kiara took note of the dark shadows under his eyes, the pallor of his skin.

"Looks like you could use some sleep too." She nodded. "Go, lie down with her. I'll keep an eye on the two idiots."

There was a feminine gasp from the other side of the camp. Bryce padded over, and Kiara had to stop herself from letting her hand touch his thick mane. He rolled his head, giving her a single look. "Good job. Looks like we're going to have some strong women finally."

A flush of pride slid through her. "It started with Zam," she said.

"That it did." He yawned. "You good if I sleep?"

"I have backup coming," she said.

"Backup?" Darcy snapped the question. "How did you get away from the Stockyards?"

Kiara waited until Bryce and Maks were lying next to Zam, flanking her. Keeping her safe even in sleep. A glimmer of blue scales under Zam's arm was all she could see of Lila. Good enough.

Kiara caught up Buttercup, apologizing for the rough run.

"She asked you a question," Steve spat through what sounded like a mouthful of blood.

Finished with her horse, at her own speed, she turned and looked at the two would-be alphas. "It was rather simple."

"Simple? Then why didn't you do it sooner?" Darcy shot a look at Steve that spoke volumes. They had wanted to get away too but hadn't figured out how.

Kiara crouched next to the spring and scooped up water for herself, then made herself busy, filling water buckets for the horses. "Because I had someone I was looking after."

"The baby," Steve said.

"No, you dumbass. I lost the baby when I was

taken by the Jinn!" She turned a glare on him. "No, I was caring for someone else. So I had to wait until he was able to travel." She was avoiding telling them just how she'd gotten away from the Stockyards because she doubted they'd believe her.

For all that was holy in this desert land, she wasn't sure she'd have believed what had happened if she herself hadn't been in the center of it.

She settled for something close to the truth, but seriously oversimplifying it. "What happened is between Ishtar and myself. She didn't tell me to pass it on to you two."

She'd seen the mage in her chamber sleeping and had moved to slip away when her voice had whispered through the night air.

She is our only hope, Kiara, protect her.

Locking eyes with Darcy first, she waited for the other female to drop her gaze, which Darcy did. Then to Steve.

"You aren't stronger than me," he growled, anger and maybe even hatred flashing in his eyes. "That was a fluke."

Kiara lifted her chin and looked down her nose at him. "You can tell yourself that all you want if it helps you to sleep at night. I don't for one second think that you're actually going to help Zam. I think you'll try to hurt or even kill her the first chance you get. But let me make this very clear, Steven," he flinched when she used his full name, "you won't just have to go through Bryce and Maks, you'll have to go through me first."

"And me."

They all turned as Shem stepped into view, Ford following him. "Me too, sheep fucker."

Steve's face all but purpled. "I did not fuck any sheep!"

Of all the things to set him off, Kiara was shocked that was it. Not the threat to his life, not the threat to his standing in the pride, but his reputation as a sheep fucker.

Kiara waited for Shem and Ford to draw close before she checked on Merlin.

Whispers between Steve and Darcy were immediate, but she didn't care. They weren't the important ones here. Not by a long shot.

10

ZAMIRA

I was surrounded by warmth, the smell of Maks under my nose, the distant smell of lion that was my brother, Lila muttering in her sleep in my arms. This was good, this was home, and I didn't want to wake up. But there was something, or someone, less than pleasant breaking through the heavy sleep that I'd been so happy to stay in.

"She can't sleep the whole day away! We have to get moving, so wake her pansy house cat ass up!" Steve's voice cut through it all, and for just a moment I thought it could be just a shitty dream, and maybe I could ignore it and go back to sleep.

"She's always been weak," Darcy's voice added weight to the bad dream. "But this is ridiculous. She fought a bunch of tiny lizards, and is exhausted enough to sleep the entire day away?"

SHANNON MAYER

I opened my eyes to see Maks staring into my face. "Hey, lizard slayer."

My lips twitched as he lifted a hand and cupped the side of my face, his thumb running over my cheek, which sent a thrill right through me. I still couldn't believe we'd beaten the odds, that he was with me.

Technically, I am still with you too. Though I suppose it's poor form to hit on your daughter-in-law.

I groaned. "Shut it, Marsum."

Damn him, he had to just be part of this still, didn't he?

Yes. You will miss me one day, little cat. You will miss having me to talk to.

Maks leaned in close. "Tell him to piss off."

I kissed Maks, speaking against his lips. "Already done."

"Hungry?" he asked.

As soon as I thought about food, my stomach snarled and hunger pangs so strong they could have been cramps shot through my belly.

"Yes," Lila stretched in my arms, jamming a wing in my face and in Maks's. "I'm starving."

"Nice to see you awake." Maks poked a finger at her belly.

She snapped at him. "How could you not know it was *Antony and Cleopatra*? Seriously, I think less of you now, you know that, right?"

"What?" The furrow in his brows made me

124

chuckle as I sat up, turned, and then assumed I was still dreaming.

Because what the hell were Kiara, Shem, Ford, and what looked like . . . "Merlin." I was up and moving, my stomach forgotten as I hurried toward the stretcher.

"What happened to him?"

Kiara was beside me in a flash, her eyes full of worry. "Ishtar. She tried to kill him and had me take his body to the graveyard."

"And," Merlin said softly, "she decided to torture me by keeping me alive."

I put a hand over his. "You probably deserved it."

"Oh, more than deserved it." He opened his one good eye. "Ishtar does not want us to help one another."

"Which means we have to stay together." I squeezed his hand.

A grunt from the peanut gallery turned me to see Steve standing there with his hands on his hips, just being a dick as usual. "He'll slow us down."

"How long it takes us to get to the Emperor doesn't matter, only that we go." I grinned. "Capiche?"

Steve shook his head. "I want to be done with you," he made a sweeping gesture that took us all in, "as soon as possible."

"Then go," Kiara snapped. "We don't need you."

Gods, she'd grown up in the last little while. "Kiara is right; we don't need you. Either of you."

He shook his head. "Not that simple. I have a message for the Emperor from Ishtar."

Darcy startled; obviously he'd kept her out of that loop. Good, let her see that he was always going to be full of secrets and lies. He was not a good man. He'd never been a good man. Which goes to show how broken I was in my own self when I was with him, to believe he was the best I could do. Kiara looked at me and I gave her a nod, seeing the same understanding in her eyes.

"Leave him behind," Steve said. "We don't need him."

Lila shot up into the air. "'Lord, what fool this mortal be!'" Sure she was paraphrasing, but it worked.

"I do know that one," Maks drawled.

Lila fanned her wings right in Steve's face. "You're an idiot. Merlin is the Emperor's son. Who if not him has more knowledge of what we are facing?"

Steve shook his head. "I'm not facing him, just giving him the message."

A low, croaking laugh rolled from Merlin. "You ever hear the saying, don't kill the messenger? That will not apply to the Emperor."

I watched as Steve's face paled. "Maybe you should just run away," I said.

"He can't. Neither of us can," Darcy whispered.

126

"She put a spell on us. If we don't do as we've been tasked—"

"NO!" Steve roared the word. "Do not tell them."

Well, shit.

I shrugged as if it didn't matter to me, because really, it didn't. If Steve and Darcy ended up cursed or spelled, that was no loss to me. If they died, sadly, it was no loss to anyone. Whatever happened to them meant nothing, not one iota of camel crap to the world, or anyone in it.

"Do what you want," I said. "We'll go at the speed our weakest member dictates, and right now, that's Merlin. That's how it works in a pride, Steve. Even you know that." I wasn't about to tell Steve that I was going to try to heal Merlin the second I had enough energy. I could do it, with Maks's help. But it was draining, and my reserves were low at best.

Goddess only knew when Ollianna would make her next play for our lives. I needed to be ready for that, not worrying about the sheep fucker.

Kiara snorted in Steve's direction. "I will pray that your death comes slowly, and with great dishonor."

"Oh," Lila stage whispered, "I like her more and more. I wish that same thing on a certain dragon. And that his wings and pecker melt off in an acid rain."

She did a barrel roll and landed on Maks's shoulder. "You're about the only male around here worth saving right now. Even if you are a Toad."

Ford, Shem, and even Merlin gave a communal "hey" that Lila ignored.

Maks shot me a questioning look and I shook my head, mouthing "later."

Kiara bent over a small fire and pulled off a skewer of lizard. "Eat, it'll help."

I didn't argue and found myself tearing through not one, not two, but three of the lizards I'd killed earlier.

The talk around me was a flow that I listened to, not interrupting. From what I could tell, Steve and Darcy had left, and Kiara, Ford, and Shem had chosen to follow with Merlin in tow in case the first two were out to cause me trouble.

"What about the younglings?" I asked around licking my fingers.

"I sent Benji and Frankie out to the hills. Ishtar seems uninterested in them, as if they don't really count." Kiara tipped her head. "It's strange."

"Not so strange," Merlin said. "Lions are her animal to draw from, but it's easier to draw from those she has ties with. And despite her taking my life-force to heal her own body, the reality is she's still weak."

I looked at him, seeing the wounds that he claimed had been on Ishtar, the wounds that the Jinn had inflicted on her at the Oracle's Haunt, and a question curled through me, finding its way to my mouth. "How was she able to take your energy in the first place? What ties did she have to you? Shouldn't you have been able to deny her?"

He cleared his throat and grimaced as though even that pained him. "Long time ago, she and I . . ." He trailed off and I doubted very much that he was sleeping. More like avoiding saying what we all heard without words.

Merlin and Ish? I wanted to bang my head against one of the oversized boulders.

"Seriously? Is there anyone you haven't fucked besides me and Kiara?" I grumbled.

"Darcy." Merlin looked up at me and gave a long slow blink that I supposed was a wink. "And Flora."

Now that one surprised me, with the way Merlin had stared after the priestess of Zeus. Not that she had returned the looks, but I'd made an assumption that there had already been a consummation of that relationship. "Where is Flora, anyway?" I crouched beside Merlin.

"I don't know," he said. "I blacked out and when I woke up, I was with Ishtar in the Stockyards."

A snort from behind us turned me around, twisting on the balls of my feet. Steve was mounted up on his horse. "Does any of this matter?"

I smiled up at him. "Yes."

"How?"

I sighed. "If I have to explain it to you, then you really are the dumbass I've always claimed you to be."

A tug along my spine, the flail reminding me that

it was indeed time to go was a far better spur than Steve being Steve.

With a quick wave of my hand, I got everyone going. "Mount up, everyone, before Steve gets his thong wrapped up so tight, he hangs himself by his balls."

I helped Kiara get the travois tied to the back of Ford's horse and took note that Ford hadn't so much as said hello. There was no way around this moment, but I wouldn't have it in front of Steve. That would only give him more reason to be difficult, and honestly with three virile male lions, all feeling the confines of being close to one another, I needed to keep things as civil as possible. At least for now.

Our new group, more than tripled in size, got moving, heading toward the Emperor's Throne. I let Steve and Darcy lead, and motioned for Lila to stay with Maks, which she happily did, chirping something into his ear as I put some distance between us.

I held Balder back so I was riding next to Ford who brought up the rear with Merlin.

"Hey, how are you?" I said softly. He'd been my rock when I'd needed it, after I'd lost Maks. Sure, I'd figured out quickly that my love for Maks wasn't going away, but in my darkest hours, Ford had been there, and he'd held me. Just that, just a love so straightforward that he could offer it to me without expecting anything in return. And I was grateful for it. He'd gone when I'd sent him—although not really willingly—to protect the others of the pride that Ishtar had taken. Ford had been the enforcer and protector I'd needed him to be in our pride.

"Alpha." He bowed his head in my direction, his voice flat and carefully emotionless. "Can I help you with something?"

My lips tightened and a flare of anger shot through me. "Really?"

He looked straight ahead. "You give the commands, and I follow. That's all you ever wanted from me."

I pulled a short riding quirt that I rarely used from the back of my saddle and swung it, smacking him across the arm. "You ass. Did you even say hello to your brother? Did you even ask how we were? How we survived?"

He shot me a surprised look, his jaw dropping. "Did you just hit me?"

"Did you really think that . . ." I shook my head, not sure how to tell him that I loved him, that if Maks had died, or if Maks had not been in my life, I could see my future with Ford. I could see us laughing and holding each other through dark and cold days. But how cruel would it have been to tell him those things, to tell him that he was second in my heart? Even if second in my heart was pretty amazing when I thought there would never be anyone in there again, never mind two amazing men.

There was no way he would appreciate that, no

way he could understand. I had to try to make him understand how much he meant to me, though. I had to get him to see that he was important. That he was meant to be here with all of us.

"Did I think what?" His voice softened and I took note that we'd fallen farther behind.

"That I didn't love you?" I wanted to curse myself for saying those words. "Ford . . . in another place . . . another time . . ." I looked away from him as the emotions flowed over me. Because I'd seen into his heart when I'd healed him, when he'd been dying and I'd brought him back. And I was pretty sure I didn't deserve his love, not like that. I'd seen the depth of his feelings and just how he viewed me, and it changed me. "Maks is my heart," I whispered. "The other half of my soul. But I see in you a good man, one that . . ." Gods, this was hard.

"One that you don't want to be with," he said simply, looking away from me.

"That's the problem," I said softly. "I want you to stay in the pride. I want you close to me for different reasons than I want Maks close to me. Maks and I are made the same, part Jinn, part shifter, and there are pieces of that no full-blooded shifter will ever understand." Ford shot a look at me, his eyes widening. I nodded, and forced myself to go on. "But that doesn't mean I can't see all the things that could have been. Does that make sense?"

Ford frowned, his hands tightening on the edge of

the saddle. "I've never felt like this about anyone, Zam. I've met other shifters before. I've been with my share of them to pass long lonely nights, but I can't seem to shake this feeling that I've always been meant to be with you. That all my life, I've wandered the desert looking for you when I was supposed to be looking for my brother. And it was you I found. Not Darcy, not Kiara. You."

I closed my eyes as the tears streamed down my cheeks, glad that everyone else had moved on ahead of us. Glad for at least this semblance of privacy. Of course, I'd forgotten Merlin, seeing as he was being pulled by Ford.

"There is an answer to this, if you care to hear it," he said from his stretcher.

I swiped away the tears on my cheeks, hating that my heart was being such a traitorous thing when I had Maks back. Just the thought of him lightened the ache in my heart, but it didn't completely wash away the literal heartache that was happening here.

"And what is that?" Ford asked. "What solution could you possibly have?"

Merlin sighed. "Did it ever occur to you that your love for her came on strong? That it was sudden and fierce? And you, Zam, did you not wonder when you saw into him how much he didn't see your flaws? That when you first met him, he was obnoxious and rude, and thought so little of you? How quickly you saw him change?"

I wasn't sure I liked what he was saying. "What are you trying to get at?"

"Well, you see, I didn't think Maks was good for you. He was part Jinn, after all," Merlin said. I looked at Ford, horror flickering through me.

"What did you do?"

"Well, not me, but Flora might have nudged him in that direction . . ." Merlin trailed off. "Because I asked her to. Because I thought Ford would be a better fit and that he'd be the steady, calming force you needed in your life to see you through what was coming your way. I thought with Ford, you'd be stronger."

There was a quiet moment while the wind of the desert swept by us, tangling my hair up, tugging at the edges of my cloak. The sun had just set and the day was bleeding into nightfall and all I could think was that Ford hadn't ever really loved me. That it was a *spell*. It hurt, as weirdly as I should have been relieved.

Because his love for me was fake.

But what I'd felt—and still felt—for him was not. Now it was my turn to look away, to hide the emotions.

"You should release him from whatever fucking spell she put on him," I said. "It's not fair to mess with people's hearts like that!"

Ford reached across the distance between us and put a hand on my forearm. "Even if it started out as a spell, it isn't now. And the spell wasn't on you, was it?"

I shook my head and clamped down on my emotions. "Doesn't matter, it isn't fair to you."

I wanted all this to be a trick, so I wouldn't feel like such a shit for hurting my friend more. Hell, he was practically my brother-in-law. I groaned. "Merlin, let him go."

"The spell is done, it dissipated. Basically, it gave him time to figure out that he really did like you, that you were good for him too." Merlin groaned as the travois hit a rock, bouncing him. I didn't feel bad, not for a second.

"Why?" The question blurted out of me. "I mean, it shouldn't matter who I end up with, does it?"

Merlin let out a sigh that turned into a low moan. "Maybe, maybe not. So many prophecies out there. I thought Ford stronger than Maks. Maks is a Jinn, but before he took on the power of a master, he wasn't terribly strong." He paused and coughed. "How long since you've read the journals that belonged to your mother?"

I shook my head and even though his eyes were closed, Merlin nodded. "That's what I thought. You should read them. The time is coming that they will guide you to your destiny."

11

Riding slowly, the early morning sun not yet hot on our backs, I knew Merlin was trying to direct me once more—I just didn't know in what direction. I only knew I didn't like how he changed the discussion from how he and Flora had warped Ford's mind and heart to be in love with yours truly, to my mother's journal papers somehow making my destiny known to me. My jaw ticked and it took everything in me not to kick the stretcher, to deliberately tip it over and throw him onto the ground.

That would teach the meddling mage to stay out of my business. Yeah, probably not, but one could hope.

"Ford, I'm sorry. I'm sorry I can't be that woman for you," I said, ignoring Merlin's not-so-subtle push to change the discussion. "I'm sorry that you think I don't care, but that's not the case at all. I do care about you, far more than I want to. Because the people around me are always in danger. They're always being drawn into fights that could end up getting them killed. And I think that if you died . . . I don't know that I would ever be the same." I finally looked at him. "You are family to me, Ford. You were from that first moment in the Oasis. Maybe not the mate you want me to be, but you are family in every other sense of the word."

Ford was quiet as he looked me straight in the eyes, the gold depths mixed with sorrow and a longing that I could never fill for him. "I don't know if I can stay with the pride. I don't know if I can watch you with him, even though I love you both. It's why I haven't spoken to him, I'm afraid I'll hit him."

I shouldn't have expected anything else, and yet it still cut into me. I swallowed hard, or tried to swallow past the lump in my throat growing with each second that ticked by. "I understand."

I didn't, not really. Because even when Steve cheated on me, I'd stayed with the pride because that's what you did. You stayed loyal to your people. I urged Balder into a trot, putting distance between me and Ford and fucking Merlin.

But I didn't catch up to the others either. Lila twisted around and looked back, saw me and flew right to me, landing on the front of my saddle. "Why are you crying? What did that jerk say?" She snaked her head around so she could give Ford the evil eye. "Do I need to spit on him? I'm telling you, all men really are assholes."

I smiled through the hurt and shook my head. "No. I just wish I understood what my heart is trying to do to me. I do care for him, Lila."

"But not the way you love Maks." She stated it simply. "Maks is special, and he fits with you like no one else, and a lot of that is all you've been through together." Lila shrugged and gave me a wink. "Much as I would have liked some cubs between you and Ford, I'll settle for cubs between you and Maks. They'll be cute little mongrels."

A quiet laugh escaped me. "Ford still loves me, and because of that, he is probably going to leave the pride," I said softly. That hurt, almost as much as him still loving me. Because I would never abandon someone I loved, not unless I had no other choice, and even then, I wasn't sure I would walk away. Hell, look at how long I'd stayed in the pride with Steve moving on to Kiara and others. I'd stayed because there were others there I loved, others I needed to protect.

I slowly straightened my shoulders, knowing in my heart what I had to do. "Lila, I need you to back me up."

"Always, you don't even have to ask," she said, "but what are we doing exactly?"

"Shem," I called for my uncle, "I need you back here, please."

Shem held his horse back and I motioned for Ford to stop. I went to the back of his horse, unhooked the makeshift travois that pulled the stretcher, and hooked it up to Shem's horse. I patted his animal on the rump and sent him forward with Merlin.

Then I turned to Ford. "You are always welcome in our pride, Ford. You have a place to come home to, to people who love you and would fight for you to the death. I can't make you stay, and I will never force someone to stay in our pride if they want to go." I took a deep breath, feeling the eyes of the others on us as Ford just stared down at me.

My lips trembled and I didn't try to stop the emotions from reaching my eyes. "I release you from the bonds of our pride. Go, find what it is you're looking for. Or stay. But if you stay . . . then you stay because you want to, not because of what could be, or what you want to be."

Lila sighed. "I second her in this, Ford. You're a good one. But if you can't be happy here, then you need to go and find your happy. Maybe bring her back when you have cubs because I think your cubs are going to be the cutest little bundles of fur." She grinned up at him from my shoulder, but he just kept looking at me.

"You're releasing me."

"Stay or go, it's your choice," I said as I swung back up into my saddle. "I won't force you either way. We want you here, but you have to want to be here." I turned Balder and we jogged to catch up to Shem who was now the back of the line of horses and riders.

"You think that was smart?" Shem asked.

"I think it was the right thing to do," I answered. "The thing is, maybe if my father had given you that option when he found out you were in love with his wife, things would have turned out differently."

"She loved me," Shem said softly, "but not like she loved your father. It took me a long time to see it and understand that difference." He glanced over his shoulder. "He's still coming this way."

I didn't look back. "Maybe you can talk to him. Without Merlin helping."

"I heard that," Merlin grumbled.

"I expect you've heard it all, ass."

Balder jogged to catch up to Batman and Maks. He didn't reach out and take my hand or anything so obvious. "How did your talk go?"

"Oh, about as good as trying to make a rock float," I muttered.

Lila hopped across to Maks. "I like Ford, but he's not you. He doesn't know Shakespeare at all."

"Is that all I'm good for?" Maks shook his head. "Pity."

"Well, and you make a good fire, you're kind to

animals, you've saved this one from herself more than a few times, you . . ." Her litany of all the good things about Maks went on for a few minutes. When she started in on his physical attributes, he held up his hand.

"Okay, enough, enough. What is all this about anyway?" he asked. I shook my head but Lila sighed.

"The males of most species could use a lesson or two from you."

"I was also possessed by a number of rather vicious Jinn, if you do recall. That's a major flaw," Maks pointed out.

"Well, good thing Zam knew how to fix that too." Lila sighed again.

After that, the usual chatter of a big group settled down. Twice Steve tried to stop us, but now it was me who wanted to keep going. The last few weeks I'd barely been able to sleep without being sucked into the dreamscape to find some other fun danger waiting for me. But if I changed my sleep pattern to one where I was sleeping when my enemies were awake, I'd have a chance at actually recharging.

Score one for the house cat.

The tug on my back from the line of the flail's handle drew me to the southwest, and I kept us heading that way. Though it seemed as if Steve was being pulled that way too. The lull of the night quieted talk, and I found myself wondering what message Ishtar could be sending for the Emperor.

Were they truly working together? Was it a temporary cease fire, or had they been working as husband and wife all these years, rebuilding their power to take back the world for their own when the moment was ripe?

All the questions and no answers that I could see. I made myself let them go, at least for now. The sun was rising and we needed somewhere to sleep. I reached up and touched Lila on the side.

"Lila, can you see if there's a place up ahead to crash for the day? A bit of shelter would be great, but I'll take anything at the moment," I said.

She bobbed her head once, then pushed off my shoulder, gone in a flash of her sparkling scales.

Maks and I watched her fly away. He moved Batman closer to us and leaned over. "What happened with her and Trick?"

I shook my head. There were too many ears and the last thing I wanted was to give Steve fodder to tease my friend. "Later."

A few minutes and Lila was back, zipping around our heads. "There's a strip of scrubby trees that runs for about a mile, and it's maybe fifteen minutes out of our way. Not the best cover, but it will work for the day."

That was better than I'd been hoping for. Now to get Steve to stop where I wanted him to.

A little manipulation never hurt anyone, right?

"Let's go," I said to Maks, giving him a wink.

Shem, Bryce and Kiara followed. I chose not to look back for Ford. If he wasn't there, I'd be hurt, and if he was there, I'd feel like a shit for not making it clearer that he could go if that was what he truly wanted.

Our group passed a slowly moving Steve and Darcy. Steve's chin drooped to his chest. I said, "Come on, we can keep going. There's no reason to stop, we can go for a few more hours." I angled us in the direction that Lila pointed.

Steve jerked awake, and Darcy narrowed her eyes at me. "You said we'd stop at the break of day," she said. "And the sun will be up in less than an hour."

Steve spluttered, wide awake now and instantly pissed off. "Why would it matter what she says? She's not running the show here!"

He had a point. I wasn't running the show. The Emperor was, but I wasn't about to point that out to him.

"I'm not going to have you run us into the ground," Steve growled, all of a sudden going against his earlier words that he wanted to move faster.

All because I said I wanted to move faster.

I bit back the grin. What a fool. I knew him too well.

"She's doing it on purpose," Darcy said. "She knows you're going to say black to her white, just because you hate her."

Well, fuck, that was not helpful, not in the least. Time to change tactics. I shrugged. "You know what,

Darcy, you're right. I'm trying to manipulate him. I'm trying to get him to stop, when I really want to move faster. But I will say, I'm impressed that he's letting you speak for him." I smiled at her. "Good job, putting him in his place."

Take that, two-timing-lying-ass-piss-poor-friend.

Darcy's eyes widened as Steve let out a low growl. "She does not speak for me. No woman of mine will speak for me."

"Ever again?" I offered. "Because I did it all the time. Nice to see you have a type."

If I'd thought that Darcy's eyes were wide before, they were nothing to what they looked like now. I'd put her in a bind that she didn't know how to get out of. If she spoke up, she was confirming I was right about her. And if she was quiet, she looked like Steve ran the show and she had no say as his newest mate —as a weaker mate than I had been. Both positions were uncomfortable for a woman who'd been her own person for so many years.

Steve gave his horse a hard boot in the ribs and scooted him forward. "I see a place to camp for the day. We can stay there."

I let him get ahead of us. Darcy brought her horse near me and Balder. I lifted an eyebrow.

"You dug your grave when you threw your lot in with his," I said softly, just loud enough for her ears. "Don't expect me to go easy on you."

She curled her lips back, showing her teeth to me,

a threat in every sense of the word. "You will never have him back."

Like Steve, she booted her horse far harder than she needed to, no doubt in part to get under my skin. They knew I cared for my mounts; all the mounts at the Stockyards had been under my care and training. "Assholes," I muttered.

Bryce moved up to where Darcy had been. "Why would she say that about Steve? Does she really think you're after him?"

I shook my head. "No idea. Probably just because—"

"Because Steve still loves you." Kiara cut me off, and she couldn't have dropped a bigger bomb.

"I'm sorry, what?" I twisted in my saddle to look at the younger lion shifter. She did not say what I thought she'd said. "That's not possible."

She frowned, looking at her hands resting on the front of her saddle. "Maybe love is too strong of a word. But he called out your name in his sleep when he was with me. I think he wants you because you don't want him. Because you defied him in every sense of the word."

Bryce let out a low growl. "That makes him dangerous in a very different way. Obsessed."

"It means," I made hard eye contact with Kiara, "that I'm not the only one in danger. I'm not the only one who has defied him."

She lifted her chin and nodded. "I know. But he's focused on you right now."

"I'll stay close to Kiara," Bryce said and held up a hand as she started to protest. "It's not that I don't think you can take care of yourself—Zam has been a good example for you of kicking ass." He paused and drew a breath, a wicked grin on his face. "It's because I want a shot at Steve, too, and if he comes at one of you . . ."

"We can all get our licks in," Maks said, also grinning.

A coughing rattle caught all our attentions, drawing us back to where Merlin was sitting up in the stretcher. "You all realize you have bigger fish to fry than a stupid lion shifter with a bad complex about women, correct?"

"Oh sure, but what's the fun in *only* going after the ones that are probably going to kill you?" I said. "Let us have our fun driving Steve mental. It'll make this trip that much better."

1 2

The mile-long strip of trees was exactly as Lila said it would be. Narrow, barely enough limbs for cover, but there were patches here and there that we could use to give not only ourselves, but the horses shade too.

As I set up a small spot to camp for the day, I caught a flash of jet-black hair as Ford stopped in another part of the strip of trees, farther down from the rest of us, but still there. Fair enough; I'd told him he could stay. I guess I'd really thought he'd just take off, go his own way.

Leave us and try to forget me and the pride.

A hand touched my arm, startling me. I turned to see Maks watching me watch Ford. "You okay?"

Two words that held a world of answers inside me, and I settled for the most honest of them. "For now."

He kissed me, gently, not a claiming of me because anyone could be watching, but just a kiss acknowledging that this was hard for me. That he was with me. Crap, was I turning into one of those people who read into every action of their mate? I shook my head.

"When do you think Ollianna is going to make another strike against us?" I asked as I went to my knees and used a flat-ended stick to dig a hole that would hopefully produce water for all of us.

Maks dropped beside me, grabbed a pointed stick and helped to loosen the ground as I dug it out. "Hard to say. That had to be a lot of energy for both the frog hatch followed so closely by the lizard men."

"And then lifting the curse off me," I said. He grunted and I glanced at him. "What?"

"I don't think she lifted that curse off you." Maks held out his hand and we switched sticks so he could dig and I could loosen the ground. "I think it was Ishtar."

I paused. "Why would you say that?"

He didn't slow his digging as he widened the hole. "Because if you were dead, Steve could have picked up the flail and carried it to the Emperor, no games, no Ollianna chasing him."

I frowned, thinking about his words. "I suppose it's possible that it was Ishtar, but I've felt her magic before, and it wasn't like that." Then again, it wasn't like I'd let Ishtar's magic touch me since she'd gained more power, since she'd gone crazy with the increase in her magic.

"I'm just saying, we don't know that it was all Ollianna. With three powerful monsters coming at us, we can't assume anything." He took one more swipe with the flat-ended stick and water bubbled up. I grabbed the collapsible buckets and carefully scooped up the water as it filled the small hole, then offered the buckets to the horses first.

Maks and I worked in silence after that, the way we had back in the beginning, back when we'd first ridden out from the Stockyards, headed into the unknown to save Darcy and the others captured by the Ice Witch. I shook my head.

So much had changed.

So much had stayed the same.

Lila swung around the treetops, snagging over-sized beetles and crunching them down by the sound of things. I made my way to where Merlin lay on his stretcher. "Let's see if I can help you," I said.

"I'm not sure it's a good idea," he said. "I think . . . I think you should leave me here."

He reached over and took my hand and a flash of power rolled between us, nothing sharp or painful, just surprising. I blinked, and then I frowned.

"Seriously? Why would you take me into the dreamscape?" I was still holding Merlin's hand, and as I tried to step away from him, I pulled him to his feet.

"Because we need to talk and there are too many ears, too many unknowns. You were very clever to realize that sleeping during the day is a way to avoid Ish and my father." Merlin didn't let go of my hand, using his free hand to rub it over his head. "We can use this to your advantage."

He tugged me and we were running across the desert, to the south. Way to the south and then to the east, until we neared a shoreline of an ocean I'd never been to. The dreamscape made it easy to cover distance. I'd give it that. Merlin slowed and pointed at a crumbled down building.

"I think that is where Ollianna is."

"How do you know?"

He snorted. "I've been in and out of consciousness for a long time. Weeks. I've been looking around, trying to figure out what I can do to help."

"And you want me to check this place out?"

"I think if you can explore it now, you can map it out in your mind and be ready to face her," Merlin said, then paused and shook his head. "I don't think I'll be there to help you when that time comes."

I looked at him, really looked at him, seeing the pallor of his skin, how thin he was, how sunken his one eye was. "Are you dying?"

"I think so. Don't bother trying to heal me. I think

this is because of my ties to Ishtar." He shook his head slowly. "She said she was killing me in part because I could still help you. That if I were to help you, you'd have a chance at making this all right." His hand tightened over mine. "Let me help you, however I can. I'm stronger here, far stronger than my mortal body."

I tightened my hold on his hand until he winced.

"You forget your own strength," he said.

I nodded. "And so do you. I won't give up any of my friends without a fight. Not even a troublesome wizard who has caused as much trouble as he's helped with."

I didn't look at him as I led the way toward what was Ollianna's stronghold. I tried not to think about Merlin dying, tried not to think about what it would mean for all of us to lose his knowledge. Instead of those thoughts, I focused on what was in front of me.

The structure was five stories tall, hundreds of feet wide, and built into the side of a cliff at the edge of the water. Made out of the same gray and brown stones of the cliff, it blended in well, and would have been unnoticeable if you weren't looking for it, especially at night.

Multiple entryways dotted the structure, but pillars held up the main opening, pillars that were carved deeply with the sinuous lines of a snake. Subtle, it was not. I went straight for that main entrance. Inside, a moaning wind curled through my hair, tugging it to the side. I made note of the intersections as we came upon them.

With Merlin, I wove my way through Ollianna's home, memorizing it as best I could.

"Is the falak really as dangerous as the Emperor made it out to be?" I asked sometime in the walk.

"Yes. Though I doubt the falak was actually being kept away by my father's presence. I think now that it was a ruse to keep his own skin intact. He was always very good at that," Merlin said.

That had been my thought too. "Which means that killing the Emperor won't significantly impact what we can do to the falak."

"True." Merlin tugged on my hand, pulling me back from an intersection. "If you get the chance, I think you should kill him. Use the flail if you can."

A soft scuttle of feet in the hall ahead of us froze me. I grabbed Merlin and shoved him into an alcove, tucking myself in tightly next to him.

Voices floated to us.

"Do you think Ollianna is correct?" The first voice was reedy, thin, and very distinct. I was sure I'd never heard it before.

The second voice was familiar. It was the old witch who ruled the Swamp. "I think she is mad with power. She thinks she's protecting us, but that child she carries is going to destroy the world. I have seen it. I cannot think how to stop her, though."

I looked at Merlin who shook his head.

But I was not that person who didn't follow her gut. A gamble was worth taking if it found us allies, if it found us a way to end the monstrosity that Ollianna was growing in her belly.

I stepped out of the alcove. The two women had their backs to me. Long skirts in black, the edges darker as if they were wet from walking in the water. Tall, slim, and both had their graying hair bound up in near-identical buns.

"And if I told you," I said and they spun around, "that we could end that monster, would you stand with me?"

The old witch's eyes took me in, her face not giving away an iota of what she was thinking or feeling. She was good. "How are you here?"

"I am not what anyone thinks I am," I said. "I have more bloodlines in me than anyone has a right to have, you've seen that, which means . . ."

"You are far more dangerous than we realized," the old witch, the mother of them all, slowly nodded. "I am Etheral. How do you propose we stop Ollianna?"

This was where things got tricky. "I need to keep this one alive if my plan is going to work." I pointed a thumb at the alcove and Merlin slowly slid out. The two witches eyed him up and down.

"He's in rough shape."

"Ishtar has a binding on him of some sort," I said. "Can you—"

"No," Etheral said. "If he is bound by Ishtar, it is only with her death that he will be freed. And that is if he isn't so tightly bound that he doesn't die with her. But that still does not answer the question. How do we stop Ollianna? If you cannot answer that, then you are of no help to us, and I can take you to Ollianna now, and gain myself favor with her."

The witch next to Etheral blinked a few times as if she were surprised by those words. I smiled. "Your friend doesn't seem to think that would be the case."

"She does not know my mind," Etheral said.

"I have a plan," I said, and looked at Merlin. "But no one else can know." I pushed him away and sent him back to the land of living, as it were. Just in case Ishtar could see through him, through whatever connection they had.

I drew a breath and faced the two witches. "It's a terrible plan, and one that will likely end in my death, but it will save the world from Ollianna and her demon spawn."

"Then tell us, so we can help. Because even if some of us die," Etheral looked me straight in the eye, "my other daughters will live, and that will be worth it."

I understood her fully. A mother's love for her children, an alpha's love for their pride, they were the same.

I opened my mouth and spun out a plan that I could only hope would be strong enough to bind Ollianna and her child tightly, so we could throw them both into a pit and be done with them once and for all.

13

MERLIN

Merlin gasped as he was shoved quite literally out of the dreamscape by Zamira. She'd looked so sad, and yet so sure of herself when she'd pushed him away that he knew he had to get back to her. He had to make sure she went where he wanted her to go.

"Merlin, what is happening?" Shem grabbed his arm which sent a powerful bolt of pain through him, stopping him from relaxing at all, stopping him from getting into the dreamscape. This was not the time to lose control of this game.

"Let go of me. She shoved me out. I need to get back to her!" He growled, coughed, and more pain blasted along his middle, reminding him of the deeper injuries that were slowly bleeding him to death. For now, it was in his best interest to be wounded.

Kiara had stitched up everything she could, but there were so many injuries that she hadn't been able to see.

Gods be damned to the seven hells and back! The voices around him were scattered and tense.

Finally, he gave up and opened his one eye. "Maks."

Maks crouched next to Zam's body while she swayed, sleeping where she sat, dreaming in the dreamscape and making whatever plans she thought to make with the witches of the Swamp. Sweet goddess, this was a terrible idea! "Is she okay?"

"She was alive when I left her," Merlin said. "What is she planning?"

Maks shook his head and took a quick look over his shoulder. Merlin followed his gaze to the sound asleep Steve and Darcy. Still, the half-Jinn lowered his voice. "To get the flail to the Emperor. We have to do that before we face anyone else. The flail is demanding it of her, driving her."

Merlin looked at the man who'd stood by his niece, fighting for her even when he'd been possessed. "You have to keep her from making whatever deal she's going to make. Do you understand?"

"It's too late. She agreed to give the flail to the Emperor in exchange for Bryce's life," Maks said. "A good bargain. It's just a weapon despite the magic in it."

Merlin groaned. "You understand what it can do?"

Maks went quiet, closed his eyes and seemed to be deep in thought. And then his mouth dropped open and his eyes flew open, a new knowledge in them. "Shit. I do now."

Merlin stared at him. "You still have the memories of those who possessed you?"

"When they feel like it," he said. Maks looked at those around and waved them closer. Lila wiggled in on his shoulder, her eyes worried as she touched Zam's ear.

"What's happening?"

Merlin sighed. "Let me explain. The Emperor wants the flail because it can break his prison, you all understand that. But the flail is more than that. It is a weapon that in the wrong hands could be used to rule all of the supernatural world. If the Emperor can make it work for him, he could control and draw on the energy of any supernatural creature alive. Anywhere. There would be no safety for any of us."

He was stretching the possibility of the weapon some, but Maks didn't argue with him.

Shem gave a low whistle. "So he can't have that flail, even though she's agreed to give it to him."

"Could she use it like that?" Ford asked quietly and Merlin turned his head to the young lion. "Could Zam use it in that way?"

Merlin shook his head. "It was always tuned to be a man's weapon, to be held by a man to rule, and all the limits on it were designed with a man's power. Maybe Maks could use it like that."

Maks was already shaking his head. "My memories are saying that there is a reason the Jinn let it go. That the flail drove them all mad when the power was opened to them. So while it might have been meant to use as a way to rule, the weapon itself did not work that way. It was too dangerous, and had too much of its own mind on how to do things. It's why the Jinn fear it."

Merlin groaned, trying to figure out how to spin this to work for him and the world. Even if the cost was Zam's life, the rest of the world had to survive. "If the Emperor was to go *more* mad, with more power, that would be worse than the falak."

Carefully, he wove a slight spell over the others, bending them to his will ever so slightly. Using their own fears to get them to see what he wanted them to see.

"Then we have to stop her from taking it to the Emperor," Shem said softly. "We have to take the weapon from her, and we have to hide it from both of them."

The pit in the middle of Merlin's stomach seemed to open up. "I'm not sure that's a good idea, or even possible. The weapon could turn on her, or whoever tried to take it."

He looked up to see Maks looking back at him, uncertainty on his face. "I'm not sure."

"Of course you aren't," Ford growled. "You wouldn't stand against her, even though it's the best thing for her."

Merlin wanted to groan but instead made himself lift a hand between the two men. "We are agreed that we need to stop her from whatever plan she's come up with?"

They agreed, all of them, even Maks and Lila, which surprised him. They loved her, and Zam was the key to stopping this madness, but not if she was herself driven mad by the flail and the power within it, and in turn handed it off to the Emperor to rule them all.

14

ZAMIRA

Trust is a funny thing, and once broken can never truly be fixed. It wasn't like a bone that once mended was stronger. No, there was always that weak spot in a relationship when trust was broken.

I pulled myself out of the dreamscape with some difficulty. The sun had nearly set, which meant I'd spent the majority of the day inside the dreamscape talking to Etheral and making plans. She was a sharp old broad for a witch. I didn't trust her, but I could read her like a book, and she was scared of Ollianna and what that idiot daughter of hers was doing.

Having learned my lesson about trusting witches, I held back some of my plan from her. Just enough that I could keep myself and my family safe.

Which brought me to this moment where trust was scattered like bread crumbs in the wind.

Merlin was asleep next to me as I pulled myself out of the dreamscape. I put a hand on his forehead, and his brow was cool. If he was right and there was no healing him, then I had to make the choice to leave him behind. I had to go forward without him.

I stood, my legs tingling as the blood flowed back into them, making me curl up my lip with the discomfort. I wove my way around the horses to find Kiara sitting with Bryce next to a small fire.

They looked good together, their heads bowed as they talked quietly back and forth. He'd be good for her, if he could get over his hang-up of wanting Darcy as his mate. Then again, I'd not seen him so much as glance in the bitch's direction. Maybe he'd given up on her finally. One could hope that he saw just what a liar and a manipulator she was.

I sat across from them. "Merlin is dying."

Kiara stood and started toward the stretcher, but I grabbed her hand. "No, there is nothing we can do. Even if we healed every wound, there is a hold that Ishtar has on him. And I think she can find us through him."

"Fuck." Bryce shook his head. "You think she's coming for you?"

"I think she's biding her time. We have to leave Merlin here. It's not the best place. But there's water, shelter and I've seen signs of game." Here came the hard part. "I need at least two people to stay back with him, to see this through."

To bury him when he finally died. To give him that much.

Kiara and Bryce shared a look and he nodded. "Okay, I'll stay with Kiara. We'll watch over him."

"Good." I stood and they followed me, a little too closely, a little bit too much to either side of me as if they were flanking me. The skin on my neck prickled. "Where are Maks and Lila?"

"They went out hunting," Kiara said. "They should be back soon."

I reached for the two closest to my heart through my connection to them and found them far closer than they should have been if they were hunting. Worry flickered through them both, and that emotion made me jittery.

I reached for Shem and found him and Ford close by too. Ford was still connected to the pride then? More than that surprise was that the four of them were in a formation that I knew all too well. A formation for taking down dangerous prey.

Only I was at the center of it.

I paused and bent as if I were tying my boot, because I had to be wrong. My own people wouldn't turn on me. Steve and Darcy? They would be at the front of the line if there was a list of people I didn't trust, but not the others. Not my pride. "You two go ahead. I'm going to check on the horses, and then—"

"No, let's talk first," Bryce said, his voice on the

edge of sorrow as he stopped behind me, keeping me flanked.

There was only one person who would have set them up for this. Only one who would try and convince them to turn on me. Even dying, Merlin couldn't just let things be.

I stood, dusted off my hands and strode back to Merlin. I kicked his stretcher, knocking him awake with a yelp that slid into a groan.

"You might be dying, but I'm not going to put up with your shit, old man. What did you do?" I glared down at him. "Because my pride thinks to take me down. As if I'm a dangerous animal. What did you say to them?"

Merlin looked up at me. "The flail cannot go to the Emperor, Zam. There will be another way to stop him, but if you take the flail to him now, it will be the end of all we know." He held out his hand. "Give it to me. If I hold it, I could use it to absorb energy, to heal my wounds."

The flail shivered, and behind me, I felt my brother tense. Apparently, this was not part of what Merlin had convinced him to do.

I did a slow turn, seeing Shem, Bryce, Kiara and Ford closing rank around me and Merlin. He knew I wouldn't kill them, and they had to know that I would do all I could not to hurt them. I looked past them to see Maks on Batman, Balder with him. Waiting. He gave me a slow nod.

He would step in if he needed to, but he trusted me to handle this on my own. I could see that in the quick glance between us.

Lila, on the other hand, shot down from above to land on my shoulder. "I don't know what you've got up your sleeve, Zam, but I trust you. Even if these fools don't."

"You agreed!" Shem snapped.

"I fucking lied to your face!" she snapped back.

They drew closer, and my heart sank. I wouldn't fight them.

Which meant it was time to run.

"Lila."

"Ready." Her talons dug into my shoulder as I shifted to my four-legged form, faster than any of my pride could reach me. Lila shot into the air dangling me above them, and Bryce jumped for me, his fingertips brushing against the soft pads of my front paws. I stared down at him, knowing that they were doing this because Merlin had convinced them that it was the best for me. Knowing that they weren't trying to hurt me, but also knowing that the only way he'd have been able to turn them was if they didn't fully trust me and that hurt . . . a lot more than I thought it would.

"Meet me at Ollianna's, Merlin. That's what you can do if you want to fucking help!" I yelled at him as Lila dropped me into Balder's saddle and I shifted back to two legs. Bryce and Kiara ran toward us, but it was too late.

I leaned into Balder and kissed at him, and he plunged forward, happy to be running even if it was the end of the day and the sun had disappeared.

Maks and Batman kept up well, and moments later, Steve and Darcy were hot on our heels. Not that they'd be able to catch up if I didn't want them to. Their horses were not as well fitted up, nor did they have the heart to run like our two boys.

I let Balder run for nearly an hour before I slowed him. By then, Steve was right pissed.

"What the fuck was that?" he roared as he yanked his puffing, heaving horse over next to me.

I wasn't about to tell him the truth, so I fudged it. "You know how it is, Steve, when it's time to make a break, you make the fucking break. Am I right, or am I right?"

Steve glared at me, and his hand went for his weapon, a rifle he held under his leg the same way I kept my shotgun.

Lila tightened her hold on my ear with one clawed hand and tangled the other into my hair, grabbing at a handful of it. "I wouldn't," she said. "I can spit my acid on you before you even get it free."

Steve's hand stopped. "I wasn't going to shoot her. I need her to . . ."

Oh, now he had my interest. Which was good, because my heart and mind were torn up with what had happened back there. Merlin had convinced the others that I had to be stopped. I glanced at Maks and he mouthed a single word.

Later.

He wasn't wrong. We couldn't show any weakness to Steve and Darcy.

"So tell me again why you are going to the Emperor?" I asked Steve, thinking he might slip up if given the chance.

Steve stared straight ahead, not even bothering to look at me. "None of your damn business."

"Hmm." I urged Balder to step sideways, away from Steve and closer to Maks. We might be going in the same direction, but I wasn't about to actually ride with my ex-husband. Gods, what a shit show this was turning out to be.

Lila did a single bounding hop off the front of Balder's saddle and shot up into the night sky. "I'm going to do some recon."

I waved at her. "Be careful." She barrel rolled and flew backward so she could wave at me.

"You care more for her than you care for your own kind," Darcy said. "It's not natural."

I snorted. "Please, you aren't my own kind and I came for you when no one else would."

"I rescued her, not you. You just got in my way, like always. Every stone we recovered was me, not you. Ish knows it, and so does everyone else," Steve growled.

My jaw dropped and I stared at the two of them long enough to see Darcy flush, even in the dark. "Is that the story you tell yourself? Do you actually believe that horseshit, Darcy?"

Steve stiffened. "Don't answer her."

Darcy's jaw tightened and I smiled at her, unable to help the laugh. "Remember, this is what you signed up for. You wanted him. Even after seeing how he treated me and Kiara, you wanted this. Enjoy it. Enjoy being ruled by an asshole who only wants you to keep his dick warm at night."

Before she could answer, Maks and I rode ahead of Darcy and Steve, putting a good distance between us. I needed the space before I swung the flail and just put us all out of our misery for having to deal with the sheep fucker.

"You showed restraint back there." Maks had the nerve to chuckle at me. "I'm impressed."

"Don't be, I thought about killing him," I said under my breath. We rode quietly for a moment. "You going to tell me what happened back there, with the others?"

Maks sighed. "The flail has more magic than even we realized. My memories are showing me it possibly being used to rule the supernatural world, but those were more theories than actual truths. The Jinn would have used it that way, you understand?"

I nodded. I did understand, Davin would have

kept the flail for himself if it had ever been a possibility he could have ruled the world.

Maks went on. "But it was always meant to be held by a man. So the abilities it would give the Emperor are different than the abilities it would give you. If it gave you any at all."

The flail shivered against my back, as if reminding me that it was there. Reminding me that it did indeed seem to have a mind of its own from time to time.

He's not wrong. The flail is not what the mage thinks, though perhaps, he thought to rule the world himself?

"I doubt Merlin wanted to rule the world," I said, then frowned. "That doesn't explain why they wanted to jump me and take it away."

Maks glanced over his shoulder, making sure Darcy and Steve were still a distance from us. They were, and they were arguing, which was a good sign.

"In the Emperor's hands, the flail could potentially give him absolute power over all the supernaturals. Merlin said he'd be able to draw on all of the supernaturals, sucking their lives away without even touching them. That is, if he can unlock its abilities, or if he even understands what the flail is capable of; he might not be able to. That was the part I didn't tell Merlin and the others because I could already see that they'd decided to take it from you."

"The flail is picky. We both know that. And again .

. . so much power in one weapon would never have been set aside by Davin. So Merlin's explanation doesn't fit. He wanted it from you for other reasons."

The flail being picky was an understatement. The flail had tried to kill me multiple times for using it, until we'd come to an understanding that I needed it, and it needed me.

His blue eyes were thoughtful. "The thing is the flail is old, and had been wielded by Jinn, shapeshifters and now you. There is no telling what it is capable of, if any of the original powers that were imbued into it are still intact even. These magical weapons have a tendency to grow and change, just like a person."

"Sentient, but not," I said.

"Exactly."

I can tell you they are all wrong about the flail. They are grasping at straws. Seeing as I am a part of it, do you want me to tell you what it's capable of, and what it's not?

I struggled to draw breath as Marsum's voice spoke inside my head. "Can you speak to Maks too?"

Hold his hand. That should do it.

I reached over and took Maks's hand. He linked his fingers with me and Marsum began to speak.

15

MERLIN

He hated to lie to Zam and the others, especially now, so close to the end game. But she'd taken the move she'd needed to take in order to get a little further. Her heart was too tangled when she had to look out for too many, and they all needed her head clear and focused on the task at hand.

He needed her oriented correctly for the last few moves.

Maks, Lila, and Zam were the three. They were the triad that would break the last of the bindings on the stones and the magic they held, and he would be there to pick up the pieces. He just hoped that she would forgive him one day for all the lies. For all the manipulation that he'd put them through.

Then again, she might not survive to be bothered

with forgiveness of any kind. Which would be as it would be.

He waited most of the night, lying quietly while the others spoke over him as if he couldn't hear, giving Zam time to get farther away. Ford was the one he worried would go after her, more than the others once the spell wore off. His heart beat for that girl, more than Merlin had thought would have happened when he'd asked Flora to nudge them together.

Finally, he could stand it no longer.

He brushed off the blanket, sat up with a groan and pulled the covering off his patched eye. "Kiara, can you cut the stitches for me, please?"

"What?" Her hands were on his arm, holding him steady as if he were about to fall over.

"The stitches. I appreciate the covering, truly, but in all honesty, they are rubbing against my eyeball."

"Wait, you were dying just a few minutes ago! And you have no eyeball, that's why I stitched it closed!" she spluttered. He turned and grinned at her.

"I'm an adept liar which is both a blessing and a curse. And an even better actor when my mind is put to the task. I am not dying, and my eyeball has grown back. Or something like that." He held still as she snipped away at the stitches and smiled as she gasped.

"You weren't kidding. You have an eye again!"

He carefully rubbed his fingers over the newly

healed orb, feeling the tingles all the way to his toes. "Exactly. Now. We have work to do. We need to gather up Flora and my daughter, and get to the other side of the desert. That is where the final showdown will happen with Ollianna." He wobbled a little as he tried out legs that had been unused for a very long time.

"Wait," Shem said, "what about the bond between you and Ishtar?"

"Well, when she drew on my life-force, I fed her the bond as part of it. That is what helped to keep me alive." He shrugged. "Also, well done turning on Zam. That was perfect."

A slap snapped his head to the side, and he went to one knee. Kiara stood over him. "We are her pride. We should never have believed you!"

He forced himself to smile up at her. "A little magical push was all that was needed. The four of you were ready to see the dark in her. Because each of you have had your doubts where she is concerned, whether it is her strength as a person, her physical prowess, or her ability as an alpha."

Each of the lion shifters looked down as he spoke.

"Maks and Lila?" Ford asked quietly.

"Neither of them believed me. Not for a second. Because they do not doubt her, my magic did not work," Merlin said. "It is why they work so well together as a team, and there was no other way for her to let the rest of us go. We need them to go on their own, to travel fast and clean."

Bryce let out a snarling growl that turned into a guttural roar that echoed across the desert. "Fucking hell!"

Kiara shook her head. "Fine. This is what happened, you have a reason for it. What is that reason?"

"She is going to need something of an army to back her up when facing Ollianna and the falak. We are going to gather that army for her." Merlin smiled as he lied straight to their faces once more. "We are going to be there when she needs us."

He paused and held out his hand as he let out a low whistle. A songbird flew in from one of the trees and landed on his wrist. He cupped his hand around its beak, whispering only one short sentence before he sent it on its way to find Zam.

"Gather the final two missing stones if you want to survive."

ZAMIRA

H olding Maks's hand as we rode toward the Emperor's Throne while Marsum spoke to both of us was weirdly comforting. Marsum had always been the asshole in my world, the one to hate beyond anything or anyone else, and yet he'd turned out to be the one to help me figure out how to save Maks.

Turned out, he wasn't the worst Jinn, not by a long shot.

So if Marsum thought he had something that would help, I would listen. We both would.

"How do you know all those things that Merlin said are wrong?" I asked.

Because the Jinn made the flail, not the Emperor. The flail was made to protect its master at all costs, even drawing in the life-force of others to rejuvenate its holder.

I looked at Maks and raised an eyebrow. "I think we already knew that much."

What felt like a sigh flowed through my head. *You are the flail's master, Zamira. Even if you hand it over to the Emperor there is a good chance it will kill him. Or try to.*

"That's good, isn't it?" Maks said.

Lila continued to fly loops ahead of us, oblivious to the conversation between the three of us. A tiny bird looped around her and I frowned. The bird was a songbird, not known for flying at night.

No. You face three superpowers in our world, and you will need at least one of them to side with you if you want a chance at stopping the other two. Zam has already figured that much out.

I cringed, and Maks blew out a low whistle. "That's asking a lot. All three have tried to kill her, to kill us, and all three are more than a few grains of sand short of a desert."

Regardless. You three are strong, but not strong enough. Not yet.

The flutter of wings drew my eyes again, straight to the sky. I couldn't take my eyes off the bird that swooped around and around Lila. Which was stupid; Lila was a predator, and the bird most definitely prey. But it didn't seem deterred. More like it was trying to get her attention.

The blast from a gun rocked the night and Lila

peeled away from the bird as it fell, and she twisted in the air.

Falling.

My heart caught in my throat and then she was back up again, low to the ground this time. She'd been missed, but not by much.

"What the fuck?" I spun Balder, already knowing who'd shot at her. We raced back toward Steve, who still had his gun in hand. And that fucker turned it on me.

"Time to take the flail," he said. "Now that your spitting lizard is dead."

He thought he'd shot Lila.

But he'd shot the bird she'd been flying with instead, and like the dumbass he was, he didn't wait to see if he was right.

I didn't slow Balder, but put my heels to him, pressing him into a proper charge.

Darcy was yelling, and from the corner of my eye, I saw her try to get around Steve, to get in between us.

But there was nothing now except to see how this final fight played out.

I'd waited a long fucking time for this moment, and I was damn ready for it.

Balder collided broadside with Steve's horse, sending it crashing over to its side. Steve's mouth was a perfect O of surprise while he fell, the gun spinning away from him.

I jumped from the saddle, through the air, and landed next to a fallen Steve. He scrambled to get his feet out from under the horse as I stood over him.

"I challenge you, Steve, for the lands of the desert, and every shifter within it. I challenge you in a fight to the death." I snarled the words and he curled his lip right back at me.

There was a scream behind us, but I didn't dare turn my back on Steve.

"I've got Darcy," Maks said. "You deal with Steve."

Steve pushed to his feet and took a half step back. "On four legs."

"Done."

His eyebrows shot up, but he didn't know that for the first time, I knew my house cat form was strong enough. I was strong enough. There was no way he could keep up with my speed. No way he could survive the blows of my claws and teeth when they were infused with the strength of the flail.

Oh, this is going to be good, Marsum all but purred. Weird, considering he was a Jinn.

Steve started his shift, and in the past, I might have waited for him. But since this was truly about who was better, who was faster, who was stronger, the ability to shift at high speed was part of that.

I stepped through that doorway in my mind from two legs to four and raced toward him as he was caught between the two forms.

I leapt, going straight for his belly, digging my

claws into his soft flesh as he finally dropped to four legs. He bellowed and roared as I clung with my front claws and teeth, then dug in with my back claws, gouging chunks of flesh out over and over.

He rolled onto his back and a paw swept me off him, but his claws didn't touch me. I was too small, and they missed. A gentle toss was all I got before I hit the ground and was running at him. Steve opened his mouth and lunged at me, his eyes closed. His fucking eyes closed!

I dropped low again and he swept toward me. I hooked one set of claws into the corner of his mouth and used the momentum of his own head toss to swing myself up and onto the back of his neck.

If this had happened even a short time before, if I'd been put in this position to kill Steve, I think a part of me would have hesitated. I would have thought about the few good times that I had with him, the way he'd told me he'd love me forever when we'd been married, the dreams that had held me to him far longer than he'd ever deserved.

If this moment had come when I'd been less sure of myself, if I'd had an iota less belief in my abilities as an alpha, I would have paused.

Not now.

I gripped both sides of his neck and tore away the flesh with claws and teeth as he bellowed in pain and rage, and then fear . . . the bellows shifted to cries as he began to beg for his life, as he promised he'd go away forever and never come back. Darcy begged for his life and the words of the two of them filled my brain the way the coppery tang of his blood filled my mouth and nose.

I found the big artery I'd been digging for, and I shredded it. Even a shifter with quick healing abilities couldn't come back from that.

My father had taught me how to kill, as well as how to survive.

Steve slowly went to the ground, blood pouring out of him, Darcy screaming in the distance.

The world didn't wobble. I didn't feel ill or nauseous. I held my ground and stayed where I was.

"Goodbye, Steve." I sat on his back, essentially making sure that he and Darcy knew that in life, and in dying, I was the alpha.

"I . . ." he gurgled and rolled, blood pooling around his mane, and I bounced off to avoid being squashed, "I never loved them."

Darcy gasped and I stepped back, taking back my two-legged form so I could look at Steve one last time. "I don't believe you ever loved anyone but yourself, Steve."

"Not true." His tongue lolled out and a deep exhale slid out of him.

"If you mean that, what was your message for the Emperor? How can you help me survive a little longer?" I asked, not really expecting an answer. I was feeling weirdly detached in that moment. I'd taken down a full-grown lion as a house cat. But more than that, I'd killed Steve, my ex-husband, sheep fucker, man whore, lying, cheating piece of shit. The emotions swirling through me were intense, and I let them flow, let them do their thing.

He gurgled. "No message."

I looked over my shoulder at Darcy. "You want him to keep suffering? Or are you going to tell me what Ishtar really sent the two of you to do?"

She was on her hands and knees, and I could see her thinking about shifting. "Maks!"

He took a step back, pulled his weapon and swung it, the curved edge sweeping across her neck before she could fully shift and turn on him. Darcy's head rolled, her eyes still looking at me, still full of light for just a few more seconds and then they dulled, the shine in them gone as if nothing in her realized that she was dead, at least not right away.

"She hated you," Steve said.

I turned back to him, surprised he was still alive. "Yeah, it took me awhile to figure that out. Made you quite the pair, didn't it?"

He looked up at me. "Not hate."

"How many times did you try to kill me, asshole?" I crouched so we were as close to eye to eye as we were going to get.

"Wanted you as my own."

I could almost believe it. "So if you couldn't have me, no one could?"

He blinked once. "Ishtar same. She wants you to love her and no other . . . she wants you safe . . . Emperor is dangerous. I was to protect you."

"But again," I poked a finger to his head. "You tried to kill me."

His golden eyes blinked heavily, and I thought he might yawn, he looked so tired. Like he was falling asleep. "Ishtar wanted you safe. Wanted me to save you from lizards."

I frowned and he went on. "Other witch offered something better."

"Ollianna?" Her name shot out of me and he blinked once.

"Yes. Offered freedom for the flail."

He'd taken a deal when he could have just protected me? "You're about to die, Steve. Any last words?"

His mouth wrinkled as if he'd smelled something bad. "I'll always be the best you had."

Another big sigh slid out of him, and there was no inhalation of breath. He was gone.

His entire body seemed to shrink as I stared at him and then his form shifted on its own, sliding back to two legs.

I grimaced and shook my head. "You know what, Steve? Fuck you. Fuck your stupid sheep loving carcass."

I couldn't help myself, I took a swing with a boot and kicked him in the side. The meaty thunk was heavy in my ears and I stepped back, not liking the sensation as much as I'd hoped. Nope, I hated him, he was a douche, but I couldn't make myself kick him now that he was dead.

I swallowed hard. "Lila, you okay?"

"Yeah, he missed me and hit that bird. It was jabbering away at me, like it had its own voice. So weird." Lila swept down and landed on my shoulder. "You okay?"

I stared down at Steve, kind of shocked that it had finally happened, that he was truly dead. But also knowing that this confrontation had been inevitable. One of us was always going to end up dead. That was where this relationship had been headed from the moment we'd met.

"Maybe." I crouched, forcing myself to stare at him a moment longer. "I'm worried that I don't feel anything. Not sadness, not grief, not even gloating that I've won. That I beat him."

"Shock," Maks said, coming to crouch at my side, "and a lot of history between the two of you. Not much of it good. Doesn't mean you wanted to kill him. Doesn't mean that you didn't want to kill him. Just means that you did what you had to do."

I leaned my head onto his shoulder. "That's just it. I wanted him dead a thousand times for all he's done, and all the hurt. And that last bit? That last *I loved only you* garbage? The *I'm the best you'll ever have?* One last game to try to hurt me, to make me feel bad for killing him. That's how well I knew him. He was trying to get me to save him even at the last moment, to play on my sympathies."

"Too bad the fight was over so quick," Lila said. "We could have strung it out for hours."

Her words made my eyebrows rise slowly and I stood, my mind ticking over a possibility. "You have a point, Lila. Maybe we aren't done with him yet."

Maks slowly stood. "What do you mean?"

"You know how the Jinn, when they died, they were made into the undead creatures that roamed the land?" I pointed at Steve. "Think you can do it to him?"

Maks blinked a few times, then closed his eyes. It took him a good minute and then he slowly nodded. "Shit, yes, I can raise the dead."

"And can you give him instructions?"

Maks closed one eye and then nodded again. "I can."

So just like that, the decision to bring Steve back to life was made. A messy, bloody, undead Steve, but a Steve, nonetheless. Because being killed once just wasn't good enough for a douche like him.

I wanted him to die twice.

"What do you need me to do?" I asked as Maks did a slow circle around Steve.

"Nothing. I just need to find that last bit of his soul and reattach it to his physical body. Then I can give him a direct command." He held his hands out, palms down over Steve's body. A deep blue smoke swirled out and drove into Steve's limbs and torso, as if he were the desert and the Jinn magic was rain being absorbed into it. Maks flicked his fingers one at a time, and with each flick a different part of Steve's body jumped and twitched until he pushed to his feet. Wobbly, but standing.

Blood coated the front of his chest and his throat was nothing but tattered flesh, the white bone of his neck visible when he turned his back to me. "You want me to send him back to Ishtar." Not really a question, but I nodded anyway.

"Tell him to kill her," I said. I knew he wouldn't be able to, but hell, it would be worth the scare on her to see that she wasn't the only one able to send assassins. I didn't believe for a second she'd sent them to protect us. She'd sent Steve and Darcy to make sure Ollianna didn't get the flail, no matter what that cost was.

Then they were to take the flail to the Emperor themselves. Of that I had no doubt.

Of course, I was not the only one with enemies on all sides. Ishtar had forgotten to consider that Ollianna might make a play for Steve's loyalties.

Maks gave a command in a language that I suspected was Akkadian, the language of the Jinn. Bits of it sounded familiar, and the words buzzed along my spine in a not-unpleasant fashion.

They reminded me of the words on my mother's papers, the few journal sheets she'd left behind.

I blinked and Steve was shambling off, heading to the east, toward the Stockyards. Naked, his skin would burn and blister in no time, the blood would call the desert insects and creatures, and by the time he reached Ishtar, he'd be unrecognizable. A veritable mess of flesh and bones.

I didn't even need to write a message and tack it to his chest. What he was and that we'd sent him was message enough.

Along my back the flail tingled, a warning that we needed to move. To get going to the southwest again, to take the Emperor his prize.

"What about Darcy?" Maks asked. "You want to bury her?"

I shook my head. "No, let the desert reclaim her. It's where we all come from. She'll feed the wildlife, and it can be the last act of good she does for this world."

I mounted up on Balder, glad for the dark night around us. Already in the distance came the bark of wild dogs. They would find Darcy's body first, and it would feed them for a few days, maybe even a week.

My stomach churned and I fought a sudden wave of nausea. I didn't realize Lila was on my shoulder until she patted my cheek. "Remind me not to turn on you. I don't want my body to feed the wildlife."

A tired, half-barked laugh slid out of me. "Gods, that was harder than I thought it would be."

"She got a clean death," Maks said, "and Steve went down fighting. It could have been worse for both of them."

He was right, and yet there was more hurt in losing Darcy than I wanted to think about. She'd been my only friend—even if it had been a lie from the beginning, even if she'd secretly hated me—for a long time. I wiped my eyes and did my best to shake off the pain. Maybe it was just the thoughts of what could have been, the friendship that I thought would see me through to the end of my life.

With a little more effort, I pushed those thoughts away, let them slide from me and said a final goodbye to them both.

Steve and Darcy had taught me how to be stronger than I'd ever thought I would be. They allowed me to find my strength. Because if they hadn't turned on me, I never would have needed to stand on my own.

I never would have found Maks or Lila, and those two . . . they were all I needed, heart and soul.

"Thank you, Steve. Thank you, Darcy, for making me the woman I am today, by turning your backs on me," I said.

Maks nodded. "Thank you, Steve, for leaving her, so I could find her and have her love that you cast aside."

I smiled at him and Lila gave a chirp from my shoulder. "Thank you for turning on her, Darcy, so she could see just how damn good she has it with me as a friend."

I laughed. "You are the best of the best, Lila."

"Speaking of," she said, "that bird was seriously trying to give me a message. But it was garbled."

"What kind of a message?" I asked. "Like a warning?"

"Nope, like . . . it sounded a bit like Merlin," Lila said. "But he shouldn't be able to use much magic, should he? When he's dying?"

I frowned. "He plays a long game, and we could very well be in the middle of one of his chess moves we can't understand yet."

"Like separating you from your pride?" Maks said thoughtfully, his eyes distant. "We move faster without them, and you have less to worry about with them behind us. Even with your brother at your side, you were more cautious. Giving him more breaks, knowing he couldn't keep up and that he wasn't a very good rider."

The wind around us picked up, swirling the smells of the desert—distant flowers, even more distant rain, and the scent of the horses all mixed together—and I tried to just think for that moment. "I give you breaks."

"Not as many," Lila said. "Because you know our strengths, as we know yours. We are tied, the three of us, in a way that you aren't tied to anyone else, not even the pride."

Lila was not wrong. "You think that Merlin did all that on purpose, to drive us away?"

"I'm thinking so. Especially if that bird had a message from him. He could have been faking how injured he was."

That didn't make sense, though, because I'd put my hand on him, I'd felt the injuries deep within his belly and how they were bleeding out. I closed my eyes and tried to capture that second in time.

Could it have been an illusion? Could Merlin have duped me once again to do what it was he thought I should? The feeling of him dying faded even as I thought about it, like a sheet pulled off a trick.

"Fucking hell," I growled. "I think he did dupe me. What does he want now?"

Lila curled her lips, twisting them into a funny pursing. "Something about the final two stones."

Maks and I shared a look. "There are only two stones left floating out there, and Ishtar is not supposed to know about either of them."

"Unless she does," I said. "And if she does, we have to stop her."

Like a bolt of lightning, understanding dawned. "He wants us to find the last two stones, the one that creates, and the one that bestows powers on others."

17

The thing about Merlin's message via the bird was two-fold problematic.

One: We were being driven toward the Emperor, and I had to do that before my promise hurt, or worse, killed me. And yeah, I did think the flail would suck my life dry if it came to me not keeping my word.

Two: Having the stones in hand when we met up with the Emperor wasn't necessarily going to make our lives any easier. If he knew we had them, I had no doubt he'd take them from me.

"What are we going to do?" Lila asked. "I don't think Merlin is wrong this time. I think finding the final two stones is smart. Better us than Ishtar or Ollianna or the Emperor."

"What do you want to bet that Ollianna and

maybe even Ishtar are already looking for them?" Maks said.

I nodded. "I think you're right. I spoke with Etheral, the previous leader of the witches, in the dreamscape. They are terrified of Ollianna, and they are willing to work with us to stop her. She knows that Ollianna is looking for more power. The stones would give her that."

Lila grunted. "You trust that witch?"

"No, not fully." I stretched my arms over my head, feeling the muscles pop and stretch. Stiff, I slid off Balder's back and walked beside him. "But I believe her when she says she is afraid of Ollianna. With the emerald stone, she's more powerful in her abilities with the reptile world, and now the falak is on its way to being born . . . even the witches have realized when they are being used."

I looked at Maks. "Anything in your memory banks about where either of the stones might have been stashed?"

His eyes closed and he swayed a bit in the saddle. I reached out and put a hand on his thigh to steady him. He dropped a hand over mine, warm on warm.

A sigh slid from him. "I can see a place, but I can't tell where it is. It seems tropical."

I frowned. "That doesn't help much. Lots of tropical places out there, both on this side of the wall and the other." Tropical would be a hell of a lot farther away than . . . "What do you want to bet the stones were taken out of here before the wall went up? So they were safe from anyone who would try to find them. No one on this side of the wall would be able to cross over. There would have been no way for Ishtar—or me or any of her minions to ever get to them. They were safe."

Maks tipped his head back. "That would make sense. And give a better chance to keep them out of the wrong hands."

"What doesn't make sense," Lila snapped, "is why the fuck Merlin wouldn't just tell us where they are!"

"He doesn't know," Maks said, his eyes at half-mast like he was seeing something inside his head. "The stones were given to those who were to protect them, and they were his most trusted people. They were the strongest, and the purest of heart when they were given the stones. They didn't tell him where they were going. Plus, for all we know, those last two stones were taken from the original protectors."

Balder gave a long low snort and shook his head as if he didn't agree with Maks. I patted him on the neck and closed my eyes. "I feel like the answer is here, that we've got it within our grasp, we just need to find it."

The rest of the night we rode passing ideas back and forth, discussing what kind of creature could be the purest of heart. Maybe a child, but a child would need a protector, and a child would grow up and become an adult—a not so pure at heart adult, no doubt.

Maybe a powerful creature like the Wyvern.

Maybe a spiritual creature like the Oracle.

There were just too many options and not enough time to check them all out.

Near dawn, we stopped to camp for the day.

Maks made a small fire and Lila brought back a pair of desert hares we roasted far past being done so Maks could eat them too. Lila grimaced as she watched me eat. "I'm glad I took the innards first. That looks terrible."

The color on Maks's face changed as he took a bite of his hare and closed his eyes. Some things would never change. He would always turn green at the thought of raw meat and Lila eating still-warm guts.

Merlin would always be turning on a dime and changing his mind.

Lila would always be my loyal friend, sister of my heart.

Balder would always run like the wind.

Maks would always stand with me, no matter what we faced. Handy that he had so much inside his head that could be helpful now, but that was an added bonus.

My family . . . I frowned, my thoughts tightening over my brother first. Bryce would always be my brother, but it was my mother who came to mind so forcefully, it was as if she were there with me, standing with me, directing me. I would always have her . . .

Journals.

I scrambled up from where I was sitting and both horses startled, snorting at me with irritation. Maks grabbed his weapon and held it out, doing a tight crouched circle. "What is it?"

"The journals! My mother's journals that no one could read because they were in glyphs! What if you can read them now, Maks? What if with all that knowledge in your head, you can read them?" I grabbed at the saddlebag that held the papers and yanked them out. What was left of them anyway.

They were crumpled and dirty, sweat- and water-stained, but I had them.

Maks put his weapon down and strode to my side. He took the first paper from me and nodded. "Yes, this is . . . they are directions. Zam, they're directions! They were done in code though, that's why . . ."

He took the stack of papers, shuffling them until he had them in an order that he seemed satisfied with. "There are some missing, though."

"Yeah." I glanced at Lila, remembering all too well the acid vomit that had preceded the loss of some of the papers. "It was an accident."

She cringed. "I'm sorry."

I waved a hand at her. "Don't fret about it. This is still more than we had a few minutes ago."

Maks muttered under his breath and pulled a paper out, then shoved it back in. "So read individually. You can see each glyph," he held a paper out to me, showing me the image of the black lion pinned on its back, the glyph I'd believed meant that Ford would die, "seems to be independent of all the others. But when you read them together, it's a message. It's a message from your mother to you written basically in code."

He sat down.

I sat across from him. "A message that will help us?"

"I think so." He waved his hand over the paper, and there was a spurt of his magic that sank into the thick parchment paper. I watched in absolute fascination as the images turned into words and lined up, the top starting with "My dearest daughter."

Maks looked over the papers, set them in order, and then handed them to me. "You read them first. In case they are personal. I think I have them in order, or as close as you're going to get with the missing bits."

I took the paper, feeling the weight of it as if they were a pile of stones, and not a note from a mother I barely remembered. A mother I'd put on a pedestal and kept there my entire life. I really hoped I hadn't been wrong about that.

I blew out a breath and started to read.

My dearest daughter,

There is no time to waste. When you read this will be when you must take action of a sort that will change the face of the desert, and perhaps the world, for generations to come.

The Emperor is a danger, but more than that, the danger will come from his wife should she ever gain back the power removed from her. He is a puppet who belongs to Ishtar, and that is something not even his only son knows. No one knows what I know, and now what you know.

Ishtar is the desert goddess. She gave the Emperor his abilities. She created the falak from mythology to give the Emperor a reason to rule—a reason to be a hero.

She is the danger that no one understands because she has hidden behind so many others. Her magic has infected those it touches. Because you and I were born of the Emperor's line, a line created by her magic, we have an immunity to her powers that no others have. It is why she hates me so, and one day will hate you too.

THERE WAS A BREAK BETWEEN THAT AND THE NEXT page that told me I was missing a chunk. I could only hope it wasn't important.

THE STONES YOU MUST FIND, THE STONES *I* HAVE BEEN *hunting for my whole life are the three you will need to*

SHANNON MAYER

stop her. The first lies with the Wyvern in the desert sands. The second lies deep within the jungles of Africa with the Changeling, and the third lies in the heart of the purest creature alive—

THE BREAK THERE WAS MADDENING. WHAT I wouldn't give to have that final creature spelled out, seeing as there was no actual place given. As it was . . . the fucking jungles of Africa?

I HAVE NOT MUCH ELSE TO TELL YOU EXCEPT THAT I DO not know if even the three stones will be enough to stop her. But she is the one, my girl. She is the one you must stop at all costs, you must take the stones from her. Give them to my brother, he can hold them and send them to safety once more. The Emperor is a puffball compared to Ishtar. He . . . my relationship with him was complicated, as I suspect yours will be as well. He is broken by her magic. When you see the one that is Shax, that is the father I knew and even loved. The other, the Emperor, he is the creation of Ishtar.

ANOTHER BREAK.

TAKE ALL YOU CAN TO STOP ISHTAR. YOU WILL NEED ALL

you have to stand against her power, and when the moment comes—and you will know when—then you must give the stones to—

THAT WAS THE FINAL BREAK. THERE WAS NO *I LOVE you*, no *you can do this*, no final words of encouragement.

I swallowed hard and turned the paper over, but there was nothing left, no more words. I handed them over to Maks to read. Lila sat on his shoulder reading along with him.

He let out a low whistle as he finished. "What do you think?"

"I think we go to the Emperor," I said softly. "And I think we let him loose."

Lila hopped off Maks's shoulder and let out a strangled squeak. "Let him loose?"

The flail shivered on my back.

Yes, I agree.

Ignoring Marsum's voice, I nodded. "I was already considering it. Let him loose, make him an ally if we can."

"Then we make a run for the other stones." Maks gave a slow nod. "He'll keep the others busy. At the very least, he'll attack Ollianna and the falak."

"That would be the hope. To them, we aren't really players in this game," I said. "Not really. Irritants at best."

"I don't think that's true, at least not about all of them," Lila said. "If Ishtar believed you to be nothing, she wouldn't have sent Steve and Darcy after you. She wouldn't have tried to control you for all those years. She sees potential in you, maybe the way she saw it in your mother."

"She sent them to help me," I pointed out. Which totally contradicted my mother's message. I held the papers, looking the words over again.

"What if," Maks took one of the papers from me and read it again, "what if Ishtar knew Steve would try to kill you? But by sending him to help, she removed the blame from herself?"

My guts twisted, souring at the suggestion, and not because he was wrong. "Fuck."

Basically, that meant even if we distracted Ollianna with the Emperor, we'd still have to watch for Ishtar—she would still be looking for ways to remove me. I worried at the inside of my cheek, holding it between my teeth. "There's a way to check on her. I could walk the dreamscape and go to the Stockyards. I could see what she's doing."

Maks closed his eyes. "Be careful."

"You're not going to try to talk me out of it?" I raised an eyebrow.

He smiled and reached for me, tugging me tightly to his side, then kissed my head. "No. It's smart to find out what the enemy is up to, even if I don't like that you'll be in danger. And I know you well enough to know you'd do it anyway."

"I can go with her," Lila said. "And if you hear us yelling, you wake us up. You're our lifeline, Toad."

Lila hopped across the ground and on the final bounce landed in my lap.

Maks tightened his arms around us both. "'My troublous dreams this night doth make me sad.'"

I smiled against him. "'What dreamed, my lord? Tell me, and I'll requite it with sweet rehearsal of my morning's dream.'"

"Let's hope it's sweet," Maks murmured against my hair. "Let's hope that—"

"*Henry VI!*" Lila said. "That was a good one."

"Fitting, very fitting," I said around a jaw-cracking yawn. I closed my eyes, knowing I was safe in Maks's arms, and fell asleep.

18

The dreamscape world was becoming far more familiar to me than I really wanted it to be. Lila peered up over my shoulder. "Strange to be here during the day, isn't it?"

"It's not really any better. Except that most of the assholes are awake which means we won't have to deal with them." I pushed to my feet, and Lila flew into the air above my head. I shifted down to my four legs and took off as fast as I could, the two of us racing toward the Stockyards.

Lila zipped along above me. "I like how fast we can travel here."

"Me too," I said as I jumped over three sand dunes at once, landing on the far side light as a feather. I kept an eye out for Steve, wondering if I'd see his shambling zombie ass on the way, but he never appeared. Relief flowed through me, surprising me. I didn't need to see him more tortured, even if he was dead. Or mostly dead. Even if I was the one who'd suggested it.

Lila and I slowed our approach when we could see the Stockyards ahead. "So, what are we hoping for exactly?"

"Any information we can use about what she's planning, if she knows where the stones are, or worse, if she has them. We'll find all of that in her personal chambers," I said. "Follow me. We'll stay close to the ground and use the shadows."

Lila dropped and jogged along beside me. We were of a size that we could have been harnessed together to pull a cart had a fairy decided to snag us.

We ducked in through the courtyard that held the horses. A smell of flesh and blood slowed my feet. "You picking up on that?"

Lila gave a little snort and shook her head. "Yeah, someone has been hurt."

The smell intensified, sticking to the back of my throat as I crept closer, ducking behind rain barrels and other buckets that had been overturned. I paused outside Balder's stall and then turned with my head cocked to one side. "Animals can see into the dream-scape and are often here."

"Yes," Lila paused and her wings trembled. "Oh no."

I turned away from Balder's stall and hurried to

the one next to him. Empty, but the third one down held the body of a horse flickering in and out. Dying.

The next and the next were the same: horses I knew and had trained, horses I'd fed and cared for were being slaughtered.

I didn't realize I was going to them until Lila tugged me away from the stalls. "You can't save them. Ishtar is doing it so no one else can get away from her."

I let her drag me backward, all the way to Balder's thankfully empty stall. I slid in and took a moment to catch my breath. "I shouldn't be surprised by her cruelty. I shouldn't be." But I was, because I remembered who she'd been before. I remembered her touch on my brow when the nightmares had come for me after the slaughter at the Oasis.

Lila butted her head against mine. "Let's see what we can find out and get the hell out of here."

I blew out a breath, trying to erase what I'd seen, and led the way once more. I leapt up to the window ledge that led into my old room. Sure, we could have walked in from a different direction, but part of me couldn't break old habits. This was how I would always come to this place.

I hopped down onto my bed and hurried across the small room to the door. It was shut, but that was easily fixed. One bound into the air and I was hanging from the lever handle. I pushed with my back feet against the wall and the heavy door creaked open a few inches.

Just enough for Lila and me to force our way through into the dim light of the hallway. I turned and hopped up for the handle on this side, once more using my back feet against the wall to get the door shut. No point in letting anyone know we were here, or that we'd been here.

Lila blinked her big eyes at me and gave me the slightest of nods as I dropped to the floor. By unspoken agreement, we were silent as I led us through the Stockyards, deeper and deeper until we reached Ishtar's inner sanctum. There were no guards, and I didn't hear or smell anything. Maybe they were all outside slaughtering the horses. I bit back a snarl, put my nose to the door and pushed it open.

Lila crept in beside me. "She doesn't lock her door?" she whispered.

"Who would dare come in?" I whispered back.

"Best jewel thief in the world?" Lila offered.

"And her smart-ass dragon sister?"

She grinned. I shifted from four legs to two. Hands would be far more helpful with this part of the snoop. I went to Ishtar's desk first and was immediately disappointed. Other than a single drawing, a picture of a black cat that didn't look all that different from me, there was nothing. I let my finger drift over it, over the green eyes and the fierce set of the cat.

I had no doubt she'd drawn this, but why of me when I was a jungle cat? She'd never seen me like that. I shook my head and let it go, knowing that a single picture didn't matter. Not now.

There wasn't a single other piece of paper, not a book, not even a scrap of a note on the massive desk. I opened drawer after drawer, only to find them completely empty.

I put both hands on the desk and leaned forward. I remembered clearly seeing all sorts of maps and paperwork on her desk the few times I'd been welcomed here. I ran a hand over my head, trying to think where else she might have put them.

"Wait for me here, keep looking," I whispered as I shifted back to four legs and hurried out of the room.

The one place that Ishtar held closer than her office was where she slept.

I'd never been allowed in there.

No one had that I knew of.

I hurried to the south end of the structure and the stairs that led down, down under the belly of the building. With my eyes, the dim light didn't bother me, and I could find my way easily. Bonus was my dark fur and size kept me well hidden from any eyes that might be looking for me.

Ishtar's smell thickened the closer I got to my destination. Spices, thick and heady, and a distinct tang of ozone, like an oncoming storm. That was new, but it smelled like her all the same.

At the bottom of the stairs the doorway stood cracked open with a sliver of light falling out of it. Like an invitation, as if she'd known I would come to her.

Fuck. I froze on the stairs and waited, listening, smelling, trying to pull up every sense I had to see if she was indeed in her room.

"Fuck." A growled word slid from a voice I knew all too well.

The Emperor.

And he was rifling through Ishtar's things?

This was more and more intriguing. If what my mother had said was true, he knew that he was not the powerhouse here, but Ishtar had let him take the fall as the one to be afraid of while she remained free.

I all but slithered down the last few steps and crept into the room. The Emperor had a small lantern in one hand and he dug through the books on her shelf with the other, knocking the books off, making no attempt to hide that he'd been there.

He'd have made a terrible thief.

I crept across the floor, keeping tight to the wall, making sure only to move when the light swung farther away from me. I reached the side of a book-shelf and tucked myself into the shadows to watch and wait. He and I needed to talk. I wasn't sure this was the right moment, but I was willing to take it if it came.

The Emperor sat on the edge of the massive bed and ran a hand over his head, not unlike how I'd done just moments before. The family connection was there, whether I wanted it to be or not.

"Where are you hiding them?" he muttered as he looked around the room. His eyes swept over me, not even seeing me within the shadows.

Another score for the little black house cat.

What did he mean by hiding them? Was he looking for the stones too? It seemed likely, but why would he think she had them?

What else could he be looking for?

Footsteps on the stairs were light, the footsteps of the woman I'd considered my mother for so many years.

Fuck. Shit. Son of a goat fucking bitch. I sunk deeper into the shadows and held my breath.

Ishtar swept into the room and slammed it open. "What are you doing here?"

"My love," the Emperor purred and leaned back on the bed. Damn, I could suddenly see a resemblance between him and Merlin. That ability to act and lie was ingrained in them as breathing.

Ishtar didn't soften, but she didn't try to hurt him either. "What are you doing here? We agreed to meet later."

"I couldn't wait." He patted the edge of the bed

and I struggled not to move. The desire to squirm cut through me. I did not want to see this. Through narrowed eyes, I calculated how far I was from the door, and if I could make it without being seen. Two sets of eyes were worse than one, especially when one set was Ishtar.

She went to the Emperor and sat beside him. "The falak is being reborn. I do not know how it is possible."

He grunted. "Ollianna was always thirsty for power. As is your daughter."

I frowned. Daughter? Did he mean me?

"She comes by it honestly." Ishtar shrugged. "My daughter is weak, though, and already has been swayed away from your teachings. That priestess has convinced her to help Zamira."

The Emperor blinked a few times, his shock apparent. Maybe he wasn't such a good actor. "She turned on me?"

"Easily." Ishtar's response was dry. "Why you think you inspire such loyalty is beyond me."

I had to agree with her on that one.

The Emperor pursed his lips and tapped the fingers of one hand on his thigh. "Zamira is still headed my way. When I take the flail, you still want me to kill her?"

Oh shit.

Ishtar was silent long enough that I knew the answer before she spoke it. "Yes. She is far too close to figuring this out. She carries four stones with her; take them."

Now the Emperor did startle. "Four? She found one of the missing stones?"

"Yes." The word was sharp and biting this time. "I am close to finding the others. One is with that bitch in the jungle. I'm sure of it."

Part of what she said was a lie. I could all but taste it on the air as she spoke. So she was stumped, was she? Good.

But who was she talking about? The changeling in the jungle then was female.

The Emperor's face was carefully neutral, which made me think he might know who the bitch was.

"Once you have all the stones," he said, "we can finally move forward together."

I almost wondered if I shouldn't bother to find the stones, leave them to stay hidden wherever they were. But if my mother thought they were important, then I needed to get them, and . . . well, maybe use them? Cast them? I wasn't sure.

"When you find them, we shall be free together." He leaned over and pressed his lips to hers. "But first . . ." He pulled her down to the bed, and she didn't fight him.

This was my chance.

With my belly low to the ground, I crept across the floor. At the stairs, I glanced back as Ishtar sat up. "No, we have much to do still."

Well, shit.

I froze.

Our eyes met.

Hers widened and I bolted up the stairs as fast as I could, feeling her magic curling toward me. She would kill me now if she could, knowing that my death here would be my death in the waking world.

I was up the stairs and racing toward the office where I'd left Lila before the magic kissed at my heels. I growled and picked up speed, turned a corner and bought myself time bolting through the narrow opening into the office. I spun, shifted to two feet and slammed the door shut, locking it.

"Time to go, Lila!" I said as I shifted back to four legs, even though my bones protested that many shifts.

"Who saw you?"

"The Emperor and Ishtar," I said as I leapt to the one bookshelf that still stood, even if it was empty.

"You don't do anything small, do you? It couldn't have been like the cook, or maybe a maid. No, you had to show yourself to those two ding-dong-alongs," she muttered as she grabbed me around the middle and flew us both high into the rafters.

The door below rattled and I pointed at the window that was now our only hope for escape. It didn't open as far as I needed, which meant we had to break it. Here's to hoping it wasn't thick old glass.

Colored glass winked at me as I raced across the

rafters and scrambled up to the window ledge, throwing my body at the glass as the door behind us blew open on a blast of magic that I felt more than saw.

Not unlike Ishtar's scream that shot down my spine as I fell out of the window, legs splayed to slow my fall.

Lila's claws once more wrapped around my middle before I'd fallen even ten feet, and then we were high in the air flying hard for the far desert. But Ishtar's magic was coming for us fast, a billowing wash of magic that would consume us both.

"Maks!" I screamed for him. "MAKS!"

Lila joined me. "TOAD!"

A splash of cold water snapped me upright, out of the dreamscape and once more in the desert leagues away from the Stockyards, sending me into a weird spiral that was discombobulating as I fought the urge to pat my body down, to make sure I was there all in one piece.

Lila spluttered and gasped, her body drenched too.

"That was intense," she said.

"What happened?" Maks grabbed me by my arms and gave me a squeeze, helping me center myself.

I quickly went over what I'd seen, and what Ishtar had said. That the Emperor was going to kill me when I took him the flail. But I wasn't sure I believed that. He'd been looking for something when I'd come upon him, and Ishtar didn't know that.

"Well, that isn't going to happen then," Lila said. "It's as simple as that."

She was right, and she was so very, very wrong.

19

"I still have to take the Emperor the flail," I said as I wiped the water out of my eyes and flicked it away with a quick shake of my fingers. Getting snapped out of the dreamscape with a bucket of water was effective but left me like water left any cat —irritated.

"WHAT?" Lila burst out, her voice bigger than before, much bigger.

I turned as she shifted to her big dragon form, looming over us. The horses snorted and startled back a bit. She bent her head to Balder's nose and brushed her snout against his. He blew out a big snort and shook his head.

"Good to see the venom shit wore off finally," I said.

"It's about damn time," Lila said. "But don't try to

distract me. You cannot possibly think to take the flail to the Emperor. Can you?"

I turned my back on her and Maks as I paced a small circle around our camp, back and forth, my mind working over what I knew. "Here's the thing: I saw the Emperor in the room before Ishtar came in. He was looking for something, several somethings."

"So?" Maks stood with his arms crossed. "That doesn't mean he won't kill you."

I thought about all my interactions with the Emperor, with all the times he could have killed me. All the times he could have and didn't. Of my mother's words, that there were two sides to him, a truth I'd seen for myself.

There was no trust between us, but maybe an understanding that I got because he was blood. I would never call him family, that would indicate some love between us. But blood understood blood in a way that I wasn't sure I could explain. "I think he wants to overthrow Ishtar. He wants the stones too, but he can't tell her that. Can he?"

Maks's jaw tightened. "I don't like what you're suggesting. You think he'd help you?"

At that, I shook my head. "Help me, no."

My original plan that I'd started putting together when I knew we had to go to the Emperor and take him the flail was still possible. In fact, I might be even more at an advantage knowing what I knew now. I grabbed my bottom lip, pinching it as I thought. "The truth is, none of the three superpowers we're dealing with want to share. Do they?"

"No," Lila said carefully as she laid her body down.

I looked at Maks. "Do they?"

He shook his head. "No. They don't. But they all see you as a threat of some sort. So why wouldn't they pair up, just like Ishtar and the Emperor are doing to wipe the common threat out?"

I shrugged. "Possible. But this is a blindside that Ishtar would never see coming. That Ollianna would never see coming. We use the Emperor, and he thinks he's using us, using me."

Maks rolled his head back so he was looking up into the bright blue sky. "The memories I have say it is possible that you could be right. It's a bold move, a risky move. We still don't know if the flail will kill him. Which will make it awfully hard to have a partner."

I reached back and touched the handle of the flail. "The flail is more than a weapon now." It shivered in my hand and down the length of my back in response. "The weapon holds an aspect of Marsum in it."

What are you trying to do?

"I'm suggesting that Marsum, whatever is left of him in this weapon, might try to hold the Emperor off long enough that he would rid himself of a weapon that is useless, then . . ."

I can try, but I cannot control it.

I'd take that chance.

Lila chuckled. "Then you would pick it up again?"

I pointed a finger at her. "Bingo."

Maks rubbed his hands over his face. "I don't know. I feel like we're missing something."

"It's not a guarantee," I let go of the handle, "but . . . it's a chance. And maybe that's all we've got now."

He sighed. "Okay, so what's the plan to get there?"

I smiled. "We have Lila to carry us the rest of the way. That will speed things up."

"And once we're there?" Maks asked.

"Once we're there, I'll go in and give the Emperor the flail." This was where I knew they would argue.

"By yourself." The flat tone of Maks's voice said it all. I grimaced.

"That's the plan."

"No." Lila and Maks spoke at the same time. Much as I'd expected. I held up my hands, palms out in mock surrender. Totally mock surrender.

"Here's the deal. We have four stones, four stones and one of them has the power of destruction in it," I said softly. "We can't let him get his hands on any of them. The flail, as strong as it is, isn't the only power we are dealing with. What about the other two missing stones? We have to find those. We *have* to."

Lila groaned. "I see a long flight in our future."

I grinned at her. "But it will be to somewhere new. Somewhere beyond the wall."

Her eyes opened a little wider and her wings perked up. "True. Do you think the humans on the other side have ever seen a dragon?"

"Not one like you," I said with a grin, knowing her little ego would love blowing human minds.

We spent the day planning how this would go. The hardest part was realizing that we had to leave the two horses behind. We needed to be able to fly fast to the Emperor, and fast away, and then to the deep jungle where horses would not be the best mode of transportation.

Maks and I rode atop Lila as she scooped the horses up and carried them off to the edge of the desert, closer to food and water. The grass was more plentiful; I had no doubt that Balder would find a water source in no time. But that didn't make it any easier to even think about leaving them behind.

Because there was something else I needed to leave besides the horses. Something that everyone wanted but me.

"I don't want to leave them behind." I turned my head so I could speak quietly to Maks over the rush of wind around us.

"I know. But you're right, the jungle is not the place for them. Remember the witches' Swamp? We were lucky, and that wasn't near as thick as what we're headed into." Maks kissed the side of my neck, a press of his lips that felt as though he were trying to impress on me his words.

It had been my idea to leave the horses behind. There were all sorts of reasons to do it, mostly to keep them safe. Yet my heart . . . ah, my heart didn't want to leave Balder behind.

The time went by too quickly, and suddenly we were there at the edge of the desert where I thought the two boys would have the best chance of finding food, water, and some form of shelter.

I found myself slowing as I stripped off Balder's tack, taking my time. Because what if I couldn't find him again? Here at the edge of the desert, he would find his way back toward the steppes of the mountains where he was born. I was sure of it. But a herdsman of the mountains or a trader would scoop him up in an instant. He was the best of the best, after all.

Free of any gear, he stood there and looked at me with those big dark eyes, questioning me. His coat was glossy and for the first time I noticed how much he was graying, his coat getting lighter as he aged. Wouldn't be long and he'd no longer be my gray gelding, but my white one. He wasn't the young horse I'd found and fought for all those years ago, the young horse that had tested my every training technique until finally he'd decided I was acceptable as a rider.

And this would be the first time I'd willingly left him behind on any of my journeys.

"I know," I whispered as I stroked his neck and up

between his ears. "But you can't come with us on this part. You just can't." He shook his head and pushed his nose against my belly. I wrapped my arms around his head and held him tightly. "Take care of Batman, and after we're done with all this . . . Maks or I will find you. I promise. And I need you to watch out for that spot I stashed . . ." I whispered the words to him. "Keep it safe if you can."

He pulled his head back and then shoved me hard in the belly. "Okay, okay." I reached for his muzzle and lifted his nose up for a kiss on the end of it. "I'll come find you. I promise."

That seemed to satisfy him, but he didn't leave, neither he nor Batman left, not even when Maks and I scrambled up on Lila's back and she lifted into the air.

Our gear was stashed between some rocks, and we'd left food and water for the horses. Enough for a day or two.

I looked back as we flew away to see Balder racing down the short slope and bolting after us, Batman close on his heels. Following us.

"Maks."

He turned to look at where I pointed and Lila slowed and did a quick turn. "Lila," Maks said softly. "Chase them back."

"Crap," she muttered even as she tucked her wings and dove toward the two horses. I expected them to run. I expected Balder to be smart.

He rose up on his hind legs and whinnied, as if he'd fight Lila for me.

She swept close enough that her wings brushed over top of him, but he didn't back down. He whinnied again, shook his head and struck the ground with his front legs, one after the other.

"What do we do?" Lila said.

With any other horse, you'd leave them behind, and they'd be glad for the break, but not Balder. Not my boy.

"Land," I said. "I have to make him go."

Lila dropped to the ground and I slid off. Balder trotted up to me, his ears pinned to his head, as pissed as I'd ever seen him. "Balder. That's enough!" I clapped my hands together and his ears popped forward. "I can't do this if you don't listen to me! You need to go, you need to hide and I will come for you, I promise. But I can't go if I know you're putting yourself in danger!"

Gods, you'd think I was a fool for talking to him like he understood clearly.

But with Balder, he'd always been different. He'd always been special. He looked from me to Maks, and then to Lila and shook his head. I reached for him and brushed a hand down the middle of his face. "I promise, Balder. I'm not leaving you forever, just for a little while. And I asked you . . . you have to keep it safe. You have to."

He shook his head vigorously, then let out a long,

low blow of air, like a big sigh. A soft nicker and then he turned and trotted back the way he'd come, gathering up Batman as he went. There was a moment that he looked over his shoulder at me, and his eyes were as full of thoughts and emotions as any person's.

You'd better not be lying or I'll kick your ass. That was the impression I got and it made me laugh.

"All right all right! But we'll be back. I promise."

As soon as we'd finished this mess. Which meant Balder and Batman would be safe from Ollianna, the Emperor, and Ishtar.

I climbed back up on Lila and Maks pulled me the rest of the way up. "He's loyal to you. You can't fault him that."

I nodded, my throat tight with the knowledge that I would probably never see my horse again. He was the best boy, and I had to leave him behind.

As we flew away the second time, the horses didn't follow us. Balder looked back a few times. I know because I did the same, but we kept moving in opposite directions.

Lila flew in the direction I pointed as the flail tingled along my spine. Without it, I wasn't sure how long it would have taken us to find the Emperor's Throne.

"You know," Lila said as we banked through a big bunch of clouds full of moisture that caught in our hair and on our skin, "Ollianna has been quiet. You think she's given up on chasing us down?"

"Don't say that out loud," Maks said. "She might be listening."

"Or fate might be listening," I said.

"You mean Murphy's Law?" Lila offered. "If something can go wrong, it will, and with great fanfare?"

I shook my head. "Let's hope not."

Around us the sky darkened, just a fraction of a degree, and the wind blowing into our faces picked up. Again, just a fraction, but we all felt it. And it was not natural.

"Lila," I said softly, "where did Trick go exactly?"

She turned her head to look at me. "He was talking to another dragon, a female that said she loved him. He told her he loved her too. That he would be with her as soon as he'd dealt with us."

Not the kind of language one used if he actually gave a shit about Lila. Or any of us. "You think he saw you?"

She shook her head. "No."

"Then I think when he shows up, we wait for him to show his true colors, and then *we* deal with *him*," I said.

A shiver rolled through her along with a wave of pain that came through the bond between us. Both Maks and I lowered a hand to her scaled side. "We're here, Lila. You aren't going to do this alone," he said.

"I know." She shook her head. "I just wish I didn't have to do it at all."

The whoosh of a body above us made me duck, and Maks grabbed me around the waist. Trick's silver and white body flew through the air. He flipped over in a barrel roll and grinned at us, as if nothing was wrong. "Just wish you didn't have to do what?"

20

I waved a hand at Trick as he and Lila flew side by side, furious that he'd hurt her, hating that he'd lied to us all. The thing was, we couldn't let on that we knew he'd been a turncoat this whole time. "We have to go to the Emperor," I said. "I hate that we have to do it, but we have no choice."

His jaw dropped open and I braced myself for a blast of lightning, but he just spluttered. "But you can't go to him. If you go to him, he'll kill you. He'll kill all of you."

I noticed that he did not say "us." Maks's arm tightened around my middle, no doubt picking up on the same thing.

Whatever game Trick was playing, it wasn't with us. He'd never truly been with us.

I just wished I knew whose side he was on. Much as I wanted to say it was Ollianna's, I didn't think that was the case, not at all. If he'd belonged to Ollianna, he would have dropped on us in the sky, raining lightning down from a distance.

"You don't have to come with us," Lila said, and the strain in her voice was obvious, at least to me. "I don't expect you to put yourself in any more danger than you already have. Whatever debt you think you owe us for saving your life is gone."

I watched his face closely, saw the quick frown there and gone in a flash. Lila was looking straight ahead, flying in the direction I gave her. I pressed against her side with my right leg and she drifted away from it. I pushed down on her back with my hand and she dropped through the clouds, listening to my silent cues. Which meant he couldn't see me directing her.

Maks kept his arm tightly around me, worry coming through loud and clear in the bonds that drew us together. There was no doubt in my mind we were playing a dangerous game with Trick.

"Trick," I called up to him, "how are the dragons faring without Corvalis? Did Ollianna catch any more of them?"

He flew down to our side, his wingtips brushing Lila's. She moved away from him without any direction on my part. He didn't seem to notice. "They haven't all been taken, but I think a few have gone missing. Without Corvalis or the gemstone to strengthen him, we are vulnerable to her commands."

"He is a monster," Lila said, "or have you forgotten that so soon?"

Trick gave a low growl. "He is our king, Lila. Your father."

"Two things I wish weren't true," she said.

Trick coasted along, but didn't say anything. What I caught was the slightest glance upward, the slightest flicker of his eyes. It was enough for me.

I pressed hard against Lila's back and she dropped, spiralling away from Trick. Maks gripped me hard and I dared a single look up, and part of me wished I hadn't.

High above us was the massive form of a black dragon I knew all too well. "Lila! Go hard, hard as you can!"

She flattened out, the land between us very different than even just a few hours before. The smell of salt water rushed up my nose. The flail warmed and shivered at the same time along my spine and I directed Lila toward the ocean.

Behind us came a massive roar followed by multiple bolts of lightning that Lila twisted and dodged as if she could feel them coming. Maks slipped, his hold loosening.

And then he was gone. I twisted, saw how close we were to the water—and the ravaged chunk of ground that housed an entrance to the Emperor's prison. I knew we could swim to it and I let go of my ride. "Lila, we're good, go, go!"

Go where I didn't know.

I shifted to four legs as I fell, landing in the water of the ocean. The ocean swallowed me whole as I sunk down and then fought to get to the surface. I clawed my way up, broke the surface and drew in a deep breath. The waves weren't strong and I could see over them to the caracal that swam through the water with me.

Side by side, we paddled hard for the shore that beckoned to us—a blasted island that was broken and torn as if it had been burned and shattered against rocks. I looked above our heads to see Lila dodging Trick and sending her own blasts his way, that sparkling acid that was so deadly.

Above them, Corvalis waited.

He waited for her to be hurt, to be killed by Trick.

"Maks, we have to hurry!" I swam harder, putting all my efforts into getting to the shore. I didn't have time to think about just what we were doing, how this was going to work, how exactly we were going to help Lila.

Unless she was with us.

Inside the Emperor's Throne.

"Lila, to me!" I yelled. "Small!"

I reached the shore next to Maks and bolted across the little bit of sand and strewn rocks, heading straight up the inclining hill, feeling a pull on my feet that I didn't understand, but went with. The slope was unnatural as though it had been placed there by someone, stacked up to make a sloppy pyramid. The sound of wings, the bellow of an enraged dragon, a bolt of lightning crashed down beside us throwing up stones and dirt, but I didn't slow, we couldn't. A split second later, Lila flew beside me and Maks, small once more.

"You hurt?" I gasped out as I bounded from one rock to another.

"Just pissed," she growled. "What's the plan?"

"All three of us are going in," I said. Which hadn't been the plan, but there was no way the two dragons could get in, not if the flail was truly the only weapon that could break the Emperor's prison.

At the top of the slope was a doorway, only it was a doorway into the ground. I didn't hesitate, but shifted to two feet between strides, feeling the pull of the flail on my back, stronger now that we were so close to the Emperor.

I reached down and grabbed the iron ring attached to the trapdoor. With a hard yank, I had it open, motioned for Lila and Maks to go, turned and one-finger saluted Trick and Corvalis, and dropped through the trapdoor.

The last thing I heard was the slam of lightning on the door itself, but it didn't give. I was not surprised about that. I mean, I'd been hoping that would be the case, but still, my plans didn't always go as I thought they should.

I landed in a crouch in the pitch black. Maks held

SHANNON MAYER

up a hand, lit with a deep orange glow as he held a flame of magic in his palm. I looked around to see a torch set in the wall. "Use that maybe."

The lightning battered the trapdoor above and then came a heavier thud along with the deep metal screeching of claws on the trapdoor. "We've got to get deeper."

Lila flew up to land on my shoulder, her tail wrapping around my neck and her fingers digging into the edge of my ear. "I hate both of them."

"Yeah, I'm not real fond of them, either," I said. I took down the torch from the wall and Maks lit it. The torch threw far more light than it should have, giving us a very good view of the room ahead of us. The space stretched out long and narrow without any adornments on either side. A perfect place for an ambush. I looked around and saw a few rocks on the floor. I scooped two of them up, handed off the torch to Maks and tossed the first rock down the long hallway.

There was a shush of something opening, just the slightest of sounds, and then a whole bunch of arrows flew out of the left side, slamming into the right side of the wall.

I looked at Maks. "Reminds me of Dragon's Ground."

"Me too," he grumbled.

"We survived that," I reminded him.

Lila shook her head. "And ended up with the entirety of Corvalis's battle dragons chasing you."

She made a good point.

I threw the second rock, bouncing it off one wall so it ricocheted several times.

Nothing popped out.

Another screech bellowed from above us. There was no time to waste. "I'll go first." I took a step and fell forward, pulled into the dreamscape by a spell we'd not seen or triggered.

Well, fuck.

21

I was still inside the Emperor's Throne, only now I was in the dreamscape which did me zero good. "Listen, asshole, I'm trying to bring you the flail. Kind of hard to do when I'm in a dreamscape!"

The laughter that answered me at one point would have chilled me, would have scared me down to my bones. But I was beyond that now. All the fucks I had to give were gone, and I was done playing nice.

I thought back to the first time I'd met him in a dreamscape that he'd pulled me into. He'd tried to convince me he was not a monster, that he was a good ruler, that he thought highly of me. He'd given me his name then, and I used it now.

"Shax," I called out, "you and I made a deal. I am

trying to fulfill my end of it. Kinda hard to do that while sleeping."

"Well, granddaughter . . ." He stepped out of the shadows of the room, both hands tucked behind his back. He was dressed in sand-colored clothes as he had been that first time, his dark brown eyes still the same, even his gray hair was braided off to one side. His skin was as tanned as before, even though I knew he'd not seen the sun for a very long time. "I thought perhaps you and I could talk in private."

I drew in a deep breath and worked to calm the anger coursing through me. I'd grown and learned a great deal in the time between now and when I'd first seen him. I gave him a nod. "Fine."

He smiled, the edges of his eyes crinkling up as if he were indeed that kindly old grandfather he'd wanted me to believe. The man my mother had thought loved her still.

"You brought dragons to my doorstep."

"They want something of mine." I smiled at him. "You know how it is with dragons, always hoarding jewels."

His eyes flashed, but I held up a hand to stop him. "I know you told Ishtar you would kill me, but I don't think you will."

He stopped moving, and his eyes rested on me. "And why is that?"

It was my turn to smile. "Because you and I both

know that if we team up, we have a better chance of stopping not only Ollianna, but Ishtar as well. She can't gain the remaining stones. If she did that . . ." I shrugged. "Who's to say she wouldn't just stick you back in here, and use you as the scapegoat again?" I was guessing, but by the look on his face my guess hit the mark, or at least close enough. I went on. "I have an offer for you, one that I think you'll have a hard time turning down."

The Emperor snapped his fingers and two chairs, a small table between them, appeared. He motioned for me to sit as if we had all the time in the world, which we did not. Not by a long shot. I could feel the fear rolling off Lila and Maks. I didn't know if they were afraid for me, or of the two dragons getting their heads through the upper trapdoor.

"The dragons will not be able to breach even the outer door. You were able to because the spells are tuned to you, thanks to your mother." He sat and waved again for me to sit.

"My mother did this?"

"Not all of it, no. But she came for a visit before you were born, when she was pregnant, actually." He leaned back in his chair and stretched his long legs out. "I don't know what she thought to find, but when she tuned the spells to let her in, you were a part of her. Hence your ability to get through without any effort."

As fascinating as I found the fact that my mother had made a trip all the way here when she was pregnant, that was not the important part of this discussion.

"Why do you think I won't kill you?" He tipped his head to one side. "You have seen both sides of me."

"Yes," I had seen the split personality he carried with him, "even if that asshole side of you showed up right now, you wouldn't kill me. Both sides are far too smart to throw away a useful tool."

The air around him tightened as I thought it would. He shifted his balance forward and there was none of the kindly grandfather left. Instead I stared into the eyes of a power-hungry warlord who would kill any in his path. "You don't think me capable?"

I waved a hand at him, trying to keep my own fear in check, seeing as my survival instinct finally came back to me, reminding me that while he'd not killed me, there had been a couple of times where it had been close. "I think you capable. I just don't think you really want to. I think you always considered me as a potential ally." I smiled at him. "The enemy of my enemy is my friend and all that shit."

"You think Ishtar is my enemy?"

"I think you hate her for helping them trap you in here. I think she believes your lies of love and wanting to be with her. I think I'm one of the few people to see you for who you really are." I put both my hands on the table, palms down. "I think that neither Ishtar nor Ollianna would ever believe that I would join forces with you."

"And you would trust me?"

I stared at him. "I think my mother trusted you."

He blinked a few times. "You think she trusted me?"

I nodded. "Yes. I have her journal. You weren't trying to kill her. Marsum neither. It was Ishtar. Ishtar knew my mother had the ability to stop her and free you. So she had her killed, and me taken so I could be raised under her hand. So that Ishtar could try and warp me, make me what she believed I should be. To turn on you." I blew out a breath. "You are dangerous, and there may come a point where we will stand on either side of a battlefield, but . . . I don't think that time is now."

The Emperor's eyes were unreadable, and his face was no better, but I thought that maybe, just maybe, there was a softening there. "I loved my daughter very much. Her mother was brought to me as a special gift, as a young girl." His eyes went distant. "She was both a shifter and a Jinn, and she'd been . . . imported." He grinned. "I didn't love her, but she gave me my best child before she ran away to her home-land, claiming she never had wanted to leave."

I had to work to keep the look off my face that

said I'd seen how much he cared for at least one of his daughters, giving Ollianna the child she wanted. But I needed him to side with me. I needed him to believe me above anything else. Even if there was much of what he'd done that I thought was deplorable.

"And my mother loved me," I said, keeping it simple, not engaging with the rest of his little monologue.

He looked away from me. "What do you have in mind? Ishtar will want proof of your death."

I touched the flail on my back. "I will free you from this prison, you will take the flail, I will do what I can to convince it not to kill you when you use it. That will help prove to her I'm gone."

The Emperor drummed his fingers on the table. "And you?"

"I think I know where one of the two remaining stones is, and I have a lead on the third."

His hands gripped the table. "And?"

"We need them to stop Ishtar," I said. "And maybe to stop the falak. I don't know about that."

He kept drumming his fingers on the table and I watched and waited. "You go for the two remaining stones, and I will prepare to face Ollianna. I will convince Ishtar that you are dead so you will have no one chasing you. I don't know for how long, but . . . it will buy you time. Granddaughter," he reached over and put a hand on mine, and it took all I had in me not to flinch, "you look very much like your mother."

I nodded. "I've heard that a time or two."

His hand tightened around mine. "Then it is agreed. We will work together to remove Ollianna and Ishtar. You will find the stones, and I—"

I slapped my hand on top of his. "I will hold the stones. They don't drive me mad like they seem to do everyone else." He tried to pull away and I held him tightly. "We have the best chance at surviving this together."

"Agreed." He gave a low growl. "I will wake you, and you will free me."

I didn't let him go. "One more thing. Maybe two."

His eyebrows rose. "Demanding much, yes?"

I smiled. "I have a novel idea. It's about those two asshole dragons up there waiting for us."

"You want me to kill them?"

I shook my head. "No, I want to kill them. But I need a little help."

As I explained my idea to him, he began to laugh. "Oh, you are a devious thing. I see much of your mother in your mind as well as your looks. It will be done, but you will owe me something."

I didn't like that, but seeing as I wasn't sure I'd survive all of this, I agreed.

"And the other?" he asked.

That one was simpler and owed to me. The Emperor grunted. "Fine, agreed. I will lift your curse once and for all. You shall have all the power and abilities that have been kept from you from here on out."

And with the two deals struck, he released me from the dreamscape.

22

I snapped out of the dreamscape with a gasp and the sound of tiny rocks hitting all around my face, the smell of old dust and musty stale air filling my nose and Lila yelling in my ear while she all but pierced the edge of it with her tiny claws.

"I'm awake. I'm awake!" I yelled as I sat up. I pushed to my feet and looked down the long narrow walkway. "Follow me, we have a deal with the Emperor."

That didn't mean it was going to be easy to get to him. Just because he'd agreed not to kill us didn't mean the prison made to hold him wouldn't try.

I took the torch in one hand, and Maks's hand in the other. "Stick close."

"Wasn't planning on leaving you," he said. "Ever."

"Thought maybe you'd want to go chat with Trick and Corvalis," I said, a half-grin on my lips. Lila was going to shit herself when she saw what the Emperor had agreed to do. Temporary, sure, but it was going to be worth the cost he'd asked of me. Whatever and whenever that would be.

Maks tightened his hand over mine. "We've been through worse."

"Don't get sappy on me, you two," Lila grumbled.

"Don't worry, we're going to handle Trick and your asshole father," I said.

She leaned out from her perch on my shoulder, so she could look me in the eye. "How is that going to happen? Is the Emperor going to kill them?"

I shook my head. "Just you wait and see, Lila. Just you wait and see."

At the far end of the narrow hallway, I pushed the next door open. We worked our way through the underground building, going deeper and deeper, until there was no sound but our breathing, and there was no feeling of the world at all, as if we'd stepped into a new realm, not unlike the dreamscape.

We set off a few more traps, avoided them all, but I was moving on some sort of weird autopilot I couldn't escape. The closer we got to the Emperor's prison, the faster I went until I was running, flat out, my hands working the traps with magic I didn't understand.

Lila and Maks were shouting, their voices distant, as they tried to slow me down. As they tried to keep me safe.

The thing was, ahead of me was a ghostly image that I couldn't unsee. My mother, heavily pregnant and leading the way through the maze of the prison, showing me where I needed to be, what traps to set, how to avoid others.

A set of stairs straight down into the earth opened ahead of me, and I flexed my hand, palm up, and wiggled my fingers, drawing the magic to me, seeing it for Merlin's work like so many of the traps had been, and dispersing it as if it were nothing but spiderwebs on the wind.

The stairs beckoned and I was moving down them, lighting the way with my own magic, the power of it coursing through me hot and ready to be used. This was what my curse had held from me.

This is what Ishtar had kept me from.

"She was the one to curse my mother," I whispered, stopping partway down the stairs. I looked back at Maks who was right behind me. "Ishtar was the one to curse my mother, not the Jinn, wasn't she?"

He closed his eyes and then slowly nodded. "Yes and no. She made the Jinn curse her, forcing their hands. It's why it didn't all come off you, even when Marsum removed the curse from you; some of it was her magic holding you back. Fuck, it would have been nice to know this!" He growled and shook his head, his frustration written all over his face. I took his hand again, the urgency to hurry leaving me.

The stone walls were tight around us, but the air was cool and moved as if a breeze blew through from some unknown place deep in the belly of the world.

I drew in a breath, but found nothing nasty, no scent of death or blood, just . . . nothing.

"You really going to do this?" Lila asked as if I could change my mind now.

"Yeah. It will be okay, Lila." I hoped anyway. I was gambling all our lives on an agreement with someone who had a split personality.

Okay, so putting it in those terms it didn't sound like such a good idea.

The bottom of the stairs spread out, leading from the narrow hall to a room that was sunken down a solid foot below the rim of the room. Like an indoor pool, that depression was filled with water. Completely unmoving black water that gave off no reflection.

I grimaced, thinking about just how we—strike that, I—was going to get the Emperor out of that unmoving blackness.

"You think he's under there?" Lila leaned forward. "It doesn't look or smell like water."

"It's a blanket of magic made with the stones." Maks reached out and pulled her back. "Don't touch it. Trust me on this. And don't swing the flail, just lower it to the surface."

I reached for the flail and pulled it from my back, glad that I didn't have to go for a swim in that black water. The handle of the flail was warm and shivered against my palm. "We can do this," I said. Speaking to a weapon, I really had cracked under the pressure.

I hope you are right, otherwise this could truly be goodbye.

There was no turning back, though. The deals had been struck, and I would hold to my word. "Just in case, thanks. And try not to kill him," I whispered. Just stick to the plan, Marsum. That was all I could think. He answered as though he could read my mind, but no doubt was just remembering.

It's not a great plan. You know that?

I shrugged. Great or not, it was literally all I had.

I held the flail out over the black reflective and oh-so-still liquid, then slowly lowered it until I was dipping the twin spiked balls into the inky darkness.

"Suck down the magic," I said. "Free the Emperor." And in my heart, I was already apologizing to the weapon, to Marsum, for giving it up. Because if I was wrong, we were all so very screwed.

My heart hammered like crazy, and the smell of my own fear mingled with Maks's and Lila's, clogging my throat. If I was wrong, we were all dead, and we all knew it.

The black mirror shimmered as the spikes slid through it, and then a groan rumbled through the mirror, and the air, deepening in sound, seemed to tighten around the flail and the black mirror suddenly let out a shriek of protest. Lines shot out in every direction from where the flail touched, like a massive spiderweb. The flail was yanked from me by an unseen force and pulled to the center of the room, the center of the black mirror. Then it began to sink. I held up a hand, almost reaching for it, because the weapon was mine.

I bit my lower lip, feeling stupidly . . . at a loss. Like a part of me was sinking into the mirror.

The cracks deepened as the last of the flail disappeared and a low laugh began to rumble through the space.

I stepped in front of Maks.

I suddenly wasn't so sure that the Emperor would hold to his word, despite my having made the deal with him in good faith. "Be ready to run," I whispered.

Maks sounded like I was strangling him. "What?"

I flashed him a grimace. "Just in case?"

He closed his eyes. "You're lucky I trust you."

"Samesies," Lila whispered.

My eyes were drawn back to the black mirror as the cracks deepened and flowed until there was no part that wasn't split into slivers. The laughter rose in volume and the shards began to tremble.

"Get down!" I yelled, and we flattened ourselves to the ground as the mirror exploded upward. Lila dropped and I shifted to four legs, flattening my belly to the ground. Eyes closed, I could only hope Maks had done the same.

The sound of tinkling glass as it fell to the ground twisted my head around. I pushed quickly to my feet, and then stepped through the doorway in my mind back to two legs. Lila flew to my shoulder and Maks stood, though he was favoring one leg.

A quick look showed a shard of black mirror sticking out of his thigh. I put a hand around it, without thinking, pulled it out and covered the wound with my palm. That other doorway in my mind, the one that held my magic, was gone.

The magic was just there, all around me.

The curse was truly lifted.

Yet, when I'd shifted, I'd been a house cat, not the black jungle cat.

I took my hand from his leg, smeared a finger over the blood still there, but there was no wound. I'd healed it with barely a thought.

Maks pulled my hand to his lips and kissed the back of it.

Lila curled her tail around my neck as if she were going to strangle me. I turned slowly, already knowing what I'd see.

The Emperor, my grandfather, stood on a dais that slowly rose out of the pit that the black mirror had covered. Those same sandy-colored clothes, deep tan across his skin, brown eyes and white hair in a braid, as if he'd stepped out of the dreamscape and into reality. Which I supposed he had.

"Granddaughter. You held to your word."

"Shax, never doubt my fucking word. When I give it, I hold true."

He startled as if he'd forgotten that he'd given me his true name. If nothing else, he seemed more stable when I used it, and for that reason I would continue to do so. Even if he didn't want people knowing.

"We have made a deal, you and I," he held the flail in his hand, glancing at it as he spoke, "I wonder if it would work for me, the way it works for you? Would it draw in energy from my enemies? Would it suck them dry?"

I nodded. "I have no doubt it would take their energy. Their lives." He grinned, and I answered it with a smile of my own. "The real question is will it try to kill you when it's done."

His smile slid. "So that much is true about it then?"

"It tried to kill me several times," I said.

"But you survived. How?"

I shrugged. "Bad luck."

He laughed. "Introduce me to your mate. I want to know who is fucking my granddaughter."

Maks stiffened and Lila let out a low hiss. "Don't you talk about them that way." Her wings spread. "Love sought is good; but given unsought is better, and they have not looked for this in each other, but they have it. Don't sully it with your shitty words."

I put a hand on her while he stood there, watching us with my flail in his hand.

"You three . . . there is magic in threes," he said finally.

I nodded. "I know. But you are bound by your own words. You will stand with us against Ollianna."

His dark brown eyes flashed. "And your curse, of course, I have lifted it."

"I can feel the magic in me different than before," I said. "That's very true."

He gave the flail an experimental swing. "I did not say I wouldn't kill you. That is something you never asked me to promise you. Foolish of you, wasn't it?"

Well, fuck.

23

Standing there within the Emperor's Throne with Lila and Maks, and facing the Emperor himself after I'd given him the flail with those words of his "I did not say I wouldn't kill you" ringing in my ears, I could do nothing but stare at him.

Lila let out a low hiss that sounded wet with her acid, and the weight of her began to increase on my shoulder. I held up a hand. "You'll crush me, Lila."

"I'm going to kill him if he dares break his word," she snarled. Next to me, Maks's magic curled against my skin, mingling with my own, strengthening me, and feeding back into him.

I kept my hand up. "You will have no one to find those last two stones, Shax."

"I could find them," he purred. "They are tuned to Ishtar's magic."

I smiled. "But I didn't bring the four stones with me. I hid them because I didn't trust your sketchy ass. Which means you have six to find, all before . . . what? What timeline are we working with here?"

His eyes narrowed, then he laughed. "Fine. You go find me the stones."

That was not the deal, but I could see that I'd lost whatever "good" side of him I'd had in the dreamscape. "And the dragons . . . you will do as you said, or I will instruct the flail to drink you down right now."

I had no idea if that was even possible, but by the way he looked at the weapon he held, he considered it was just that.

"Fine. Go. Fight the dragons. I will meet you in three days, sundown, on the water's edge where the falak will rebirth into the world."

Oh, all the questions I had burning in me, but I didn't dare voice a one of them. I took Maks's hand and backed out of the chamber, found the stairs with my feet and kept backing until I could no longer see the Emperor. Then I turned and we ran.

The interior of the throne was riddled with the traps we'd set off, that I'd walked through as if they were nothing. I saw them now.

Acid.

Flame.

Pits filled with spikes.

More magic than I could shake a fist at with spells

varying from those that would knock you out, to those that would pull all the air from your lungs.

"How did we get through this?" I asked, slowing to look at one of the pits and the spikes filling the bottom.

"You led us through," Lila said. "It was like you knew exactly where to put your steps, and we just followed."

I barely remembered what I'd done, like it was a dream where I'd followed my mother, a dream that I couldn't quite grasp. But was it my magic, or was it the pull of my grandfather to save him?

We reached the first narrow hallway and once more the sound of the dragons at the top battering at the trapdoor met our ears, only now the sound was deeper, the ground shaking with each blow.

"The prison no longer holds," Maks said, his blue eyes worried. He looked at me, one brow raised. "I assume you have a plan?"

I crouched down. "Can you blast the door open so Lila and I can fly out of here? We'll draw them off the door and then you can get out. After that we'll need backup."

Maks stared at me. "What did the Emperor give you?"

Part of me wanted to surprise them both, mostly because Lila was going to flip her shit, but maybe this wasn't the moment for surprising them. "A one-time deal. I'm going to shift into a dragon to fight at Lila's side." Before Maks could protest, I held up a hand. "I tried to get you in on the deal, Maks. Because three against one is far better. But you . . ."

"I don't have a connection to the dragons like you seem to." He let out a slow sigh, his jaw ticking. "Be careful. Both of you."

"You're going to fire at them from the ground. Use whatever you can to help tip the scales in our direction," I said, and finally looked at Lila who'd hopped off my shoulder and sat in front of me. Her jeweled eyes just stared at me. "What?"

"You're going to fight at my side, in the sky?"

I nodded. "Sisters."

Her bottom lip trembled. "They could kill us."

"The Emperor could kill us," I pointed out. "We need to deal with Corvalis and Trick or we'll never get the final two stones, Lila. And we have the greatest Jinn in the desert standing with us." I looked at Maks and smiled. "Together, we can do this."

I grabbed Maks behind the neck and pulled him in for a hard kiss. He didn't hold back, and for that moment, I breathed him in. Only for a moment, though, because we had to hurry. The falak was growing stronger in Ollianna, and it wouldn't be long before it would be free to wreak havoc on the world.

"One super-baddy at a time," I said.

Lila nodded and then grinned. "Starting with a super-baddy dragon daddy."

Maks laughed. "Okay, let's do this. We should

really be far more serious going into a battle of this size and danger."

"Meh," I flopped both hands and shook my head, "life's short. Let's laugh at the assholes."

The three of us crept toward the trapdoor. I counted the timing between the blows and it was pretty set. "Ten seconds between. As soon as they blast next, blow the hole open for us."

I shifted from two legs to four and prayed the Emperor was truly going to hold to his word. He'd said that I needed to be high in the air, that I needed to be dropped for the dragon he woke in me to emerge. "Ready."

Lila flew above me, reached down and tightened her talons around my middle. "Ready."

Maks nodded. "Ready."

The next blast hit the ground of the throne and Maks stepped up, his Jinn magic swirling hard and fast, slamming into the trapdoor . . . and doing nothing.

Twice more he hit it, with no effect. I held up a paw. "Wait. It could still be tied to me. I might have to open it."

Lila put me down and I shifted back to two legs. "This is going to be a quick change, you ready?"

Maks grabbed my arm. "All three of us. We'll push it open faster that way."

I nodded. We waited for the next blast from above. But it didn't come.

"Shit," I whispered.

"They know we're here," Lila said. She clung to my shoulder, shaking, but I didn't think it was in fear.

She was ready to fight, all three of us were.

I looked at them, my best friend, and my mate. "On three."

Maks and I lifted our hands in tandem and when my palm came in contact with the trapdoor it buzzed with electricity. "One."

"Two," Maks said.

Lila clenched her claws around my shoulder. "Three."

Maks and I pushed on the door, flinging it open as Lila began to drag me upward. I shifted to four legs and we shot into the air, just dodging a bolt of lightning.

That went straight for Maks.

A look down confirmed he was on the ground but moving. He'd somehow dodged out of the way, barely missed by the lightning if the scorched ground was any indication.

"Gnat, don't do this!" Trick yelled. "You need to give us one of the stones, then we can trade for the emerald stone."

Lila kept flying up, higher and higher. "No!" she yelled back. "You're a liar. You're no better than Corvalis."

The massive pitch-black dragon that was her father swept across our path through the clouds. "Do you feel ready to die, you miserable excuse for a dragon?" Corvalis boomed the words.

"Now, Lila," I whispered. "No matter what, don't catch me."

There was a single tremor and she let me go, and she shifted to the dragon she'd been born to be. She let out a bellow and then I had to pay attention to my own flight.

Or fall as the case was.

Legs splayed out, I fell fast. "Come on, there's a dragon in there!" I whispered. My words whipped away from me.

The Emperor had said to fall, but there had to be more to it than that.

I stared at the oncoming ground, at Maks watching me fall, ready to try and catch me. But I needed wings if Lila was going to survive this. I had no doubt she could take Corvalis, but not if Trick helped.

A bellow of pain rippled from up above and then several bolts of lightning lit the sky and all I could think was that she needed me, more now than ever.

And my body shifted, slowly at first, and then faster and faster, shimmering and twisting until I was no longer a house cat, or a jungle cat, but something I'd never have thought was possible.

I snapped my wings out wide, catching myself before I fell any farther. A glimpse down and Maks grinning up at me said it all.

I was a dragon. A bitching, big-ass dragon!

Black and green scales caught at the edges of my vision as I swept upward, my own magic curling through me, rising to meet the challenge of two dragons. The power of the desert, the power of the Jinn ran in my blood and I embraced it, weaving it with the strengths I'd found along the way, turning it into a new weapon. I flew as hard as I could, not realizing how fast I was going until I was on top of the battle high in the clouds.

Lila flew between the two male dragons, her talons digging in hard to her father's talons as they spun in a circle, their mouths snaking at one another, taking chunks out of their hides. Blood fell like rain, and Trick threw lightning at the pair.

And he hit Lila. She bellowed, and clung to her father, the bolt going through them both at least, though it hit her the worst.

All of this was in the few heartbeats that it took for me to see them before body slamming into Trick.

His eyes were wide with shock as they locked onto me, but it was too late for him. I clawed my way across his body and was on his back in a flash, slashing and digging at him, fighting not like a dragon, but like a cat. I dug my back talons into either side of his spine and dragged them through the muscles that worked his wings. "You cheating, lying asshole!" I snarled as I went for his neck.

"Who are you?" he bellowed as he rolled in the

sky, spinning faster and faster, trying to throw me off even as we fell. Lightning tried to hit us, but we were moving too fast.

"Your fucking nightmare!" I snarled as I gave one last dig with my claws and then let go as he rolled, throwing me into the sky even as he slammed into the ground with a boom that left him completely still. His neck lay across a protrusion of rock that left his head dangling at a strange angle. By the way his chest rose and fell, he was unconscious but not dead. Not yet.

I beat my wings, getting my balance, looking for Lila and Corvalis in the sky. But they weren't there. Hearing a roar below, I twisted around.

Lila floated in the air, out cold, just above the ground, Maks's magic wrapping around her, protecting her with one hand as he fought off Corvalis with the other. He'd stirred up the desert wind, turning it into a twister that pushed Corvalis back, keeping him at bay.

Barely.

I let out a roar, a challenge in any language, dragon, lion, cat, or human. Corvalis turned and glared at me. His ability was one not unlike the flail. He could absorb his opponent's abilities and strength. I just didn't know if that was before or after his opponent was dead. I was hoping after death.

My magic curled through me, stronger than I'd ever felt it. I formed and aimed it like a spear, then sent it flying faster than any bullet from a gun straight for him.

Grinning, Corvalis caught it with his front talons, crushing the threads of magic as if they were nothing. "Best you got, pussy cat? You might look like a dragon, but you're as weak as you were before."

A low rumbling hiss slid from me. I couldn't check on Lila even through our bond. "Why don't you come and see, bitch, just how weak I am then?"

With his wings spread wide, Corvalis made a formidable dragon, but I'd faced him before, and I was banking on him remembering that. But I didn't have the flail any longer strengthening my claws and talons.

He didn't know that, though.

And I had the high ground. I tucked my wings in tightly to my sides, turning my body into a missile with a hell of a lot of weight behind it. Talons outstretched, I thought of the desert hawks and how they'd tangled with one another.

Corvalis didn't slow but grinned up at me.

Only he didn't know what I was capable of. He didn't understand how I fought.

We were ten feet apart when I rolled in the air, slid under his belly and raked him the length of his body.

Scores of long wounds sliced through his hide, a spray of blood fell, but no guts. I'd been hoping to completely open him up. I kept spinning, snapped my wings open and turned as he slammed into me, knocking the wind from me.

"I'll kill you and take your magic too!" he bellowed in my face, the smell of dragon musk thick in the air, clogging my throat.

"You can try!" I yelled back, snapping my teeth at one of his eyes.

I kept my wings close, forcing him to hold us both up as I clawed and dug at him. He was doing the same, only not as well. I snaked my neck in for a bite and caught him at the base of the throat. He yanked his upper body out of the way, swung back and wrapped his talons around my neck and squeezed.

Shit.

I twisted and fought, but there was no getting away from him and with each movement, he tightened his hold further. "I will never be defeated. Certainly not by some mockery of a dragon!" he roared.

A shadow passed over us and the air around us thickened as if a storm were brewing. Lightning bolted down and cut through Corvalis's hold on me. I was thrown backward, but the lightning didn't touch me, skating across my scales as if it didn't dare hurt me.

As I fell, the magic that had given me the shape of a dragon slid off me, like sloughing a skin that was not my own. Well, shit, that didn't last as long as I'd been hoping. And with Trick back in play, Lila was in danger.

I fell, four legs and a small house cat once more, limp from the battle with only one hope.

That Maks would catch me.

And together the three of us would stop Corvalis and Trick.

24

I fell from the sky, my black fur fluttering in the wind that swept past me, and knew that if anyone would catch me, it would be Maks. If he saw me anyway.

Even as I thought it, his magic spun around me, slowing my fall until he lowered me to the ground at his feet.

"Get up, Zam, you have to see this." Maks held his hand out and I forced my body to shift back to two legs, knowing that any wounds I had would heal in the transition, no matter how bad it hurt.

I bit back the scream that wanted to fight its way through my bruised and torn muscles, through the gashes I could feel on my belly and thighs, healing them as I shifted, but at a cost. Wounds I'd barely felt as I'd fought.

Maks took my hand and pulled me to my feet. "Look!"

I did as he said, tipping my head back. Lila was above her father, her magic all around her. Not just her magic, but Trick's too. I looked away to see the storm dragon still on the ground, his neck still at that strange angle. Dead or knocked out, I wasn't sure which, but the storm magic wasn't coming from him.

"What happened?"

"I think she has her father's ability to absorb other dragons' magic," Maks said.

I looked at Trick again, not seeing a rise or fall to his chest. "She took his magic then?"

"I think so. She landed on him before she flew up to you and snapped his neck." Maks's hand tightened on mine and I felt him draw on my own abilities. I relaxed and let him, knowing he had more practice at using magic as a weapon than I did.

Unless . . . I pulled a little magic toward me, picked up a stick and let the magic flow over it, bending and turning it until I held a bow in my hands. I picked up another stick, lengthened it and put a tip on it. It had been a long time since I'd shot a bow and arrow, but I was willing to try.

Pouring my magic into the weapon, I lifted it, sighting down the length until Corvalis slid into view, dodging Lila but not well.

I breathed out and released the arrow. Powered

by magic, it shot through the sky and drove into Corvalis's side, exploding on impact.

He bellowed and fell, his wings collapsing on themselves. Lila followed him, raining down blow after blow, until he hit the ground.

The earth beneath our feet shook, and I reached for Maks to steady myself. Lila landed next to her father, put a foot on his shoulder and when he whimpered, she reached down and twisted his head, snapping his neck.

She stumbled back and let out a roar that rattled the air around us, beating at the air in my lungs like a drum. I put a hand to my chest, holding the sound there, and hearing not only the triumph in it, but the grief and the pain. She was not a killer. She'd not wanted it to come to this between her and Trick, or her and Corvalis.

Her jeweled eyes blinked a few times and then filled with tears as she took a few steps toward me, shifted to her smaller size and flew into my arms. I held her close as she sobbed, clinging to me. Maks circled us both, holding us tightly.

There were no words to say, because it was not all right. Killing her father had been a necessity, killing Trick kept us all safe, but making it happen didn't make it all right.

A slow series of claps from behind us slowly turned me, even though I knew who it would be.

The Emperor strolled toward us, the flail strapped

to his back as it had been to mine a short time before. "Well done, granddaughter. Truly, you fight like you do not care if you die."

Lila trembled against me, again in anger, not fear. I held her tighter. "I fight for those I love. That means I fight with everything I have, even unto death."

Maks took one hand and waved it between us and the Emperor. Black flames shot up from the rock cutting off the Emperor's approach, a literal line drawn in the sand between us. "No closer. You've made it clear that not killing any of us was not part of your promises."

The Emperor laughed. "I will tell you this. When the time comes for us to fight, it will be glorious. And your little flames will mean nothing, Jinn master."

He gave me a wink, thumbed his nose at Maks, turned and walked away, down the slope toward the ocean. I hurried after him in time to see him drop a hand into the water, and a burst of magic flow out of him. From the depths came a creature that made no sense to me. I could not decide if it was an animal of mythology or just one from the depths.

More coils and tentacles than anything else, attached to a brilliant red body that was large enough to eclipse a decent-sized fishing boat. He stepped out onto it as if it *were* a boat and the creature swam away with him. He turned and lifted a hand, three fingers in the air. "Sunset on the third day or our deal is off."

I lifted him my own personal salute. "One broken promise and our deal is off, Shax." He flinched and I wondered if he regretted giving me his name. Or if it reminded him of someone he was once, before whatever corrupted his mind took over.

Maks pulled me back from view. "Holy shit, what the hell is that?"

I shook my head. "No idea. Not sure I want to know." I tightened my hold over a now-quiet Lila. "Holy shit indeed. Lila, are you physically hurt?"

She bobbed her head once and a small whimper slid from her that I think was a yes. I pulled on my magic, weaving it through her and closing the wounds as easily as if I'd been doing it all my life. Strange to have such access to so much strength and power. She let out a sigh and promptly fell asleep.

"What now?" Maks said. "We can't leave this rock. The goddess only knows what kind of booby traps are in the water itself. And if there are more of those things . . ." he waved a hand at the shoreline where the Emperor's beast had risen from the depths.

He wasn't wrong, and we needed to go farther east yet, well into the human lands.

"Until Lila wakes up, I think we're stuck here," I said softly. Lila grumbled in her sleep and stretched out in my arms so her belly was up to the sky and her limbs were flopped in every direction, like a veritable rag doll.

Maks leaned over and scratched her belly with one finger. "I can't believe you were a dragon."

"Me either," I said.

He took my hand, lacing our fingers together. There weren't really words for when your mate suddenly turned into a creature they weren't supposed to be able to turn into.

"At some point, we should talk about it," he sighed, "but how about not right now?"

I leaned into him and he slid his arm around my waist. "Yes, agreed. Not right now."

I could still feel the Emperor's magic inside me; that was worrisome. Did it mean he'd put some sort of hook into me, under my skin so he could track me? Or maybe so he could control me?

Yeah, I thought both were a possibility. Ones I'd not taken into consideration when I'd made the deal with him, mostly because I knew that I had to make the deal. There was no other way, so what did the cost matter? We would have all been killed if I'd not made that deal. I was sure of it.

Of course, now that the fight was over and we'd all survived one more step, the cost was more than relevant.

Shit.

I started back across the rock face, up to the crest of the island. The bodies of Corvalis and Trick were hard not to notice. Maks let go of my hand and went straight to Corvalis. He lifted his right hand, twisting it at the wrist, and the dragon's head turned to face him, eyes flat and dead.

"What are you doing?"

"Just taking a precaution." Maks's magic curled through the dragon's mouth and wrapped around the upper fangs. With a pop, he pulled them out, and tucked them into his pouch on his hip. "Just in case."

I stared at him. "Just in case what?"

"There are spells and magic that require dragon fangs," he said. "Maybe we won't need them," he rolled his shoulders as if stretching them, "but I'd rather take them and not need them than the other way around."

I went to Trick and laid a hand on his side. What words were there to say goodbye to someone you thought was a friend, but turned out to be a liar and a traitor? I leaned into my hand, feeling the residual warmth from his side. "You chose poorly," I said. His mother was right not to name him after the dragon hero that she'd considered. He'd have sullied the name with his treachery.

"We just wait then?" Maks asked.

I sat, then lay flat on the ground, so I was looking into the sky. "We wait for Lila to wake."

Maks lay beside me. "Middle of the day, good time for a nap."

I closed my eyes and yawned. "Think we need to take turns sleeping?" I said the words, but I was already sliding under the spell of fatigue that wrapped itself around me.

He mumbled something but I was already gone, snuggling against him, holding Lila between us.

For the first time in I didn't know how long, I slept deeply and without stepping into the dreamscape. At one point, I jerked awake, panic flooding my system as if I'd been running.

"Just sleep." Maks curled his arm tighter around me and I did just that.

My dreams were normal, I mean, they were nightmares to be fair, but just that. Regular nightmares of death and total destruction without a dreamscape to fear I would die in, or to come out of barely rested.

Hours stretched by before the rough ground of the rock we were sleeping on finally outmatched my desire for sleep. I yawned and stretched until my muscles slowly relaxed and loosened their hold on every knot that I'd been clinging too. I slowly sat up. The light had shifted, nearing dusk. Hours indeed. We'd gone into the Emperor's Throne in the morning and now had slept a good portion of the day away.

"Did you spell me?" I asked Maks. He yawned as he sat up.

"Not a chance. I was too tired. Passed out right after you."

"At least we know they are really dead." I stood, still holding Lila. She'd been hurt the worst and even with being healed had needed the sleep more than me or Maks.

Lila stirred in my arms, rolled and opened her eyes; her claws dug into my arm as she faced the very still form of Trick. I didn't try to put her down. "He . . . he told me that he cared about me," she said. "But he was a liar, just like my father."

"I wonder why he let us through the Dragon's Ground that first time," I asked, more to myself than to Lila. But she answered anyway.

"He told me up there as the battle started," she said. "I asked him the same thing and he said he didn't want to kill me. He felt bad because I was so weak and he didn't want to be the one to kill the Gnat. So he let us pass thinking my grandmother would do the job, or some other dragon."

Maks stepped up beside us. "And when he came to help?"

"My father sent him, seeing that I was sweet on him." Her voice was tight, not with tears, but anger. "He was sent to keep an eye on us, to find out where the stones were. They wanted them all, hoarders of jewels that they are."

I took a few steps back from Trick. "What do you want to bet that Corvalis was still in thrall to Ollianna? Not that he wouldn't have attacked us, but if he was coming for the stones, he wasn't just looking for the emerald."

Maks gave a low grunt of agreement. "That makes

sense. He might have thought he was free of her, but . . ."

"I don't feel bad for either of them," Lila said. "Neither of them deserved my love."

"No, they didn't," I said.

Maks reached over and took Lila from my arms and held her out in front of him. "'She's beautiful, and therefore to be wooed; She is woman, and therefore to be won.' Don't you ever forget that, Lila. You are worth fighting for."

She burst into tears, huge gulping sobs, and threw herself at Maks, wrapping herself around his neck. "Damn you, Toad. You aren't supposed to make me cry!"

"You don't know what play? Excellent, I finally won!" He gave her a hug and she hiccuped a laugh.

"Of course, I know that. It's *Henry VI*, Toad." She climbed to his shoulder and wiped her eyes, deliberately turning her back to Trick's body. "We need to get off this rock."

"Please don't shift on top of me," Maks said.

Lila grunted, let him go and shifted beside him, going to full size as fast as I shifted to my house cat form, then bumped him with her hip. "Fine. But that's only because you said nice things."

Maks climbed up on her back first. "I'll keep that in mind."

Lila turned to look at me. "You coming?"

I drew in a deep breath and nodded. "Yeah, just thinking about what we're going after next."

"The changeling?" she asked.

The bitch in the jungle, if Ishtar was to be believed.

I took hold of the base of her wing and pulled myself up onto her back. "Yeah, the changeling in the middle of a jungle with a stone she probably won't want to give up."

25

Lila flew us across the open water between the continents easily with no one chasing us. What a shock that was.

Maybe Ollianna thought the Emperor had killed me. That was possible. Then again, it might just be that we were far enough out of Ollianna's range that her power couldn't reach us.

That seemed more likely. Until she had my head on a pike, I didn't think she'd believe me dead. I smiled to myself, taking that as a weird compliment.

"You told the Emperor you didn't have the stones," Maks said, startling me out of my thoughts. "Is that true?"

I swallowed hard. "I knew that if I walked in there with them on me, he'd try to take them. So I stashed them before we left."

Lila let out a low whistle and shook her head. "Why didn't you say anything?"

"I didn't think about it until the last minute," I said. "And then everything was happening so fast that I didn't have time to even mention it."

We banked through a cluster of low-hanging clouds that smelled of rain and left a good amount of moisture clinging to our hair and clothes.

"So . . ." Lila drawled out that one word, "do we have a plan?"

I grimaced. "Not really. I know very little about changelings. Maks, you got anything in those memory banks of yours?" I looked over my shoulder at him.

He closed his eyes and his chin dropped to his chest as he began to speak. "Changelings—they aren't shifters. They are created when two infants are exchanged. Usually a human child and a fairy child but not always. The term can be applied to any infant taken from its home and swapped with another. Which means that we could be looking at literally any kind of creature that walks under the sun." He opened his eyes and shook his head. "Not a lot of help."

It was and it wasn't, he was right about that.

There had been one picture on Ishtar's desk, a picture I'd seen in my mind when the Emperor and I had been connected. When we'd been talking about finding the other stones.

The image of a large black jungle cat. But did that mean she knew about the other stones? Did it mean she was looking?

"I can feel you tense up, you know," Lila said. "What did you just think of?"

"Hang on, let me see if I can put the pieces together," I said.

The Emperor had talked about my grandmother, his concubine, that she was from a distant land. That she'd been brought in special for him.

Bloodlines.

What if she . . . what if she'd been stolen specifically for the Emperor? And another child from the desert had been put in her place? Wouldn't that make my own grandmother . . . a changeling?

My heart began to beat harder as a burst of adrenaline rushed through me. The pieces were there, I could almost see them.

From where, though, had my grandmother been taken? A lush forest, a lush jungle . . . the darkest parts of the jungle to hide a large black cat? "Lila, we need to scent for green, living things, for the most lush part of the jungle."

"Okay." She curled through a burst of wind and dropped us lower through the clouds. It was only then that I saw how far we'd come. We were flying south, along the coastline of what had to be Africa.

I leaned over her side to get a better look.

"Talk to me, Zam," Maks said. "I can't help you if I don't know what you're thinking."

The words fell out of my mouth as I tried to explain what I was seeing, what I was feeling—that it could be my grandmother that had been given the last stone. "Of all the people out there who would want to keep the Emperor imprisoned, who better than one who'd been forced to give him a child? One who hated him?"

"What about the Jinn bloodline, didn't that come from your grandmother's side? How could she have been brought in from the jungle?" Lila asked. "Not to be the devil's advocate here, but your reasoning doesn't make sense. I mean, it's close but . . ."

A shiver ran from the top of my head, down my spine to the soles of my feet. "I can't explain it. I just know that it's right. Maybe it will make sense when we see it."

Maks cleared his throat. "Could be that we are facing a Jinn shapeshifter then," he said. "And if it was a changeling for a changeling, it would be a female Jinn, like you, Zam. Powerful, able to adapt and use more magic than any male Jinn."

That trickle of a shiver turned into a raging river along my back and I started to shake. That was it.

That was what we were going to face in the jungle, a Jinn of more power than any we'd yet seen.

I blew out a slow breath. "Then let's go find her."

Maks held out a hand. "If it's a Jinn, and we're

right about that, then I can find her. Or him. Perks of being a master now."

His hand began to glow with the deep blue magic that was his unique blend, a color that hadn't happened until after he was freed from the other masters.

The smoke swirled around his fingertips and then shot out in five different directions.

It didn't take more than a minute for him to open his eyes and point. "It looks like you were onto it. There is a Jinn, and she's to the south, and farther to the west."

Lila banked her wings, adjusting our flight path. "So this Jinn we are looking for, will she strike first, do you think?"

I looked out past Lila's shoulder toward the swath of green that we approached. "Probably."

"So we're going in stealth mode?"

I blew out a breath. "One more heist."

Maks pointed out exactly where he was picking up on the other Jinn.

"Does it seem strange to you that two stones were given to Jinn?" Lila asked as we circled high above the treetops, looking for a place to land. Which wasn't going to happen. I could already see there was no space large enough for Lila's wingspan.

"Yes," I said. "It seems damn strange, but I—"

A burst of vines shot up out of the trees, straight up for us, unfurling at a speed that Lila couldn't dodge. They were thick with suckers covered in a sticky substance that I could see even at a distance.

I held tightly to her, a quick plan coming to me. "Let it drag us down, Lila!"

"WHAT?"

"When we get close to the treetops, we'll all shift," I said. The vines whipped around, tangling around our middles. "Don't show them our hand. They can't know we have magic."

Them.

Yeah, I wasn't betting on a single Jinn holding the stone, whatever the stone was.

If it was the stone that allowed for creation, there was literally no telling what we'd be up against. And if it was the stone that bestowed gifts of power on others, that wasn't much better.

The vines tightened around us and I struggled not to struggle. "Maks?"

"Yeah?" he grunted.

"Feel like Jinn magic to you?"

"Nope."

"We're in trouble, aren't we?"

"Yup." He wiggled his hand and a tiny flow of magic swirled around us, sinking into my skin. "But that will keep the vines from sticking when we shift."

One good thing, but I had a feeling it wasn't going to be enough when it came to dealing with this changeling, whoever and whatever it was.

The treetops were coming up faster and faster.

"Here we go," I said as the first whiff of the jungle trees curled up my nose. A blend of green living things, along with green dying things, and in the smack middle of it, the smell of jungle cat.

The first branch touched Lila's belly, and she shifted first, gone from beneath Maks and me. I twisted to the left as I shifted, taking a full-on dive into the trees. Of Maks all I caught was a glimpse of tawny hide as his caracal form plunged into limbs.

Goddess keep the two of them safe. I didn't even have Marsum's voice in my head to encourage me. Funny to think I missed it.

Vines snaked around me, but they slid off as Maks's magic held tightly, keeping the suckers from staying on us.

Branches and leaves slapped at me as I reached for something to slow my fall, my claws slicing through the thin foliage until I dug into a tree trunk, sliding a bit but finally stopping. But that was only a brief second as the vines shot toward me.

"Fuckers," I growled as I pushed away from the trunk toward another branch, found my footing and started running. Using the treetops, I raced away from the vines. "Maks, Lila!" I called out, knowing I would pinpoint myself for those I was running from, but needing Maks and Lila to be able to find me.

From my left came the flap of wings and Lila was there, racing along my side. "Where's Maks?"

I slowed, turned, and looked back. The vines had

stopped about thirty feet behind me, and in their grasp, they had Maks.

All wrapped up and struggling for his life.

A snarl ripped out of me as I raced back the way I'd come. I knew a trap when I saw one. I knew bait when I saw it.

It didn't matter. This was Maks we were talking about, and I'd come too close to losing him too many times to just keep on running.

As I got closer to the vines, they came at me and I swatted at them, my tiny claws doing very little damage. But they pulled back as if I'd taken a machete to them. They reminded me of the vines the Emperor had used to absorb energy and that only spurred me on harder. If they were draining not only Maks's life, but his life energy for themselves . . . I couldn't let that happen.

I tore into the vines, and they fled from me. I didn't understand it, and I didn't care why it was happening. I only knew that my claws and teeth were as sharp and as deadly as they'd ever been.

For a house cat.

I snarled as I got closer to Maks, and he was released from the vines completely.

"A trap," he gasped out. All over his body were marks where the vines had dug in and bled him. They hadn't been strangling him, they'd been draining him.

"I know." I pushed him toward the upper

branches, even as I wove my magic around him, healing the hundreds of tiny wounds. Any one of them on their own would have been no big deal, but together . . . he groaned as I closed the last one. "Lila, take him up, circle around."

"You can't do this on your own," Lila said. She looked around us. "This place is dangerous, Zam. And it's not the desert. None of us know it."

For the first time, I tried to take my jungle cat's shape, opening myself to that larger feline and all it offered. There was a moment of hesitation in my body, as if it wasn't sure, and then it flowed over me. "I think I have to do this on my own. Maks is hurt, keep him safe. I'll come back here when I've got the stone."

"And if you don't?" Maks's eyes fluttered. "What then?"

"Go find Balder," I said. "And ride as far as you can ride to get away from all the madness."

I butted my much larger head against his, letting my magic flow over him. It wouldn't give him his energy back, but the tiny wounds were gone. "Go." I could see that Lila wanted to argue with me. "If you could be made into a jungle cat, you could come with me."

She grumbled. "I could rain acid down on them."

"That won't help us find the stone." I grinned up at her, showing off my fangs. "Go. I'll be okay."

She launched into the air, swung down and

grabbed a half-passed-out Maks and peeled away from the treetops.

I watched them go, watched as Lila shifted to her larger form. Just like my own bigger size, it had a place and time.

Turning back, I slunk into the jungle, the branches and shadows hiding me and my near pitch-black fur. The rosettes under the black helped me slide through as though I were a shadow and not a predator.

All the way to the ground I went, landing on the soft mulch of many leaves, small bodies of creatures long dead, and wet earth. The pungent smell rose up my nose and I blew it out, trying instead to find the scent of jungle cat.

I padded forward, using the shadows of the trees for cover, working my way carefully deeper into the jungle as I searched for what it was I was looking for. A stone I didn't really want, a way to stop the monsters who threatened my family and my home, and maybe some understanding of my own past.

I wasn't sure that any of it was possible.

Which was why I'd sent Maks and Lila up and away. If I didn't come back, I knew they'd look for me.

But I had to try.

The snap of a twig behind me and I flattened myself to the ground and held my breath.

No more sound, but as I lay there, not breathing, I struggled not to jump up and run forward.

Because there was a jungle cat passing me by, a female who for all intents and purposes could be my sister.

Or my mother.

26

I couldn't stop the trembling in my body as I stared at the jungle cat stalking past me. I couldn't even tell why I thought she was my mother. If it was the way she moved, or the smell that rolled off her that was part desert, part jungle cat, I couldn't be sure.

"Stop!" I all but fell out of my hiding spot. She spun around, teeth bared and a snarling growl rippling from her lips. "Stop, please!" I lay on my belly, being as submissive as I dared, all thoughts of the stone flying from my head. "Mom?"

I swallowed hard and let the shift take me from four legs to two. "It's me, Zamira."

The jungle cat stared at me, eyes as green as my own, her voice with the lilting accent that came from living in the desert. "I am not your mother."

I closed my eyes, tears pooling in the corners of

them, more disappointed than I could put into words that this jungle cat shifter was not my mother. And even though I'd seen my mother's death in the dreamscape, even though I'd had to live through it, I couldn't help but believe maybe it was a lie to keep her and me safe.

"Are you sure?" I mumbled into the dirt, breathing in the moist air of the jungle floor.

Okay, yes, it was a stupid question, a child's question, but I couldn't help it. I lifted my head so I could look the cat eye to eye, but it was no longer a cat but a woman.

A very old woman. Her hair was braided off to one side, jet black shot through with white strands that reached nearly to her waist; her skin was pale as if she hadn't seen the sun in a long time. Or maybe she'd spent more time as a jungle cat than she spent on two legs. Green eyes stared down at me, fathomless as they swept over me. "I am quite sure."

I didn't know if I should push to my feet, or if I should just lay there and cry. Stupid, so fucking stupid when there was so much on the line, so much—

"Granddaughter," she said. "You are my granddaughter."

Slowly, ever so slowly, I raised my head. "Are you sure?"

Her lips curled up into a tight smile. "Quite. I pass on my stamp of coloring in both two and four legs.

Come. I want to know how you broke the curse that was put on your mother."

She turned and strode away from me. Old she might have been, but she was hardly frail. I scrambled to my feet and hurried after her. She was the same height as me with a similar lean build. Leaner though, as if she'd burned off all the excess fat on her body.

"Why are you here, granddaughter?" She didn't turn to ask me the question. I made my way to her side as she pushed her way through the jungle.

I opened my mouth to answer her, to tell her the truth, but found myself pausing. "Can you tell me about my mother, first? It might answer the questions I have that brought me here."

She slowed and looked at me. "Your mother was a wild one, the blend of my bloodlines and her father's made her so strong, strong enough to rule in his place. That's what he wanted, you know. He wanted a child that would be able to stand against his bitch of a wife." She sighed.

All thoughts of this woman being the changeling, of getting the stone from her if that was the case were gone. Gone with the need to understand my own past.

"But the curse on her, you knew about it?" Why, why would a mother not fight to keep a curse from her own child? I didn't understand.

Those green eyes looked through me, and she

lifted a hand almost as if she would touch me but dropped it before she made contact.

"Yes and no. I agreed to have her jungle cat kept from her to keep her from learning to fight—it was meant to be temporary. I thought to protect her. I pushed her toward the lion prides, thinking she would find humility there, and she found only death and a child that was born a runt."

That was like a slap and I fought to keep my reaction from showing. She went on. "Ishtar cursed her with an early death. She cursed her that any child she had would carry the same troubles, that the curse would become a part of the bloodline. I didn't think you'd survive, to be honest."

Troubles? That's what she wanted to call what I'd faced in my life?

She pushed aside a series of hanging vines and the view opened to a waterfall cascading down to a crystal-clear pool. The sounds of voices mingled with the calls of birds and animals. "What else do you want to know about your mother?"

"Did you love her?"

Those green eyes were sharp. "She was my child, and it was my duty to give birth to her, nothing more."

Nothing about love there. I thought about the Emperor, and what he'd said. That he'd loved my mother the most.

She'd been the child he'd wanted.

Even if he was a crazy motherfucker, I could at least understand love. I couldn't understand this disconnect.

"So, no love."

"I gave her life," she said. "What else should I have done?"

I didn't even know my grandmother's name and I realized I didn't need to. She was not family.

"Well and good, at least I know where I stand with you," I said, regretting deeply the tears she'd seen on my face only because she would equate them with weakness, which I was not. Love didn't make you weak; it gave you the strength to dig deep.

"Would you like to meet—"

"No." The word rippled out of me, harder than I wanted it to. "You are part Jinn?"

She stiffened. "I care not to think about it, but yes, I am. My mother escaped to the jungle during the purge, before the wall went up."

I nodded and that piece of the puzzle clicked into place. "Then you know I carry the same power."

"You cannot access it. I made sure of that. My daughter was too unpredictable, just like her father. Just like your grandfather, ruled by emotions and not reality. It was the one thing that Ishtar did that I was glad for." She sniffed and waved toward the pool. "You have cousins."

Two men and three women stood, similar build, similar coloring to me and my grandmother.

I was just one of many. Weird to think that I'd always wanted to be part of a pride, to fit in with all the golden-haired and -eyed lions, only to have it offered to me and feel nothing but wanting to be just me. Dark green eyes, black hair, skin the color of the desert sands.

Did they have the strength that I had in the magic of our bloodline? I was about to find out.

"Merlin asked you to hide a stone for him, one of Ishtar's stones. It either holds the power of creation itself, or the ability to gift abilities to others." I stood a few feet from her as I spoke, enough that I had room to shift if I needed to. "I need it now to keep our world alive."

She snorted. "Just like your mother, so grandiose in your daydreams. You know, she once . . ."

Her words trailed off in my head, like a buzzing of gnats that I couldn't get away from. She wasn't going to give me the stone. She was going to act like she didn't even have it.

The question was what would I do to save my family?

Anything. I started out across the small clearing, heading straight toward the others, the ones who were my cousins.

I didn't need to know their names. As I approached, I saw the way they watched me. Curious, but not afraid.

That was a mistake.

"Which one of you is your grandmother's favorite?" I smiled as I asked. They laughed and looked at each other, and they all pointed at what had to be the youngest girl. She was petite by the standards that our body type seemed stamped with. I motioned for her to come close to me.

And she did. Fool that she was.

She stepped close and I pulled her into a hug. "I'm sorry."

"What?" She tipped her head up at me, confusion in every line of her face. I spun her around so her back was to my front, my one knife I still had on me pressed to her throat. I backed us up as she squawked and struggled against me. Not for long as I pressed the blade against her skin.

"The stone," I said.

My grandmother had her hands up toward me, magic curling out. I flicked my fingers at her, brushing it away as if it were nothing. "The stone for her life."

"You are mad!" she screeched. "Just like him, just like—"

"Shax," I said. "And if I am mad like him, then I will be mad like him, but at least I know the importance of love. Of family."

The girl in my arms stopped struggling. A dry laugh escaped me. "Do you understand that she does not love you enough to give me the stone?"

"Gram?" the girl whispered. "Please, she's hurting me."

The old woman stared me down and shook her head. "No. Love is not the answer."

I tightened my hold on the girl and whispered in her ear, "Do you believe that?"

She whimpered. "No."

With a quick shift of my hold on her, I pressed the blade against a different part of her throat. "You were to be the one to take over guarding the stone one day, weren't you?"

Another whimper. "Will you leave if I give it to you?"

"NO!" The old woman launched at us, her knife thrown ahead of her. Not aimed for me, but for her granddaughter.

I yanked the girl out of the way so she fell without injury, and took the blow to my upper arm. The knife cut in deep, hard against the bone. I snarled and shoved my grandmother back.

Goddess of the desert, what was it with my asshole bloodline? Could I not have one grandparent that wasn't homicidal?

"You would kill those you are bound to protect!" I circled her, switching my knife to the other hand, gripping the handle.

"To keep the world safe from the Emperor! To keep him imprisoned!" she roared back at me, fear in every line of her face, in every staccato move of her body.

I pointed the knife at her. "The Emperor is free, Ishtar is on the loose, and the falak is about to be reborn! I am fighting for my family. I am fighting for those I love more than anything in this world!" The words poured out of me. "You don't even have that! You don't fight for anything, you cower in this place, hiding!"

Her eyes widened and her face paled. "I am not a coward."

I shook my head, and lowered the knife, seeing in her a path that could have been mine if I'd run from my destiny, if I'd let the hurt and broken heart Steve had handed out to me rule my life.

I would have ended up like this.

"I don't want to fight you," I said. "I don't want to hurt anyone."

Those green eyes that could have been my own narrowed. I held my hands out to my sides, not submissive, but not fighting. "I could have killed your granddaughter. You threw the knife to end her life."

My grandmother's lips tightened. "She was the wrong choice to protect the stone, that she would give it up so easily."

"To protect her brothers?" I tipped my head but didn't take my eyes off the old woman. Interesting that none of my cousins had come at me from behind. "There is no sin in that."

A snarl rippled past her lips, showing off her overly sharp canines. "There is sin in not doing your duty."

For just a moment, I could feel my father's presence as if he were standing right there with me. Duty was something he'd understood, something he'd lived day in and day out, and it had cost him his life, protecting those who could not protect themselves.

"I have a duty to those I am protecting, not just my own family but our world," I said softly. "Do not make me kill you for that duty, old woman."

Her other grandchildren were sliding away from my side, shifting to get behind her. Two of the boys motioned for me to hold my ground.

The girl was gone, disappeared.

My grandmother tensed, muscles quivering as she prepped for a shift. I shook my head. "Don't. This is a bad idea all around."

Her shift was fast, as fast as my own, and she was in the air, paws outstretched and mouth open wide. I ducked and rolled out from under her, came up with my knife and sliced her through her side. She hit the ground hard, stumbled, looked at her side as though she couldn't believe I'd actually cut her.

I kept her circling with me, drawing her closer and closer to the grandchildren that were my cousins. Cousins who didn't seem all that fussed about turning on their grandmother. It made me wonder where their parents were.

A snarl rippled out of her as she launched herself at me again. This time I caught both front legs, just above her paws, just held her there. "Don't make me kill you." I grimaced. "There has been enough death in my life, that I . . . for once, I don't want to watch someone who is family—even asshole family—die."

She shifted back to two legs, and I tightened my hold on her wrists to keep her in place. Her magic rose within her, along her skin, and mine rose to meet it. Like seeing two cats check each other out, to see who was stronger, the magics circled one another, testing, pulsing.

"You are not strong enough to beat me," she growled. "Just like your aunties. They weren't strong enough to beat me."

My jaw dropped.

"You killed their parents? Your own children?" All I could do was stare at her, the horror of her words sinking into me. Under my skin, my magic flowed faster, spinning through me. Showing me how to take her.

Because she would keep on killing. She would keep on hurting others.

Only I never got the chance to follow through; I didn't have to.

Her grandchildren took care of it for me.

2 7

I held my maternal grandmother tightly, my magic and hers pushing on one another, testing before there was any real fight. The jungle seemed to exhale around us, the thick canopy and thicker underbrush rustling with movement.

"I think you're going to regret your actions," I said softly, shoving her away from me, straight into the arms of her other grandchildren. One of the men caught her and she relaxed into his arms, thinking herself safe. He held her while the other next to him grabbed her head and snapped her neck in a move that was just like Lila killing Corvalis.

Her jaw went slack and her eyes that had been narrowed at me widened ever so slightly before the light slid out of them.

An inglorious death for a woman so very afraid of the world.

I looked at my cousins, not sure what to say. From the shadows of the jungle stepped the girl, the youngest of the group. She approached me, her hand clenched over what I knew would be the stone.

"I don't want to guard it," she said.

"Why?"

"Because it makes people crazy, just like you said." She rolled her hand over and opened her palm. In the center lay the smallest stone, only it wasn't a stone so much as a shard. A shard of blue, as if chipped off the stone the Wyvern had given me.

Two sides of the same coin, destruction and creation. I was sure of it.

I held my hand out and the girl dropped the blue shard into my palm. "Thank you."

"We should be thanking you," she said. "Grandmother would never have turned her back on us without you here. You gave us a chance to free ourselves."

I clenched the stone in my hand, feeling the power in it, feeling the jungle seem to breathe around me again as if it knew that I held the shard. I shook my head. "She guarded the stone for a long time. It seems to drive even the best crazy."

I tucked the shard into my leather pouch on my hip, shifted from two legs to four, and ran to the edge of the clearing where I paused. "I battle for the world," I said. "Wish me luck."

"Maybe we will meet again, cousin," she said

softly. "I wish you the luck you will need to survive, to meet again and talk of family."

They held up their hands to me, the body of our grandmother lying between us. I mimicked them, feeling the tie between us tighten. Family.

I turned my back and ran for all I was worth through the jungle, racing against time. We had one more stone to find . . . and only a vague idea of where it could be.

I found the big tree that we'd tumbled down at the very beginning of this excursion. One ginormous leap I'd never have done in my smaller form, and my big claws dug deep into the bark as I leapfrogged my way up to the top branches. Once there, I shifted again, this time to my house cat form. Lighter of foot, I scrambled up to the very top of the tree where my jungle cat form could never have stood.

A shadow passed overhead. "Lila!"

That shadow paused, swung around and headed my way. There were no vines reaching for her, though I could feel them as if they were a part of me, as if through the stone there was a connection still to the jungle. "A world of creation," I said softly.

Looking out around me at the treetops and the distant mountains, the sounds and smells of this place that hummed in my blood, I could believe this was where the world had begun. And a part of me was sorry to leave it.

Lila's talons closed around me and lifted me high

above the canopy. I didn't scramble up her leg, but instead stayed where I was to watch the jungle slide away behind us.

"Zam, are you okay?" Lila bent her head down to me. "You're crying."

I blinked a few times and scrubbed at my face with my paws. "I'm okay."

At least I thought I was. The pull of the jungle on me was stronger than I'd thought it would be, now that I was leaving.

"I want to come back here, one day," I said, more to myself than to Lila or Maks. I pulled myself out of Lila's talons and with a turn of her body she helped me get onto her back. Maks sat quietly, pale from the blood loss. I shifted back to two legs and wrapped myself around him, holding him tightly. He leaned back against me and I put my cheek to his.

"Was it hard to get the stone?"

I closed my eyes. "Harder than I thought."

Maybe another day I'd tell them what happened, but for then and there, I needed to keep it a story that was no one else's but my own.

"Where to next?" Lila asked, seeming to understand I wasn't ready to talk. "For the last stone?"

I opened my eyes but kept my chin on Maks's shoulder. "What is the purest soul? That is still the issue."

Lila hummed quietly to herself and then she all but stumbled in mid-flight. "*The Tempest!*"

I looked at Maks and shook my head. "It wasn't a Shakespeare quote, Lila."

"I know. I know! But I was thinking through the plays, thinking about how to stump Maks and I got one, but I think, I think it answers the question."

"Well, go on, then," I laughed. "What is the quote?"

"'A puppet show in real life. Now I'll believe that unicorns exist, and that there's a tree in Arabia where the phoenix lives.'" She paused. "We've already found the phoenix in the Oracle. What if . . . what if, the purest animal is the unicorn?"

"Shit," Maks breathed out the word. "I think she's right. It makes sense."

Lila looked over her shoulder. "But I've never seen one. Last I heard, they all had their horns cut off so they could hide from other supernaturals. They were being used and killed too often because of their purity."

My stomach rolled with the thoughts that wrapped around me. "Or that's what we were told because their horns had so much power in them."

Maks put his hands over mine. "The last herd was seen in the steppes above the desert, but that was a long time ago, hundreds of years."

"It's a place to start," I said. "We can pick up Balder and Batman and find the herders I bought Balder from. They might know something. They'd have the stories at least to start with." I tried not to think about what would happen if we failed, if we didn't find the last stone. Would we still have enough fire power to take out Ollianna and the falak? Would it be enough to stop Ishtar? Finding a unicorn, though, that was not going to be an easy task. Not by a long shot.

Gods, I didn't know and that was the worst of it, the not knowing.

We flew straight through the night and into the next morning before we were back on familiar ground. Literally, we flew over Dragon's Ground.

"Wait," I said. "Lila, what about your grand-mother? She's a seer; would she help us?"

Lila slowed her wings. "I could use a break." On a spiral, she coasted to the ground, not far from where the wall had resided for so many years. The wall that was now broken, the spell shattered, allowing super-naturals to come and go as they pleased.

Lila landed, and Maks and I slid off. I divvied up what was left of our food stuffs between Maks and me. "Sorry, Lila, not sure there is enough for you."

She shifted down to her smaller form and flew up to my shoulder. "You can carry me for a bit."

"Fair enough." I held up a stick of dried camel jerky and she took it, chewing right in my ear.

Maks leaned against a tree, his eyes closed. "This is not how we should be going into battle. Drained, tired, injured."

"You mean like we usually do?" Lila said around a mouthful. "Because let's be honest, it's not like we've ever gone into a fight knowing we were all at our best."

She chattered at Maks, and they began to trade Shakespearean insults, each one worse than the last. The words flowed over me, and I found myself staring at a spot beyond the trees, a slim opening between a large boulder and a tree that had to be a thousand years old by the way it was bent and gnarled. In that space thrummed an energy I felt under my skin.

I gave a slight bow at the waist. "Amalia, lovely to see you again."

Laughter rolled out around us and Lila shot up from my shoulder, shifting to her larger form in the blink of an eye, putting herself between us and the laughter.

"Oh, granddaughter, you are home!" Amalia appeared slowly, as if she stepped through a bank of fog. Her pearlescent scales were as stunning as before, creams and whites and silvers like the grand dame she was.

Lila didn't stand down. "Grandmother, I am not here to stay."

"I felt the death of your father," Amalia said. "We all did."

There was a moment when I thought Lila would shrink and duck her head, but she held it together and stood a little taller, spread her wings a little wider. "I know. I killed him. Him and Trick."

Amalia blinked at Lila. "Then you are the ruler of Dragon's Ground now."

Lila shook her head. "I am here only because we need guidance. You are one of the few true seers left in this world, and we are on a desperate hunt."

I stepped back and Maks moved up beside me. This was Lila's moment, not ours.

Amalia sat back on her haunches. "As you are my leader, I cannot deny you help."

"I am asking, not demanding," Lila said. "Even now with my father dead, I know I am not welcome here. I know that taking the emerald stone away has caused a rift between the dragons." Her voice hitched. "A rift that caused someone I thought was my friend his life."

I swallowed hard, my throat suddenly tight at the thought of Trick. I could all too easily imagine the pain Lila was going through as I had walked that path with Maks, not knowing if I would have to kill him at the end of it.

Slowly, the old dragon bowed her head. "The cost of coming into your own—"

I watched as Lila's shoulders and head drooped, as if the words of her grandmother would weigh her down. That was a whole lot of nope.

I waved a hand, stopping her. "No. This was not Lila coming into her own. This was the three of us pitted against a dragon who has had it in for her since she was born. Lila came into her own years ago, you just didn't want to see it. No one wanted to see it."

Her grandmother looked down at me. "I see, little cat, you have also found more than you bargained for. Your life is not yet your own, and I don't think it ever will be." Her eyes were sad and thoughtful. "If Lila leaves now, she will never be accepted as leader here."

"I don't want to be the leader, Grandmother," Lila said. "I will protect my people. I will be the guardian they need, but I will never lead."

Chills swept through me at her words, and I was so, *so* proud of her. Not for turning down the call of a leader, but because it was what she wanted. No one was asking her to turn it down.

Again, her grandmother bowed her head in acquiescence. "Then a boon I give you. The creature you seek is far closer to your heart," she pointed a claw at me, "than you could have ever realized. You are matched with him and he has seen to your soul and found it worthy of his gift."

I frowned up at her. "What do you mean? I've never met a . . ." My words trailed off, and those chills from before? Yeah, those came back in waves so hard that my knees buckled, and I went to the ground.

White noise rushed through my ears. I was sure Maks and Lila were talking to me, but I couldn't hear them. All I could see was my life and my one constant through it since I was a young woman.

Me and my horse.

My horse who was smarter than any other, who seemed to understand me speaking even though he had no reason to. My horse who had more speed and stamina, more heart in him than was possible.

My horse who had fought for me, and me for him to the literal walking of a line between life and death.

My horse . . . who was not a horse. My horse who I had left behind to keep him safe from the dangers we faced.

"We have to go." I stood and stumbled toward Lila. Maks helped me because my legs were shaking so hard. All this time, all this time . . .

And so many more things made sense.

The times I'd survived when I shouldn't have. When I'd been able to find Balder and he was able to find me.

We were in the air and flying hard toward where we'd left the horses before Maks's voice really penetrated my head.

"Zam, is Balder in trouble?" He turned me toward him.

"No." I paused and shook my head. "Well, maybe if someone else figures out what I just figured out. He's the unicorn, Maks. Balder is a fucking unicorn."

A s we flew away from the jungle, back to where we'd dropped Batman and Balder off at the edge of the desert, I made myself ask Maks the question I'd been avoiding.

"Maks, talk to me about the falak. What do your memories say?" I forced the words out. "I mean, if Ollianna kills Shax, and the falak has no fear of anyone, what happens? Does the world really end?"

He leaned his head against me, and his breathing slowed. The words that flowed from his mouth did nothing to ease my worry, not one bit.

"When the falak came before, it devoured the land. Thousands of feet long, its coils would literally wrap a city up and crush it with as little effort as breathing. Fangs as big as trees, venom that flowed like a river from its mouth and a desire for nothing more than filling its belly with anything it could find.

It pulled dragons from the sky, and scattered any whose power might thrwart it."

My guts twisted up. "That's all? Well, that's not too—"

"It ate magic, and the supernatural creatures even far from it began to fade, their very life force being sucked away just by its mere presence within the world."

Lila blew out a breath. "We could—"

"It had only one weakness, and that is lost to all but the Emperor."

I held still, waiting. "Maks?"

"Yes?"

"That it?"

He lifted his head off my shoulder where he'd rested it. "Yeah. I think so."

There was no disputing that the falak was bad. We'd always known that. But not . . . goddess on a mangy donkey, we did not have the fire power, the magic, the knowledge to deal with a creature like that.

We had to kill it.

If it didn't kill us first.

After that, there wasn't a lot to say, or maybe we were all just too wrapped up in what we'd learned, and how it impacted all of us. Or maybe, just maybe we all realized right then how bleak our path ahead of us was.

Fuck.

Lila flew to the edge of exhaustion to get us to where we'd dropped Balder and Batman off. She circled once, and my heart couldn't handle it.

The horses weren't there. Of course they weren't. I'd known they would go deeper into the steppes. That had been my plan and hope for them. I'd taken the jewels and stuffed them into a crevice near where I'd left the horses. Because honestly, if we died trying to get the final stones, what did it matter if someone else found them? The world would be done.

With a light hop, Lila landed, and Maks and I were off her back in a flash. I shifted to four legs, taking my jungle cat form, and Maks followed my lead. "Stay here!" I yelled over my shoulder at Lila.

We needed her rested for getting us all the hell out of here.

I bounded up the rocks, Maks keeping pace in his caracal form. He scented the air. "They were still here last night. But there is something else."

I drew in a big breath, catching wind of something deadly. "Fucking Ollianna!"

I scrambled to where I'd buried the stones at the top of the slope. The flat stone I'd laid on top was undisturbed, and I flipped it off and dug through the loose soil until I found the leather wrapped bag. I grabbed it in my mouth and nodded at Maks.

I was going to fucking kill them all if they'd so much as harmed a hair on either horse. Mind you, the plan was likely to kill them all anyway.

Up the slope, we scrambled, following not only the smell of the horses and lizard men, but the hoof-prints as well. More than hoofprints; soon the tiny scuttles of small lizard bodies turned into bigger feet, more human-like.

We turned on the speed, running full tilt down the far side of the slope, leaping over rocks and divots, letting gravity help us along.

A whinny full of fear shrieked ahead of us.

Faster, we needed to go faster. I flattened out, digging deep into whatever reserves I had left, thinking about Balder giving his all.

Even if he hadn't been a unicorn—and shit, I still had a hard time seeing him that way—I wouldn't have left him to this if I'd had any choice in it.

Maks and I hit the bottom of the slope, skidded, dug our claws in and turned hard to the left down a narrow alley. I didn't have to know this place to feel the walls closing in and recognize a funnel when I saw one. The first of the lizard men came into view.

There were about thirty of them, not so many as before, not by a long shot.

But they had the two horses cornered.

Balder was on his back feet, striking out as the lizards shot forward, trying to get at his belly to disembowel him.

I dropped the bag of stones and literally leapt into the fray, hitting the first oversized gecko in the back, driving him to the ground, my fangs buried in his neck as I crushed it with one bite. Maks shifted to two legs beside me, using his weapon and its long reach to do damage while the creatures still had their backs turned, while they didn't realize they were about to get pincushioned.

Claws and fangs, blade and blows, we had half of Ollianna's creatures dealt with before the rest seemed to realize what was happening. When they finally turned, they had their backs to Balder.

That was not a smart move.

As I took out two lizard men at the knees, he shot in, grabbed one by the connection between shoulder and neck and shook him until his neck snapped and he went limp.

Hooves entered the fray, the sound of bones snapping not slowing Ollianna's attack at all. They had no choice, they were under her power, but I could see it in them, the desire to run.

They knew they were all going to be killed.

Maks whipped his curved blade through the air, taking two heads at once, and killing the last of them. "Check the horses. I'll finish any that are still breathing."

I shifted to two legs and ran to Balder. He stood there heaving, flanks soaked with sweat, blood on his lips. I wiped the blood away, then wrapped my arms around his neck. "Thank the goddess we made it in time."

He gave a soft nicker and dropped his head so he

hugged me to his chest. I swatted his shoulder. "Why didn't you tell me you were a unicorn?"

Balder pulled back and those big eyes blinked at me with an innocence that I didn't believe, not for a second.

The way he'd wanted to battle the White Wolf came back to me in a rush, how he'd challenged the creature.

How he'd reveled in the battles we'd galloped into.

"I'm not letting you go. You're my horse, even if you are a unicorn." I grabbed him by the nose. "But why didn't you tell me?"

Batman nudged me from the other side, and I ran my hands over him, checking them both for wounds. Other than a few scrapes and cuts and a whole lot of sweat, they were fine. Dehydrated, by the way their skin reacted to a pinch test, but that could be dealt with.

A nose bumped my back and I turned to Balder. Maks stood back, giving space for this moment.

A girl and her horse. There was no bond so strong and I felt . . . honored that he'd stayed with me all these years.

His nose stretched out and I cupped his muzzle. He pushed farther until we were nose to nose, breathing in each other's air. An old trainer's trick to allow a horse to smell you. Only I was breathing in Balder's air, and with that warmth, my eyes closed.

Images flickered to life inside my head.

A gangly-legged solid black colt next to his pure white mother, her horn glimmering in the sunlight.

Someone in a cloak offering the mare a bright purple stone, asking her to protect the magic within, the words muted as though from a long distance away. I couldn't tell if it was a man or a woman under the cloak.

The mare dropping her nose to her colt's and the images grew stronger. The need to protect the magic, to wait until the right one came along to share the magic with. The trust that would be placed on that child of one of the last unicorns. And the stone sliding into him, settling inside his chest.

Tears pooled in my eyes as I watched the mare lay down her life for her colt, not in a battle, but to give him all her strength to live as long as he would need to live. The tears slid down my face as he gave up his horn, watched it fall to the earth and disappear into the mountain steppes in order to keep his identity safe.

And then seeing me for the first time as I haggled with the traders he'd allowed to capture him. Wondering about me.

Thinking I was okay as long as the treats kept coming.

I laughed. "Treats? That's all I am to you?"

He blew a deep breath and winked at me. That smart-ass horse winked at me.

Another big breath out and I saw him carry me through battles that made his blood sing, that he secretly loved because he didn't have to hold back his strength or speed. I let him be all that he could be and never questioned him for it.

And then came the first time he'd gifted me with an ability through the power of the stone. When I'd found Lila and rescued her, he gave me a connection to her.

Then when I'd tried to send him away in the Swamps, to keep him safe, he'd gifted me with a connection to the fairy folk.

Other little things were there too, my added stamina and strength for fights I should never have had, my gut instincts . . . the ability to walk in the dreamscape as deeply as I'd needed to.

He'd seen me there one of the first times I'd walked the dreamscape, seemingly asleep. But he'd been there, carrying me through so much, just waiting for me to realize just how important he was.

More than all that was the same gift he had, one that he'd give no one else.

The ability to carry any and all of the stones without their power corrupting me. Balder had been the one to give me that, not my connection to my mother, to the Emperor, or to my father.

My horse.

"I always knew how important you were, you

donkey." I held his head tightly. "You're family. Long before this moment."

A sensation flowed over me, one of agreement, but also that none of the gifts could be taken back, so he had to be careful about what he handed out. I rubbed his forehead and he leaned into my hand. "You will fight with us then?"

He bobbed his head once.

Maks was at Batman's side and his horse leaned into him. I looked at Balder through narrowed eyes. "You gave him more speed, didn't you? So he could keep up with us?"

If horses could look smug, Balder did in that moment. He flipped his lips at me, then shook his head side to side so his mane flipped back and forth. No true words came to me from him, but the sensations were strong. He liked Batman, and more than that, he liked Maks and wanted them to stay with us.

So he figured they'd need to keep up.

I glanced at Maks. "He likes you."

"I'd hope so," Maks said. "I did help you save him from the ophidians."

Balder stomped with a front foot, then bowed down, welcoming me onto his back. "Just a minute." I hurried back to the neck of the funnel where I'd dropped the bag of stones I'd collected.

For just a moment, I thought they'd be gone, that my shitty luck would turn on me again.

But they were there, waiting for me. I scooped

them up and peeked inside. All accounted for, and add one more to that mix, and we were off to the races.

Or at least, we were off to see the wicked witch of the south.

We had all the stones we were going to have.

Now it was time to battle Ollianna, hope that the witches kept their word, and that the Emperor would be able to stop the falak.

Because if he couldn't . . . we were all in deep shit that there would be no escaping.

29

KIARA

The desert was quiet, hot, stifling with the lack of wind. More than that, Kiara couldn't help but feel the pull toward the Stockyards as they rode nearer to the only place she'd known as home. Her eyes swung that way, and in the very far distance was the shimmer of heat waves rolling off the buildings she'd called home for so long.

She wanted to believe that Merlin was telling them the truth. She wanted to believe that going south to help Zam face Ollianna and the falak was the way to do things.

But that pull toward the Stockyards . . .

Was it a true pull toward home, or was it something else? Was it Ishtar trying to fool them yet again, or was the sensation something deeper, an instinct she needed to listen to?

Kiara had spent her life believing that Ishtar was their guardian, the last one to look out for the Bright Lion pride, only to find out that not only had she been using them, but that Steve had been . . . Kiara pulled herself up short, her big paws padding silently across the shifting sand over the hard-packed earth.

Her nose wrinkled as she caught wind of something . . . rotting. Dead, but lion.

Heart hammering, she made herself take another deep breath, because it wasn't just any lion, but one she knew all too well.

Steve.

Something moved in the distance, heading straight for the Stockyards with purpose. The wind shifted again and she crouched as if he would turn and see her. But he was focused on what he was doing, or where he was going.

She glanced over her shoulder to see that Merlin, Ford, Shem and Bryce had carried on. They were swapping out horses as quickly as they could, and the four lion shifters used their legs for much of the travel, but Kiara could see there was no way they'd make it to Ollianna's place in the south in time.

Not even if they all had horses. Not even if they all were healthy, which Merlin was not despite his miraculous recovery.

"Hold," she called out.

The men paused and turned as if startled she'd spoken at all.

She hated that she'd turned on Zam, that her fears about her friend and only true mentor had surfaced and Merlin had used it against her.

"What is it? Are you hurt?" Bryce trotted back to her, and she had to admit her heart hammered for a different reason. She shook of the spurt of attraction, needing to focus on what was in front of them, not on a slim chance of the future.

"Not hurt. But you and I both know the place Merlin wants to get to, there is no way we'll make it in time. And if we do . . . what do you want to bet that we'd be used as cannon fodder or worse, bait? Or worse even than that, blackmail?" She shook her head. "There has to be a better way to help Zam." She turned and looked at the Stockyards.

Bryce moved up beside her. "What are you thinking?"

Kiara tried to put a plan together the way that Zam might have. What would be the boldest move? The one that . . . "We could keep Ishtar busy," she said softly. "We keep her attention here, and not on whatever Zam is doing." She looked at Bryce. "She'd do it for us."

Slowly he nodded, and then he looked over his shoulder to where Merlin sat on one of the horses. "He won't want to stay."

"He's not part of our pride," she said. "He can stay or go as he pleases."

Merlin frowned, not hearing them, but, of

course, their eyes were on him as they spoke. "Ishtar could kill any one of us, and she could force us back to her side to drain us of our energy," Kiara said softly. "But if we go into that battle, we are all surely dead."

Bryce leaned into her, giving her not only his warmth, but literal support. "I'm with you. We stay here, try to keep Ishtar busy, keep her eyes off Zam."

Surprise filtered through her. "You used to argue with everyone," she said. "I like this side of you better."

He gave a chuffing grunt. "Being caged showed me some humility. Nearly dying offered me a chance to look at what I'd do different."

She fought not to cringe. His path had been a hard one, but it had given him a far better outlook on life than if he'd had it easy. Maybe if the pride was handed to him, he would have turned out like Steve.

Speaking of . . . she turned and looked at the figure lurching forward. "That's Steve out there. I'm thinking he finally pissed Zam off enough that she killed him."

Bryce looked at where she pointed with her nose and took a deep breath. "I'll be buggered. He smells dead."

Shem and Ford joined the two of them, and for just a moment she felt a connection to all three men, a connection that warmed her from the top of her head down to the tip of her tufted tail. Ford looked at her, his eyes as gold as any other lions', only framed with all that dark hair.

And Shem, lean as a whip and old enough to be her father but still handsome, still full of wisdom and surety.

Not a harem, but her pride, and that connection to each of them, that trust was what Zam had been trying to make happen. But it couldn't, not fully, because Zam was only part lion, as much as it killed her to admit it; she would always be a little on the outside of their species. Kiara's heart skipped a beat as she understood Ishtar's games. "That's why she kept us apart."

"What?" Bryce looked at her.

"If a pride is truly connected to a proper alpha, they are far stronger than if they are all individual. That's what Ishtar was doing all those years, keeping you wounded, keeping Steve at all of us, even encouraging him to mess around on Zam. I heard her once tell him that he was the pride leader and he should do as he pleased. And she encouraged Zam to challenge him, all the time." Her words tumbled past her lips. "But a true pride, one of full-blooded lions connected together, following a single alpha, she can't touch that. Ishtar can't break through those bonds. That's why she never came at the prides before the Jinn attacked!"

She wasn't even sure just how that all had come to her, but she felt it in her bones. Like a story her mother had told her when she'd been a cub, before she'd been rescued by Zam, before she'd been fooled by Steve and before she'd lost her own cub. A story she could half remember about prides sticking together and being stronger for it.

That was why they'd stood against the Jinn all those years. Why they'd been the protectors of the desert.

Shem slowly nodded. "That is true. A proper pride following an alpha they have all committed to by blood and by bond cannot be broken. Bryce?"

Bryce was already shaking his head. "No, it isn't in me anymore. I am not the man I was. Ford?"

Ford sighed. "Nah, I'm too fucking lazy to be the boss."

Shem laughed. "And I am too crazy. But I see one I would follow. One with a heart that would defy the odds."

Ford looked at her and nodded. "Me too."

Bryce leaned into her again. "I see you, Kiara, and would follow you as alpha of the Bright Lion Pride."

Shivers racked her body as each of the men pledged to follow her as the alpha.

Her.

Kiara.

The girl no one wanted. The girl who Steve thought was stupid.

The girl who Zam never stopped believing in, even if she'd stopped believing in herself.

She lifted her head and the desert wind swirled around her, tugging at her, daring her to do what she was born to do. Kiara opened her mouth and roared, the sound echoing out to the Stockyards, and farther, calling any lion within the vicinity to her, calling them to battle at her side, against Ishtar.

The sound echoed and echoed and she looked back to see Merlin smiling. "I thought you'd be angry that we're staying, instead of going with you."

He shrugged. "I'm a go-with-the-flow kind of guy."

"Bullshit," she said.

Merlin shrugged again. "Look, I'll be straight with you. From the beginning, I've been trying to run the show and look at how that's done. Maybe I'll just roll with this, see what happens."

Kiara gave him a slow nod. "Then you'll stay and help?"

"As surely as if you were Zam herself." Merlin gave a bow from his waist. "Besides, I think my Flora is almost upon us."

They all turned as a pair of horse and riders galloped from the north toward them, skirts flying in the wind. Not just Flora then, but another woman too.

Kiara stepped up and roared again, this time a direct challenge to Ishtar.

The desert wind carried the sound, and from the

Stockyards there was a burst of flame around the edge of the buildings.

So be it then, the battle would be on them soon.

Let her come at them, unified as they were now as a pride. Let her see who the real queen of the desert was and let her tremble before the strength they held together.

30

ZAMIRA

The flight to the south was . . . quiet. No one chased us, no one threw spells at us. No traps, no enemies. I knew they were out there, waiting, watching, and my skin crawled with that knowledge.

Basically, all of it weirded the shit out of me.

We'd avoided the Stockyards by a good distance, to be on the safe side. I found my head turning toward that direction, though, as if something would tug me there.

"You thinking about Steve?" Maks asked, no doubt seeing the direction I stared. I laughed and shook my head.

"No, I was just thinking that . . . that I have to face her soon." I sighed and tipped my head toward the Stockyards and Ishtar. "Assuming we survive these first two battles."

Maks tightened his arms around me in a fierce hug. "You mean to take the Emperor on as soon as we finish fighting Ollianna and the falak, don't you? To take him by surprise?"

I bit my lower lip and nodded. "The Emperor won't be expecting it. Hopefully he'll be injured from the fight. That will help us." Again, there was an assumption there would be injuries to the Emperor, enough to turn the tide in our direction. I mean, if the falak was killed, there was no worry about keeping the Emperor alive. Right?

Right.

On top of those thoughts, I was wondering why Ollianna's creatures had gone after Balder. Did she actually know what he was? Did she know that he held one of the stones, or did she figure out that I'd left the powerful jewels behind? I chewed on the inside of my lip. "If Ollianna knew not only where to find Balder, but that he was a unicorn, who would have told her? How did she figure it out?"

Lila banked her wings on the wind, turning us to the right. "Could she have just figured it out? You know, gotten a hint and puzzled it through?"

"We didn't, and he's been with us all along," I said. "I mean, the only clue we had was that 'purest of heart,' which yes, sounds like a unicorn. But they've been unseen for as long as I've been alive. And we got that clue from Merlin. He wouldn't have given her any such clue." *MIA* as my father would have said.

Unicorns hadn't been plentiful, and the only time he said he'd seen one was when he'd first landed on this side of the wall, sent in to help.

Only he hadn't known he was being dropped off because "they" knew he was a supernatural, and his superiors didn't tell him. There was no one in danger, or at least not immediate danger.

Maks held out a hand, palm up. A tiny puff of smoke flowed over his palm. "There are other seers." The smoke curled up until it turned into the Oracle —a phoenix. The smoke pooled in his hand and then swirled around once more, forming another figure of myth—a gryphon. Then another—a three-headed woman. "Any one of them could have given her a hint. Does it really matter?"

"It matters because she'll try to kill him, to get the stone out of his chest," I said.

He closed his fist and the smoke slid off his fingers, caught up in the wind all around us. "Shit, I hadn't thought about that."

I had. It had been almost all I'd been thinking about since we'd found the horses in the narrow cut. They'd been chased down, stuffed into a corner, and I had no doubt they would have eventually been over-run. Maybe Balder could have done something, given Batman a gift that would have allowed them to both escape, but I wasn't sure.

The easiest way to take whatever stone he had would be to kill him and rip it from his chest.

Lila flew with both horses held in her talons, gripped as carefully as she could. "I'm going to need a break soon."

I looked over her side, taking in just where we were and actually recognizing it. "We aren't far from the Blackened Market. Let's land near there."

Yes, I knew it was a dangerous place, but they would have food and it wasn't like I was dealing with Davin again.

At the speed we were traveling, we were well within our time frame, and would make it to Ollianna's lair by sunrise the next day.

Lila flew down until she was just north of the market. "Why do you want to stop here?"

"I want to see if it's still thriving," I said. More than that was a promise I'd made months before, a promise to find the missing dragon babies. I was no Tracker, but I was a damn good thief, and if anyone could find something that had been stolen, it was me.

As soon as we landed, Lila shifted and I tucked her inside my shirt where she could sleep. A quick mount up on the horses—all right, one horse and one unicorn—and we were off at a quick pace. The two boys were fresh and they danced forward.

Or maybe they were remembering being here, chased by ophidians, fighting for our lives.

We passed by the edge of the Blackened Market, and there was no movement. Maks shaded his eyes. "It'll still be up and running, just not here."

The buildings that had lined the strip of trading in goods, weapons, foods, slaves, and baby dragons were decrepit, as if they'd been left empty for years and not a week. Had it only been a week?

I blew out a breath. "We have to come back here, Maks. We have to find them." I loved that I didn't have to spell it out. Maks knew exactly what I was talking about.

"We survive these next few days, and I'll follow you anywhere you want to go," he said. "Let's survive the week first."

"Fair enough. Though I must say your belief that we might not all survive this is somewhat disturbing." I smiled at him, but he didn't smile back, and that made my own mirth slip away from me. "Maks?"

"I don't think we'll all survive." He closed his eyes a moment as if he were listening to a memory he had that was not his own. "The last time the falak was destroyed . . . those who faced it were all killed, all except the one we know as the Emperor. He was the last man standing and he rewrote history to make himself the hero. But he didn't do it on his own. He'd needed four others."

Four.

I swallowed hard. "You, me, Lila . . . and Balder. We could be the four this time that he sacrificed in order to survive." A shiver that didn't fit in with the desert heat slid down my spine and settled in the pit of my belly. "Are you sure?"

He looked over at me. "Sorry to be the bearer of bad news. It only just came to me."

"Maybe Davin's memories are fucking with you," I said. "Let's say that's the case for right now. How about that?"

Maks did smile then, though it was as fake as smiles came. "Do you have a plan?"

I considered what we were up against. "What do you think about taking the amber stone again?"

His face was thoughtful as the horses jogged along under us. Balder gave a low snort and bobbed his head up and down. Agreement from the unicorn. Maks held out his hand and I slipped him the amber stone. The one the Jinn had used to keep their hold on the desert.

"What does it do?" I asked.

"It amps up my abilities, making them stronger," he said, a grimace on his face. "But I can feel it worming its way into me already, urging me to be violent." He dropped the stone into his own pouch and his face relaxed. "That's better."

"No wonder Davin lost his marbles," I said. "If he was already power hungry, adding that to the mix would have just pushed him over the edge."

Maks nodded. "What about Lila?"

"I doubt she'll take the sapphire stone," I said, brushing my hand over the pouch. "I can use it. The cold will be good with reptiles." Only I found myself thinking about the stone the Wyvern had given me and how I'd used it to wipe out all the frogs, stopping their hearts. Could I do that again? Fuck, it had almost killed me last time, and that had been frogs. Simple creatures that didn't fight back all that much.

"Good call." He looked ahead of us. "You think Ollianna will send ophidians toward us again?"

The thing was I didn't think she would. I closed my eyes, letting the movement of Balder lull me into a doze. I pushed myself into the dreamscape, opened my eyes and let out a low hiss.

"Balder! Do you see this?"

He gave a sharp snort. I couldn't believe what was in front of me. The entire dreamscape looked as though it had been lit on fire. The mirror of our world was breaking into pieces.

"This cannot be good," I said, then urged Balder into a gallop, knowing it was not in the real world. We raced over the short distance between where we were and where Ollianna was.

Before we even arrived at her seaside villa, her cries filled the air. Screams.

She was in labor.

I bit down on the inside of my mouth and snapped myself out of the dreamscape. "We have a chance," I said.

Maks looked at me nothing but trust in his eyes. "What's happening?"

"She's in labor. I don't know for how long but . . ."

I swallowed hard. "If we go now, we could take her by surprise. Her witches will side with us."

He reached over, took my hand and brought it to his lips, kissing the back of it. "Then let's kick some lizard ass."

We leaned into the horses and they took off, running flat out, their legs and necks stretched as if they were truly racing for a prize. Lila dozed off and on inside my shirt, which was good. I could feel her exhaustion even through our bond. The miles slid by and I fed my magic into Balder, and saw Maks do the same for Batman, giving them the energy and stamina to keep going.

To keep running.

The hours slid by and the day turned into night. Midnight came rolling around and with it the smell of the ocean.

We eased the horses back to a trot. I slid off with my hand supporting Lila, groaning as my legs tingled from the sudden impact on the bottom of my feet, body sore from the full-speed gallop we'd been riding. I jogged beside Balder as I pulled out not only the water but the oat and camel fat balls I kept for them. I shoved the energy balls into his mouth, then held the water skin up so he could drink while we jogged along.

A distinct sense of gratitude flowed between him and me. I patted him on the neck. "Least I can do."

Lila crawled up to the top of my cloak and gave a

jaw-cracking yawn. "I thought we weren't going to get here until the morning?"

A scream cut through the air; a scream that made the hair stand all along the back of my neck.

Lila stiffened, her head snaking out and twisting around. "Is that Ollianna? It sounds like her."

"Yes, still in labor, I'd guess," I said. "Do you three trust me?"

Lila squeezed my shoulder with her claws. "Of course."

"Always," Maks said. "What are you thinking?"

I blew out a slow breath as the plan formed fully in my head. "I think I can get in there on my own, I can get to her, I can . . . I can kill her before the child is born. She'll be very weak, and very focused on the baby. Etheral and the witches will help. We had a plan for them to help me get into her sanctuary."

Goddess, even as I said the words, I cringed inside, my guts twisting. Even knowing that the child was a monster that would be bent on destroying the world, even knowing that this moment could give us the best chance at stopping them both, I could see all too clearly in my head my flail crashing down on the body of small child. Knowing it was a monster didn't take away from the image and my bile kept rising.

We were at the top of a cliff overlooking the structure built into the rock wall. I'd traced my steps through it, and I knew exactly where Ollianna's room was, knew exactly where she'd be giving birth.

I knew where I was going and I knew I could get there faster on my own without worrying about Lila, Maks, or Balder.

"Can you do it, though? It won't be a single blow," Maks said softly without recrimination in his voice. "A blow for her, and one for the child."

Before I could answer, the decision was answered for me. A woman's cry of joy split the air followed by the first cry of a child.

The child that would change everything.

"Well, shit," I muttered, standing on the cliffs above Ollianna's seaside hideaway, listening to not only the sound of the ocean, but the newborn wail of a monster that would eat the world whole. Just fucking fantastic.

The falak had been born if that cry was what I thought it was. A child of a witch and the Emperor himself, a monster invoked. I rubbed my face with one hand, frustrated.

The plan I'd had wasn't terrible, but a very small part of me was glad that the choice had been taken from me.

I didn't want to kill a child, even if that child was a monster. Did it look like a monster? Somehow I doubted it. Call me cynical, but if I were a betting woman, I'd bet the child would look like an angel with pink cheeks and huge eyes that would beg me to spare it while it stabbed me with some long venomous tentacle attached to its ass. I shook my head. My imagination was getting the better of me.

"We wait then?" Lila asked.

It was my turn to nod. "We rest here, and we wait on the Emperor."

There was no fire for us, no țuică to ease our worries, and nothing to say as the night crept over us. We faced our greatest battle on the morrow. Part of me thought it was stupid to wait, we should go in now when Ollianna was exhausted from giving birth and just lay waste while we could, but the other part . . . the other part didn't want to kill her.

"If you see any reptile around, kill it," I said. "We don't need her eyes on us."

Balder stomped a foot and blew out a low snort. He flipped his nose, pointing at the cliff and the structure built into it. I stood and went to his side, ran my hands over his neck. "You got an idea?"

He shook his head and a sensation of calm flowed over me followed by the warm tingling I recognized now as magic.

A gift, he was bestowing on me a gift.

I licked my lips and held a hand up, palm to the sky, not understanding what he'd given me. No magic pooled around my hand, no flame or lightning bolt danced over my fingertips. I raised my eyebrows at a him. "You going to tell me what it is?"

He gave a low nicker, the sound rumbling under

my hand still on his warm hide and he shook his head, a sensation flowing from him to me that I would know when I needed to know. The only other image he gave me was one of my flail. The flail I'd given to the Emperor.

Basically, it was a surprise then.

"More effective if I know," I muttered. He bunted me with his nose and snorted as if laughing. I loosened his girth, took his bridle off and then did the same for Batman.

Balder lay down with a grunt, tucking his long legs under him. Batman followed his lead. Maks and I sat next to them, leaning against their warmth, Lila curled up on my lap.

"It's not really that cold out," she said.

"No, but imminent death does bring its own special kind of chill," Maks drawled. He draped an arm around my shoulders and stared up at the sky. "'Cowards die many times before their deaths.'" Lila snorted.

"Try again. *Julius Caesar.*"

He smiled as he stared upward, his profile calm despite what we were facing. "'The sudden hand of Death close up mine eye!'"

"Oh, that's a good one," I murmured, looking up to the stars with him. "Lila, you know it?"

"Give me a minute," she whispered, then repeated the verse over and over. I leaned my head on Maks's shoulder, letting the moment wash over me while

345

Lila struggled with the lines.

"Damn it!"

"Does that mean I win?" he asked.

"No, it means that you win only if I can't stump you on the next one." She scrambled from my shoulder to fly a loop around us. "But where is that one from?"

"*Love's Labour's Lost*," I said, feeling the title had more meaning than just a play's title, at least to us. Love . . . we'd all fought for it so hard. What if we lost tomorrow? What if we didn't all come out of this? I pushed to my feet, my guts twisting with the possibilities and I didn't like most of them. "I'm going to circle around," I said. "You see if you can stump him."

Lila grunted. "Already on it. I fight for the honor of my people against this man who thinks he can out-Shakespeare me."

Maks laughed, even though I could feel his eyes on my back. "Did you just use Shakespeare as a verb?"

"Hell, yeah," Lila said to him, but her eyes were on me too. They knew me too well, enough to let me have my space even while they both worried.

I should have been tired, exhausted by the hurried run to the south. I should have been resting, should have, should have, should have. I walked until I was a solid mile from camp. The sounds and smell of the ocean filled my senses, and I drew them in. I could die tomorrow. I could lose Lila, or Maks, or Balder, or Batman, or all of them, and I wasn't sure I could survive and not lose my own self if one of them greeted death.

I closed my eyes and imagined the doorway in my mind between one shape and another. Only it was not how it had always been.

I could see the two forms offered to me, my house cat form, my jungle cat form, and now a third. A third that made my heart pound, and I couldn't help but wonder just why it was being offered. What had I done to deserve this?

Was this the gift from Balder?

"No, it is a gift from me. My last gift to you. Again, it won't last long once you use it, but use it you can."

I spun on my knees, yanking the knife I carried free of its sheath. The Emperor stood about twenty feet off to my left. "What? Why?"

He approached slowly, and I didn't lower my knife. He motioned for me to put it away.

I did not.

A smile creased his face. "So you have seen there are times I am a right bastard, and times like now that I am not?"

"Uh, yeah."

His smile seemed genuine, if tired. "It is the problem with Ishtar working her magic on me, to make me more powerful. To make me a mate worthy of her own power, only it backfired on her." He sighed and sat on a large flat rock across from me. "It split my mind. Shax is my name, the one that I was born with. The Emperor is the asshole who craves power above all others."

I stared hard at him, still not lowering the knife. Just in case. "So? I still can't trust you."

"For now, you have an agreement, and even that dark side of me recognizes it."

For now. That could mean five minutes or thirty seconds after the battle, he could turn on us. His eyes were on mine and he gave me a slow nod as if he could see that I understood.

"Right now, we can discuss what will happen tomorrow," he said. "I can take Ollianna. I've no doubt about that."

I frowned. "How do you know that?"

"She tied herself to me in a way that . . . was foolish." He frowned.

In my head, I could see the two of them in the dreamscape, her demanding a child, a child of power even if meant spreading her legs for her own father.

"You mean because you fucked her?"

His head shot up and his brows furrowed. "How do you know?"

I finally lowered my knife. "The dreamscape is a funny place. But that doesn't answer why you think you can take her down."

"When those with strong magic fuck, as you so delicately put it, the stronger one can draw on the life-force of the weaker. It's about trust, but Ollianna does not understand. Very few people do." He looked at me. "It is why we must keep the stones from Ishtar."

I blinked a few times, seeing Merlin's face as he'd told me Ish had drained his life-force. "That's how Ishtar took him."

"Took who?"

"Merlin," I said, seeing the injuries in my mind's eye. "She nearly killed him."

The Emperor snorted. "She isn't the stronger one. Not with so many of her stones missing. His mother was . . . well, let's just say that she was stronger even than Ishtar."

I'll admit, my jaw dropped, implications slamming into my brain. "But I thought he was dying. Shit, I thought he would have died after I left him behind."

"Doubtful." Shax scratched at his chin. "He has learned to manipulate people to an extent that I'm not sure he would even recognize if he was lying or not. He breathes his twists out past his lips without thinking."

Trust, that was what this all came down to. "So I can't trust him, either, that's what you're saying?" I wasn't sure that I would even trust Shax's determination of not trusting Merlin. Talk about getting all twisted.

"Probably best to keep him on a short leash. The

same with me. The same with any powerhouse around you." He sat looking at me, and I at him.

"So you take Ollianna. And me, Maks, and Lila take the falak?"

His jaw worked side to side. "The falak will be monstrous. You cannot hesitate."

"You didn't answer me," I said. "That's how we will split our forces?"

I could see in his eyes that there was something he didn't want to tell me and that sent my fear into a sharp spike that made my own mouth dry. "Spit it out. Just spit it the fuck out."

He laced his fingers together and set his clasped hands between his knees. "Ollianna will try to take your Lila friend. And the witches, despite your agreement with them, will eventually turn on you, which Maks can handle. Which leaves you facing the falak alone."

Well.

That did not sound like a party I wanted to go to. "And if you're wrong?"

He shrugged. "Then, of course, the three of you can tackle the falak together." His eyes were sad.

I stared hard at him, wanting nothing more than to shake him. "And why should I believe any of this?"

"Because despite our rather rocky history, you do indeed remind me of the one child that I loved beyond measure. I chased her from my home to keep her safe from the darkness in me, and Ishtar tried to corrupt her as punishment. Her own mother didn't want her because she was a reminder that she'd loved a man she should have hated. Through it all, her heart—your mother's heart—was true, she was . . . she was a good person." He looked at me with such sadness in his eyes that I wanted to believe him. "I couldn't save her. Maybe I can help keep you alive, something she would have wanted."

Again, my jaw wanted to drop. Not because of his nice words, but because they were so out of line with so much of what I'd dealt with. The urge to take his hand flowed over me.

The hand that had rested on Balder's side.

I put down my knife and held my hand out to him, not knowing what I was doing, not really.

Goddess of the desert, Balder had given me a gift.

And I was about to use it.

32

The dark of the night held as I stood in front of my grandfather, thinking that this was a turning point for us. Knowing Lila and Maks weren't far back at camp helped me center myself.

"I believe you," I said as I took the Emperor's hand. His eyes shot to mine, shock filling them, but I didn't let him speak as I gripped him tighter, pulling him close enough that I could see the shadows under his eyes. "I believe that your mind has split. I believe that you think you are the only one to stop the falak. I believe that you think you can take Ollianna."

There was only the slightest flicker in his eyes, like a partial blink that he couldn't quite control, or a flinch around them. Like he thought he had me. I put my other hand over top of the first, pressing into his flesh. "I believe you loved my mother."

He closed his eyes. "I did. So much."

"I believe you believe all of this. But I see you for who you are," I said, digging my nails into his flesh, pinning him to me. "I see you for the monster you've become. That you will turn on me and mine when we are injured and open to being killed easily."

The Emperor's eyes flew open and he tried to drag his hands back, but I dug my fingers in. "You won't beat them without me!" he growled.

"That is what you believe." My voice was strangely calm as the new gift Balder had given me flowed through my body, the image of the flail thrumming in my veins. "I believe we will win."

A pulse of energy tried to roll out of him, like a shock wave to blast me back. I saw it as if it were a living weapon and I *sidestepped* it.

He reached for the weapon strapped to his back, then his arm slumped, and he held it trembling at his side. "Take the flail and kill me quickly. I can't hold that other side of me back. He would have turned on you mid-battle. He would have tried to rule with Ollianna and take control of the falak. Do it quickly, for the world depends on you now, guardian of the desert."

I reached across him and took the flail from his back. The handle warmed to me and I stared down at him.

"You knew it would come down to this, didn't you?"

"Suspected," he whispered. "I suspected."

I held the flail out, the spiked balls hanging toward his hands. He lifted one palm and cupped the side of the flail without so much as a whimper.

"Take it all," I whispered, and the power of the Emperor coursed through his body and into the flail. He fought it, three heartbeats in.

The Emperor tried to yank himself away, but the flail dug in, and I held fast to the handle. "Drink him down, all of him!"

The flail shivered and pulsed, the twin balls glowing with a soft silvery light as they swallowed down not only his magic, but his life.

And it was then that I considered what had made him mad. What had turned him into a monster.

The magic.

"Only the magic!" I yelled. "Only the magic, Marsum!"

His body bent backward, his one hand still holding the flail, gripping it, blood dripping from his flesh.

Still trying to save the monster, huh? Marsum's voice was thick with amusement. ***We aren't all redeemable. But maybe this one . . .***

The flail pulsed twice more and then slid away from the Emperor's palm with a wet sucking noise.

I took a few steps back, so that I was ready to swing the weapon if I needed to. "Marsum, you took it all?"

Every last drop. It won't save him, you know. It will only give him a measure of sanity before his death.

I lowered the weapon as my grandfather sat up, his eyes confused as he touched his head. "Then a moment of sanity is what he'll get. At the very least, he can explain himself."

Shax turned to me, and yes, in that look between us, I saw him for the first time. Just as a man, not an Emperor, and not a mage.

"How am I still alive?" He held out his hands and turned them over. "Or did you already face Ollianna and the falak and die?"

I snorted. "You are alive. You have no magic. For all intents and purposes, you are a human."

His face paled, and in the darkness, it was obvious this was not the answer he'd been looking for. "I am . . . powerless?"

"Yes." I sighed. "It was all I could do."

"You could have killed me," he pointed out as he pushed to his feet.

"Well, seeing as I just watched my grandmother die —crazy ass that she was—I didn't feel like repeating the move twice in one day. Okay?" I didn't move from where I was, unsure if I wanted to lead him back to the camp, unsure of just what to do with him.

He frowned and scrubbed a hand over his face. "She was before Ishtar. When I'd been powerful, but not the Emperor."

"Did you really love her? Or my mother?"

His smile was more than a little pained. "Your mother I loved to the moon and the stars. Your grandmother, I . . . I loved her the best I could at the time. I have not been a good man. You know that, I'm sure."

I snorted but let him go on.

He ran a hand over his head. "Ishtar wanted a child of power. That was why she made me her mate. And I believed her when she said we'd be more powerful together. She gifted me with ability after ability, and they made me dangerous, deadly, and worse, they started to break my mind." His eyes skimmed over me. "Sometimes those gifts came for what seemed like all the right reasons. To keep people I loved safe. To keep those I was to protect safe. But that power in me kept growing and growing. And then it was too much, and I could no longer contain it all." He sighed and closed his eyes, squinting as if the memories hurt him.

We stood across from each other and I didn't know what to say. He was no longer the Emperor. The falak was out there waiting, as was Ollianna.

"You should probably go," I said. "There's nothing you can do to help now, and if you try, you'll likely get killed."

Shax sighed and shook his head. "Powerless is not something I'm sure I know how to be."

"Just stay out of the way tomorrow," I said, not unkindly, then turned and walked away.

A mile walk passed by far quicker than I wanted it to, and when I finally found my way back to the campsite, Maks and Lila were both wide awake and waiting for me.

"So," Lila cleared her throat. "You want to tell us what happened out there?"

I looked from one to the other and then took note of where they were looking. Reaching up, I touched the handle of the flail. "He's dealt with."

I had no doubt the Emperor had come early to set up a trap for me, Maks, and Lila. No doubt this would give us a better chance.

I went to Maks and leaned into him, pulling him into a hug. Lila flew up and I pulled her in between us. "Everything in me wants to leave you two behind, to make sure you're both safe," I said softly.

Lila opened her mouth and I shushed her. "But that's not how it works with us, not anymore. Where I go, you go, and where you go, I go."

Maks kissed my forehead. "So glad you finally realize that."

A smiled ghosted its way across my lips. "Which means we are going in tonight, undercover. It will give us a better chance. All three of us are small enough, and I know the way."

Maks tightened his hold on me and then gently let me go. "You have a plan?"

I nodded. "The witches will keep Ollianna busy, giving us time to kill the falak."

That was the deal I'd made with them. Of course, Etheral thought we were going to let her keep the emerald dragon's stone once Ollianna was dealt with.

Balder butted me with his nose and I circled an arm around his head. "Unless you can shift, you aren't in this battle, my friend. Stay here with Batman."

He snorted and bobbed his head, and an image floated through my mind of him and me facing Ishtar together, a sandstorm billowing around us. Chills flickered up and down my arms making the hair stand on end. "Yeah, I think you're right."

I kissed him on the nose, stepped back and shifted to four legs. Four very small legs. Lila swept down to the ground beside me and trotted along the cliff edge. Maks was on my other side and kept pace easily as a caracal.

"You know," Lila said, "it's pretty here. Maybe we could come back sometime."

She wasn't wrong, the scenery was stunning, and I really had barely noticed it with all that we'd been dealing with. The sound of the ocean waves washing up over the beach, the cries of the sea birds as they settled in for the night, salty crisp air and a hint of magic in every breath I took. Pretty, and I could understand why Ollianna had come here to birth her little monster.

I took the lead, hurrying, finding a way down the side of the cliff, using ledges that switchbacked. Where we got stuck, Lila helped out, lifting us down one at a time.

There was no banter between us like normal going into a fight. No last Shakespeare quip.

Too much was riding on this fight, and we needed it to be over quickly.

I took us into the castle built into the cliffs through an upper window. I hopped through, and they followed, silent. Maks's tufted ears swiveled and then he nodded.

All clear. Again, I led, finding my way through the huge structure easily. It was exactly as I remembered from the dreamscape. I had to ask Shax when I saw him next if him breaking free of the prison had broken the dreamscape, or something else.

Something like the birth of the falak.

I shivered, sniffed the air and then flattened myself against the wall. Lila and Maks did the same, hiding in the deep shadows as a trio of witches hurried across our paths. If they'd been looking for us, they would have found us easily, but their heads were down and bunched together and their voices were thick with worry.

"Does she really think to take on the Emperor? How can she?"

"We have to be ready for anything."

"But if Etheral—"

That was all we heard and then they were gone. I waited for a solid minute before I bobbed my head and started out again, navigating our way to the bottom level of the castle. There, I turned and took us away from Ollianna's sanctuary, sniffing the air as I sought out another witch.

I found her in a communal room with four other witches. Stopping at the doorway, keeping Maks and Lila behind me, I let out a yowl that made the women jump. But not Etheral. Her eyes found me, and she gave a slow nod. "Daughters. We welcome a new child this night. Let us go and celebrate with our young queen."

The other witches startled and then slowly nodded, smiles on their faces that were not smiles really but the mere baring of teeth. Feral. Wild.

Deadly.

Etheral turned, her long green skirt flaring. The other witches were already turned, and I hurried forward, setting myself right behind Etheral who motioned for the others to precede her.

Lila and Maks were at my side in a flash.

Etheral made a movement with her hand and a light spell settled around us. "They cannot hear us speaking now. Where is the Emperor?"

"He sent us in first," I said, barely above a whisper. "I have the flail and Ollianna will not expect us tonight."

"She does not expect you at all," Etheral drawled.

"She announced your death yesterday at the hands of the Emperor."

"I'm a cat," I said. "I've got a few lives left in me."

The witch laughed. "Well then, try to use this one to kill the child. It is growing already. There is little time."

"Does it look . . ."

"Like a monster? No, it does not." She sighed. "Already her beauty makes eyes tear up, and she charms all those who see her. They cannot see *through* her."

I swallowed hard. "You saw through her? To what she really is?"

Her eyes were wide, dilated, as though she were hunting. "I did. She is monstrous to look at, cat, and more than that, she is hungry for this world and all it holds. I can see it in her face, even while she tried to coo at me, tries to make me believe she is not to be feared."

She was also technically a cousin of mine, family. Fuck me upside down and sideways, this was not going to be easy, even if the child was easy to kill. I had to remember what Maks had told me, what his memories had given us in terms of understanding the falak's nature.

We paused at the top of the stairs that led to Ollianna's sanctuary.

"Why is it always the deep dark shithole?" Lila

muttered as we stood at the spiraling stairs that would take us into the belly of the castle.

"Because that's where the monsters live," Maks said softly. "In the deep dark shitholes."

I hurried down the steps after Etheral and her witches. Five witches to hold Ollianna, five who hadn't been charmed by the child.

My jaw ticked, and the adrenaline coursed faster as we drew closer to the bottom.

The stairs suddenly stopped and I kept tight to the wide skirts of Etheral, using her as our shadow to stay hidden from the eyes we were dodging. I motioned for Maks and Lila to stay to the wall by the stairs where the dark was thickest.

"Ah, Ollianna, you look tired, child," Etheral said as she swept forward. I stayed with her, Maks and Lila guarding our rear. I had no doubt that more witches would come when Ollianna realized it was an attack.

Maks had the amber stone, that would help, and though Lila had refused the sapphire stone as I'd known she would, she had Trick's ability with lightning. That would be a surprise for them.

I reached for the bonds between the three of us, and tightened them, pouring my love for the two of them into it. Because Ollianna would try to take Lila from us, of that, I had no doubt.

"Mother, I thought you would never come to see me," Ollianna said softly.

Etheral stopped moving and to my left was a child's bed. A soft coo rolled out of it. The gurgle of a child far older than a few hours.

"You are my daughter, and I will always do what I can to provide and care for you," she said and leaned forward, blocking Ollianna's view of the cradle.

This was my moment.

I leapt up and over the edge, landing quietly within the bed in a crouch, unseen by any but the child who stared at me with huge eyes. Eyes of silver and gold, jewel eyes. An angel child fallen from the stars above could not have been more beautiful and I understood that no one could stand against her.

Except that I could see that she was no beautiful child.

Her image wavered, that child of the stars morphed into a coiled serpent with scales of dark gray and brown flecked with green. The eyes were the same, but the mouth was no perfect cupid's bow, worthy of a thousand kisses. The falak's mouth opened and four tongues shot out toward me, one wrapping around each leg, yanking me close.

There was a pull on my energy, and I shook my head. A weak pull, barely enough to do anything to harm me. I opened myself to the flail's power and reversed the flow, such a simple trick, and one that the child was too young to understand. Or too new.

Or so I thought.

A soft mewl escaped her mouth, the tongues tried to loosen, but I held on. This was not going to be the fight of fights the Emperor had made it out to be. It was not the fight that Merlin or anyone made it out to be. Hell, did Ollianna understand how weak her child was?

She'd believed her child would be a superpower too—we all had.

Yet, it looked like . . . that was just another lie. But why? What was the reason behind making the falak a monster that everyone feared, that everyone wanted to kill or maim? What could it possibly be?

Even as I thought that, the energy exchange equalized. She wasn't trying to eat me.

Images flickered through my mind, the way they did with Balder, and I recognized the falak's attempt to communicate with me, even as I drained its life away.

The desire to sleep, the desire to not be afraid, and she was always afraid. Afraid of the Emperor. And afraid of another—the one behind the Emperor.

He'd killed his friends first and then he'd killed her, the falak. She was not a monstrous, oversized demon, but he'd killed her because he'd been afraid of what others would realize.

She was the balance.

Light and dark.

Good and evil.

She was knowledge incarnate.

Not the devourer of all that we cared for, not the destroyer of the world.

She brought the understanding of the past that other oracles wouldn't give or didn't understand. The falak understood it all, held all the knowledge, and that was why she was feared.

The best I could wrap my brain around was that she was like a library of the universe encased in a single body when she was reborn. A form of a goddess that was neither evil nor good nor chaotic. The falak, just *was*. And that in itself was dangerous. Want to know how to end the Emperor's reign? Consult the falak.

Kill Ishtar once and for all?

Consult the falak.

She knew what everyone had done, knew their hearts and their intentions, just as she knew mine. Her mind was infinite in its stretch, and even reborn into a new body, she understood clearly what was at stake for this world should the powers that be take control of her abilities and use them.

They would either use her or kill her. And death, while not something that would end her existence, was still something she feared. Because what if in one moment, or one life, she no longer could be reborn?

Then it would be over for her.

All of this swept over me in a flash, heartbeats that stretched, and it was fucking overwhelming.

Like listening to someone who talked too fast, but what they were saying was important and your mind struggled to keep pace.

I formed my own question. What about those who would control her and try to make her into a weapon?

The flow of energy between us balanced out further, neither taking.

They needed to be stopped, those who would use her. She was not meant to be a weapon for anyone.

What about her mother?

Not her mother, a vessel, a vessel of madness now that she'd glimpsed into the all-knowing that the falak had been unable to keep from her while in her womb.

A mortal mind could not contain all the falak held.

There was a shout above us, a cry from Ollianna.

"Kill the child now!" Etheral screamed.

So many lies, so many deaths that had led to this. Lies from the Emperor, lies from Ishtar. From Merlin and Ollianna. I saw the creature in front of me, understanding clearly that Balder had gifted me with the ability to communicate with her, to not be torn apart by the vastness of her mind.

And I believed her. She was one of very few not lying.

You are like an oracle then? I asked. *To be sought by many, but found by few?*

A resounding yes came through and I bowed my head, knowing what I was being asked to do. I was a protector, a guardian of the desert. And the falak was a creature of the desert.

"Maks, do you trust me?"

"Always!"

"Lila?"

"You seriously have to ask right now?" Her strangled answer made me smile.

I stared at the child. "Then away with you and me."

She slithered to me and wrapped around my middle as I shifted into my jungle cat form.

The cradle snapped under my increased weight.

I twisted around as the child clung to me, whimpering.

Across the room, the witches held Ollianna to the wall, but barely. "Do not kill her, Zam, please!" Ollianna shrieked the words.

And I set the world on fire with mine.

"I won't. But you need to stop the others from doing just that. And you need to give me the stone." I locked eyes with her. "You trust my word, Ollie. You always did."

There was a moment I thought she'd turn on me, and then the stone shot through the air. I jumped straight up and caught it with my mouth.

"Protect her," she said, her voice strangled. "Protect her and I will guard your escape."

I nodded, then bounded across the room in a few short leaps and raced up the stairs. Behind us, the witches below battled their short-lived queen.

Booms of powerful magic shook the ground and the falak clung harder yet to me as the screaming began. The witches might have tried to come for me, but Ollianna was strong, even without the emerald stone. Strong enough and devoted enough to a child that she'd wanted above all other things in this world, that none of them came for us.

Neither Lila nor Maks questioned what I was doing. Not one question and I loved them more for their trust.

We burst out at the top of the stairs as a handful of witches headed our way. Maks shifted, stood, and slammed the surprised women with a blanket of black magic that pinned them against the wall.

"Go!" he yelled, and we were off and running with me in the lead once more. Three turns and four doorways later, we were out on the sand, racing across it. The child clung to me harder, head buried against my neck.

Just like the last time, so much death, but no protector then.

Warmth rushed through me, a connection I wasn't sure I wanted with a child that everyone sought either to use for her knowledge, or to kill for knowledge, not understanding the power she carried was not earth-shattering, at least not in the physical sense.

Lila shifted into her larger shape as Maks and I ran through the thick sand, scooped us up and swept us to the top of the cliff in the blink of an eye. I scrambled up to her back and shifted to two legs. The falak slithered down under my shirt, against my chest, still clinging to me.

"The horses, Lila!" I said as I fumbled the green stone into the pouch at my side. Six stones, I had six of the stones.

But would it be enough to stop Ishtar? Fuck, who was I kidding. I didn't know what the hell I was going to do with the stones. Jesus Christ on a spitting camel in a goddess-damned sandstorm would have a better chance of defeating her at this point. At least he had some higher power looking out for him.

Me? No higher powers here.

"On it." Lila swept across the cliff tops and bundled up Balder and Batman.

The falak looked up at me with those jeweled eyes and images rushed through my head. Images of a timeline that didn't make sense. A timeline that brought tears to my eyes.

Truth, Balder had given me the gift to see truth through all the lies, to finally understand my world in a way that no one else could have ever shown me. I clung to Maks, connecting him to the images, him and Lila.

She gasped and Maks stiffened as the timeline spooled out, so different than we'd all been told, so skewed.

I bent forward, tears coating my cheeks as the falak's truth—the real truth—rocketed through us all.

33

KIARA

The lions ranged around Kiara on sands to the south of the Stockyards, restless, ready to fight Ishtar the moment she stepped out of her sanctuary. If she dared.

The power surging through her pride—goddess, how that made her blood pound, *her pride*—as they waited outside Ishtar's domain. Other lions had come to her call.

Queen of the desert.

A roar bellowed out of her and the others answered. The smell and sound of lions filled every sense in her body.

Merlin was the only one who stood out, and he rested near the back of the pride with the horses.

She turned her head to check on him. He'd been so close to dying. So close, and yet it had been a lie.

And that above so many other things bothered

her in a way she couldn't quite put her finger on. He'd said so many things.

Claimed the flail couldn't go with Zam.

Claimed they had to stop her.

Claimed that Ishtar had hurt him.

Flora and the girl, Merlin's daughter, were off to the side and she found her feet taking her to them.

Flora's sharp green eyes watched not the lions ranging around her, but the wizard that Kiara would have said she cared for, the wizard that Flora loved. Didn't she?

The way she watched Merlin, Kiara suddenly wasn't so sure.

"Flora, what bothers you?" The words were careful, crafted out of a necessity not to tip her hand. Already she could see that making Merlin an enemy was a terrible idea.

"He is . . . not the same," Flora said softly. "It is like . . . he is the man I remember from my youth."

"My father—the one who I thought was my father —" the girl at her side shook her head, long dark waves of tresses catching the wind, "he said that Merlin was as broken as he. That I should not trust either of them."

Either of them. The story had been brief, only that this girl was Merlin and Ishtar's daughter. That she'd thought the Emperor had been her father and had trusted him as such. "The Emperor said not to trust Merlin or himself?"

"Exactly," she whispered. "I was to go to Ishtar. To stand with her against the others."

Kiara didn't so much as twitch. She didn't know who to trust. Did this girl mean that Ishtar was the least dangerous then? Sweet goddess, that would change things drastically.

"What did he say exactly?" she asked, still pitching her voice low as the tension in the desert began to rise. A slight turn of her head and she felt her throat tighten.

The desert rose behind them, a sandstorm that had no natural place in the world, lights of red, blue, and brilliant flashes of lightning turning the inside of the sandstorm into a show of deadly colors.

"Flora?"

"Sweet baby goddess," Flora whispered, "I was right. He was in on it all along."

"Who?" she roared, not sure where to turn, where to face.

Flora looked at her as she raised her hands, power circling around her and her staff. "I have no words of safety for you, young queen. Your reign may not last long caught between two powers like these."

Kiara's eyes swept the desert and her heart sank, and at the same time her fur rose along her spine. "To me! Guardians of the desert. To ME!"

The lions came to her. She looked to Flora.

"We're going to die here, Flora."

Flora's eyes hardened. "But until we stop breathing, we will give them hell."

The priestess slid off her horse and turned and faced Merlin, the young girl at her side. They faced him and he shook his head.

"Flora. Please don't do this. I really don't want to hurt you."

Around them, creatures rose from the ground, creatures of the desert manipulated by his power.

Twisted and dark, they looked like a combination of gorc and some sort of oversized lizard men. Huge and hulking, they were covered in natural body armor. Unlike gorcs, they were fast and moved like lightning with both teeth and weapons. And there wasn't just one or two of them. With each minute that passed, more and more seemingly climbed out of the ground.

These new creatures lunged at the lions, pressing them inward. Not Jinn, not gorcs, but creatures that had qualities of both. And they were attacking them all.

"A trickster in the end, how many people did you fool? I thought these lizard bastards were Ollianna's!" Flora spat the words at him as magic swirled around both women as if the other monsters had not just arrived.

"They were my idea that I presented to her," Merlin said as calmly as if they were discussing the weather.

Kiara moved to Flora's side, pressing her body against the woman's legs, giving her not only her presence but her energy, understanding clearly that if Merlin died, all this stopped. Flora stood a little taller.

"I fooled all of them," he said with a strange trace of sorrow in his eyes. "The world needs a hand to guide it, Flora. You've seen that. I can be that hand. I was born to be that hand."

"This is madness!" the girl screamed. "You can't do this!"

Kiara didn't quite understand, and then she did. "The jewels."

"He'll take them from Zam, then face Ishtar and take the rest," Flora said.

"No, no." He waved his hands. "You don't understand. She'll fight Ishtar first, and because Ishtar truly loves that girl, she'll let Zamira win, thinking she'll be doing the right thing. And then I will kill her. It's easy to do."

Kiara snarled. "No."

"No?" Merlin tipped his head to one side and lifted a hand, power crackling around it. "No? You think that if I break her heart, she'll have the strength to fight me? You think that if she sees her entire pride —her whole family—killed by Ishtar, she'll be able to stop? You think that if she sees her man and soul mate split down their spines, she'll have it in her? I've been watching her all along. I've seen her strengths and her weakness. I played you all, and you thought I was here for you. I've pushed and directed from the shadows and you all did my bidding."

Flora gasped. "And before?"

"You mean before we arrived here?" Merlin smiled. "Yes, all of that was a game I was bent on winning."

He flicked his fingers at the girl, his own daughter, first, blasting her into the air, end over end. She hit the ground with a thud and didn't rise again. "I schooled even my own thoughts, just in case my father was watching—which he was. In case Ishtar was watching—which she was. I even let my heart love you a little, Flora." He flicked his fingers at her, and she crossed her staff in front of them both, blocking the strike. "So the world would think I had changed. The world would forget who I truly was, and will always be."

Kiara snarled and leapt at the mage, going not for his throat, but his legs. She caught an ankle and snapped it with one bite and then something shot through her body, freezing her in place. The crack of bones, the sensation of warmth pooling around her paws, and she knew her injury was bad.

So very bad.

Bryce's bellow filled her ears as she slid to the ground, struggling to breathe. But her eyes were locked on the storm.

All around her the cries of pain slipped through

her mind as she rolled to her side. The sandstorm drew closer. Hands cupped her face, but she couldn't look away from the storm.

"The storm rages, and we find hope in it," she whispered. "Look to the storm. Bryce." She turned his head without looking at him, the sound of her own blood in her lungs thick in her ears.

Kiara forced herself to her feet and bellowed out a welcome.

A booming roar answered back, and everyone froze. Twisting around the sandstorm, not one, but two dragons burst out of the swirling mass.

The black dragon was as large as the blue and they flew side by side, wingtips touching.

She didn't know how it was possible, but she knew who that black dragon was; she would know her no matter what form she took. The dragons paused, back-fanning the air with their massive wings surveying the ground.

The black dragon's eyes seemed to rest on her for just a moment.

Then the two dragons, they shot forward into the battle.

Not toward Ishtar and the Stockyards.

Toward Merlin.

34

ZAMIRA

The falak's memories of the world before, of the reason for the wall—Merlin had created the wall to make it so he could slowly take over, so he could work the world to his bidding in peace with the other superpowers locked away and out of his way—of the twisted connections between Merlin, Ishtar, and the Emperor . . . all of the truth had broken what was left of my desire to hold anything back.

We'd flown hard, fast, from the seaside of Ollianna's, heading north with Maks's power pushing us from behind. We needed to reach the Stockyards. I could feel my pride there, and it was where Ishtar waited.

And if Ishtar was there with the jewels she carried, Merlin would not be far.

Time slipped away as we flew, and I knew we had to hurry, and hurry we did.

We were going into battle physically exhausted, but there was no choice. Too many lives were on the line. The whole damn world was on the line.

The Stockyards were drawing close when we found a sandstorm blocking our path. Which meant only one thing.

Merlin was making a move now—I was sure of it. He didn't expect us here yet. He didn't expect the Emperor and Ollianna to go down so fast.

He didn't know that the falak had told me all his dirty little secrets.

How Merlin had planted false memories in so many people. How he'd done it all so he could be the new Emperor in truth, to take all of Ishtar's power.

But I knew now, and that knowledge had to be enough to help me stop him.

"Maks, you can cut us a path through the sand-storm?" I yelled to be heard over the sound of the wind and sand swirling hundreds of feet high and miles wide. All to block us from the Stockyards.

From those I was born to protect.

"You got it!" he hollered over the roaring wind. Lila had dropped him and the horses off and he worked his magic—literally—opening the storm like popping a door in the middle of it. "It's strong," he yelled. "If it's really him, Zam, and this is his strength without the stones . . . I don't know if we can stop him even with them."

Fuck, that was not what I wanted to hear.

"We go in hard. He doesn't know that we know," I said. The falak tightened around my chest. She whimpered, terrified. Of course she was. I knew who'd really killed her the first time. And why.

Fucking Merlin and his fucking games.

"Lila, I'm going to shift."

"Jungle cat?" She looked back at me and I shook my head.

"Dragon." My last gift from my grandfather. Fleeting, but it was there, and I would use it.

"Bitch, yes!" She spun, throwing me off her back.

I fell and let the shift take me. The flail went with me as it did, infusing my claws and teeth with even more striking power. Only I didn't expect the falak to damn well *absorb* into me.

I touched my chest where she'd laid so quietly. "Hey, what are you doing?"

Staying safe.

She's not wrong. She's far safer with you than somewhere out there.

"Great. Now I have two voices inside my head."

"Ready?" Maks yelled from the ground.

"Never readier!" Lila yelled back.

The ground rumbled and Maks pulled the sandstorm apart, or at least, made an opening. I could feel the strain on him, could feel the effort it took just to do that. "Let's do this, Lila!"

We winged forward, picking up speed as we hit the edge of the storm, the particles of sand smacking into us, biting, but not near as bad as it would have been without Maks.

I focused on Kiara, knowing she was on the other side, knowing she was with Merlin. Fucking Merlin!

Lila and I popped out of the storm as the bellow of a lion greeted me. I opened my mouth and roared back in tandem with Lila.

We were home.

Only home was a fucking mess.

Besides the storm, the desert was littered with creatures that didn't belong and they were attacking the lions that Kiara had drawn to her. Goddess be damned, she'd done a good job.

Merlin was in the middle of it, acting innocent.

"Fucking douche."

I reared back and then shot forward, going straight for him. One bite, even he wouldn't survive that.

And he'd never see it coming.

Only he did.

I went straight for him, and he flung up his hand at the last second, smashing me with a blow to the belly that flipped me onto my back and I skidded across the desert. I took out a whole slew of his creatures, rolling over them, squashing them flat.

"You okay?" I checked in not only with Lila and Maks but the falak too.

"Good!" Lila roared as she battled the creatures that would overwhelm the lions.

"Killing things!" Maks yelled back.

I am with you. Do not be afraid.

What she said.

Only there was every reason to be afraid.

Every person I loved, every reason for my heart beating strong was here on this battlefield and that was every reason to be afraid—not for myself, but for them.

"Zamira, give me the stones! Ishtar has raised this storm to kill all those you love!" Merlin shouted. "Whatever she has told you is lies! You know her, you know the games she plays!"

Lies. Lies were all that came from his mouth. I shifted as I ran toward him, taking on my jungle cat form, using it to dodge the creatures. I didn't bother to stop to fight. I didn't use the stones. That wasn't how I was going to take him down.

That had never been how I was going to stop him.

I ran toward him while those I loved were slaughtered beside me, not stopping to help them.

Shem was the first I saw go down, his throat severed by a blade from a lizard creature.

Then Ford as he was taken down by something that looked like a misshapen Jinn.

Kiara crawled on her belly toward me, stabbed in the back. Like Bryce had been.

I kept running, tears streaming down my face as I closed the distance between me and Merlin.

I am with you. Do not be afraid.

Bryce leapt in my way, taking down a full-grown gorc, but was grabbed by another, his body skewered ten times over. I roared as I ran, the pain of their lives being stripped from this world was everything.

"I can save them, Zam, you just have to give me the stones. Their lives surely mean that much to you." Merlin stood so quietly in the middle of all that blood, all that chaos. That smile on his face I thought had meant he had a secret joke, and, of course, I'd been right. He'd just never planned on letting me in on it.

Flora lay at his feet, blood pooling around her as she heaved for breath. "Do not give him—"

He bent and covered her mouth with his hand. "Don't listen to the old lady."

Her body shriveled under his hand, aging in an instant. Still alive, but old, and feeble.

I slid to a stop and circled him. "I know you for what you are, Merlin. Merlin the Monster. That was the name they gave you all those years ago. Your mother was a monster, and you're *just like her.*"

He seemed genuinely surprised. "How did you know that?"

"You are the one who took the stones from Ishtar,

for yourself. But you got caught by your father. And you spun a tale to keep yourself from taking the blame because you can't stand for people not to believe you are the hero." I kept circling him, waiting for my moment. Knowing it would come. Trying not to think about all those dying around me.

Trying not to feel their deaths, even though every fiber of my being cried out to save them. Tears streamed down my face, through the anger, through the storm.

For the first time, I understood my father in a way I never had before. Not only was a protector often asked to give their own life, but the lives of all they loved to protect a greater cause.

I closed my eyes and I used my own magic to change the scene around us. "Now you will see, Merlin, what I know."

The world around us shimmered as my power wrapped around us. The Emperor's bloodline ran strong in me, and I used it to create my own dream-scape, changing what Merlin saw. Bending reality just enough to hopefully throw him off balance.

Merlin spun as the desert opened around us, spreading out in sweeping sand dunes, and a bright blue sky. The Oasis popped up around us as if it grew on the spot, and the bodies of my father, my pride lay scattered at our feet. The site of a battle that had changed my world. Fitting that we should be there as I changed it once more.

"Merlin. As guardian of the desert, I call on you to pay for the crimes you've committed."

"You cannot beat me. Give me the stones." He held his hand out. "And I will end Ishtar."

"You broke her mind on purpose. You broke her mind so I would fear her. Just as you broke the Emperor's mind. You couldn't have anyone remember the truth about you. Which is why you made sure that everyone feared the falak. So that if she was ever reborn, we would all be sure to kill her. To kill the memory you feared the most."

His nostrils flared. "I never told you the falak was female." Around us the dead rose with a flick of his fingers, skeletal lions that clacked and clattered. "You have done as your mother suggested, though, and you brought me the jewels. Pity you can't just hand them to me like a good girl."

I stared at him. "You . . . you wrote the papers, didn't you? The journals that were supposed to be my mother's?" Goddess, would the lies never end? The words from what I thought were her hand rushed over me again. That I was to give the stones to her brother, that he would deal with the power in them. All wrong, all of it.

He shrugged. "I did what I had to do."

Another thought hit me. "And the unicorn? Did you tell Ollianna it was a unicorn that held the last stone?"

Merlin smiled then. "Just in case you failed, I

needed a backup. Someone else to get the jewels for me." He shook his head. "Enough questions. Time for you to die, Zamira. You are stronger and more troublesome than even I thought you would be."

The dead he'd raised raced toward me, and I knocked them down, the swipes of my paws enough to take them out easily. But they were never meant to hurt me, just distract me.

"Where did you find the last stone?" He snapped his fingers and the Oasis was gone.

We were outside the Stockyards once more, only the storm was gone. Quiet.

Death was all I could smell. Bodies ripped and shredded.

I am with you. Do not be afraid.

I was shaking as I tried to find Lila and Maks. And couldn't. I couldn't feel them, and I didn't dare look. "You think that killing them will break me?"

"I know it will." He smiled and crouched, snapping his fingers, stripping me of my jungle cat form and forcing me back to my house cat form. "I know that you are so tied to them, that their deaths will crush you. They will take you to the grave with them. It is a weakness to love like that, to let yourself be so bonded to another that their death leaves you wishing for your own demise."

I let the pain wash through me, like breathing through an injury, let myself feel it, let it flow on past. Let the calm flow with the tears. The falak's energy beat inside my own, and through her, I saw the truth.

And with her knowledge in my head, I was not afraid. Merlin wasn't the only one who could make another believe a lie. I bowed my head, and spoke softly, "You're the only family I have left, please . . ."

I crouched and let him scoop me up. Let him hold me to his chest as though I were a defenseless kitten. "Ah, Zam, you made the right choice. Give me the stones."

He thought I was nothing but a mere house cat.

Boy, is he in for a fucking shock.

Marsum was not wrong.

I went from complete stillness to an absolute tornado in Merlin's arms, clawing and biting, tearing through the flesh of his chest and neck, my strength infused by the power of the flail. Blood sprayed as he tried to pull me off him.

My fangs found the artery in his neck and I shredded it, found the artery in his upper arm and opened it too. I found my way to his back and bit down hard over his spine as I shifted to my jungle cat form. My fangs slid through, crushing the bone, shattering them.

The moment stretched, and I knew how to kill him. The falak showed me what would end his life.

A powerful blow slammed into my side, and my lungs collapsed, but I didn't slow, I was almost there even though I couldn't breathe.

They are all with you, all those you love. One last blow, guardian of the desert, and we will be free of his machinations.

I scrambled up his back as he screamed at me, screamed my name, his magic spooling around me as my fangs found the back of his neck. I bit down hard, driving them through the flesh and into the bone as something akin to fire lit along the edge of my fur, the heat driving into me.

I closed my eyes, readjusted my hold on his spine and yanked for all I was worth. There was a moment I thought I wouldn't be strong enough, that I thought I wouldn't be able to do it.

But then, his head popped from his shoulders—literally the sound was a huge sucking pop—like knocking a flower off its stem. His scream cut short and the tension in his shoulders slid away.

Only then did I stop, and feel the pain rocketing through me.

Only then did his magic fade.

I am with you. Do not be afraid.

Her words were there but I still could not find Lila or Maks. "MAKS!" I shifted to two legs, forcing my body to heal as I did so. I fell to my knees and gasped for all of five seconds before I pushed up, and ran past the bodies, seeing them still there. All those I loved.

Dead.

It wasn't an illusion.

None of it was an illusion.

"BALDER!" I screamed for him, then saw him, head bowed over a body. His own hide was scored with wounds, blood dripped to the ground in a slowly growing puddle.

I didn't understand. It didn't seem that bad. The fight had been swinging in our direction, it was all an illusion. Wasn't it?

I stumbled when I reached Balder and went to my knees. Maks was still breathing, but barely.

"Did we win?" Maks looked up at me and I nodded as I struggled to keep it together.

"He's dead."

He coughed once and I ran my hands over his body. I didn't understand how he was dying. What had happened?

Oh shit.

"What? What is it?"

Merlin must have tied his life to them. So when you killed him . . .

A tremor crashed through me as though I'd been hit by lightning. "Oh sweet baby goddess, no."

Balder dropped his head to me, his nose on my shoulder, then went to his knees, lying down. The one place I trusted the jewels to be was with him. He'd swallowed them whole before we made the attack on Ollianna's sanctuary, and now . . . the jewels dropped one by one out of his chest until they sat in a glittering pile at my feet. He bumped me again.

An image of me pressing the stones together, of that being enough. I didn't hesitate, scrambled to press them together, using the magic in me to wrap around them. They pulsed and danced and merged into a single multifaceted, multilayered stone, easier than anything I'd done so far.

As if this was what they'd been waiting for all along.

I held it tightly and poured my power through it as I reached for my connection to all those I loved, to all those I was bound, heart and soul, to protect.

And I found them, their souls close as if waiting. "You all aren't getting away from me that quickly."

The falak wrapped around my wrist, and Balder leaned into me and the images flowed between us, a different kind of trio. Three, three, three.

That was what the Oracle had said what seemed like forever ago.

Three.

Always three.

I wove the magic wide like a net and cast it over my people. My family, and I breathed for them, I clung to their souls, refusing to let them go so easily. We'd all fought too fucking hard to be pulled apart now.

A bolt of lightning cut through the sky, and all

around me, the hearts I wasn't sure I could live without started beating again. One by one, I felt them connect to me, felt them sit up, felt them look around and wonder what the fuck was going on. I smiled even as I slumped, even as Maks caught me in his arms.

"Zam . . . I was dead."

"I know," I said. "But I've already decided I can't live without you or Lila. Which means I had to bring you back or die. Wasn't ready to call it quits yet." I leaned against him.

The stone in my arms was about half the size of a football, and I cradled it in one arm.

From the Stockyards came a stiff breeze.

And a shock I wasn't sure even I was ready for.

Ishtar walked toward me, her skirts billowing out around her legs, her hair braided off to one side. Chin held high still, even now. Even though she had a blindfold over her eyes.

None of that was terribly surprising. But who walked with her was a bit more of a shock.

I couldn't help the glare that settled over my face. Could no one follow orders? "Hey, I thought I told you to stay the hell out of this fight, old man."

Shax walked with Ishtar, leading her by the hand across the open ground between the site of the battle and the Stockyards. "Ah, well, when I saw your compassion for me, I thought perhaps you would show it to her as well. I do care for her, and I know you do as well."

I wanted to tell him to stuff it. That she'd killed my mother. That she'd at turns tried to have me killed in her madness, and had thrown me and my friends—my family—into danger without any thought of what it meant to her other than to have her power back.

I bowed my head as my emotions raged from the need for wiping her off the face of the earth, and making sure no one else tried to pull the kind of tricks she and Merlin had concocted for all those years.

Lila grabbed the edge of my ear, small once more. "What do you think?"

"I think that there is not enough compassion in this world of ours," the words were thick in my throat. "That even though I have every reason to hate her, maybe I can help instead."

I pulled the flail from my back. "Can you take all that power in?" It pulsed against my hand, shivering. That was a definite yes. "Even the stones?"

Another shiver. Well, shit.

I held the flail in one hand and dropped the multicolored stone to the ground, then slowly lowered the spiked balls onto it.

The spikes dug in deep to the stone. The colors were the first thing to disappear, then the stone itself was crushed, shattering as the last bit of power was drunk down.

The falak peered up out of my shirt, watching the dragon on my shoulder, then gave her a tiny wave with one super small claw-tipped hand. Lila stared down at her and frowned. "Don't get comfortable. That's my spot when it's cold out."

I hefted the flail, ignoring the two tiny dragons— seeing as that's really what the falak was, just a different kind of dragon, one whose ability was knowledge instead of spitting acid.

I closed my eyes. The stones' power thrummed through the weapon.

I already knew what I had to do, could see it as clearly as anything in my head. "Thanks."

It is the safest for the world. The falak's voice whispered through me, but I was not the only one who heard it.

Lila bobbed her head and Maks nodded. Balder bumped his nose against my back. Well, at least we were all in agreement.

"Shax, I don't think this is a good idea," Ishtar said, her eyes still blindfolded.

"It's a surprise. You'll love it." He held up her hands to me, and I lowered the flail onto her palms.

"Just the power from the stones," I whispered.

The flail dug in hard and she screamed and pulled back with a blast of energy that sent everyone tumbling away, end over end, and even kicked the flail off, detaching it from her hands.

Not killed, just flung far away.

I stared at her, at the blindfold that hung around her neck instead of covering her eyes. Well shit.

"It was always going to come to this," I said. "Always. Despite Merlin's machinations, you had your own. You killed my mother."

"The Jinn—"

I pointed the flail at her. "You made it happen. You hated her. You knew she could do what I'm doing now."

Ishtar shook her head and the stones glowed within

her belly. "No, she could never have done what you did, Zamira. She wasn't strong enough." Not strong enough. Her eyes met mine. "Are you strong enough to do what must be done? To finally say goodbye?"

My lower lip trembled as I dropped the flail to the ground. Only the falak was with me, and through her eyes, I saw the truth of Ishtar. I saw her heart.

And in the end, it is only what is in the heart that truly matters. It is only those you love that matter. I walked toward her and held out my hand. "It has to be me, doesn't it?"

She went to her knees. "Before the stones' power takes me again. There is no separating me from them the way you saved your grandfather. Though I think that in itself is a great punishment, for him to have no power, and to live with it for however long the desert lets him live."

My lip kept up its damn trembling, and for a moment, I couldn't see her through the blur.

"Don't cry for me, my girl."

"You were my mother," I whispered.

"Not a very good one."

I closed my eyes and went to my knees beside her. The knife in my hand felt heavier than the flail ever had as I pressed it to her belly, cutting it open with a quick strike. There was no blood. Of course, she was a goddess.

The remaining stones poured out of her, pooling between us.

Her eyes were on mine even as they faded. "I will never truly be gone. I will be there in the sandstorms and the oasis, in the death and birth of every creature the desert owns. You always knew that. I am the goddess, and you are one of my many children."

"This is the Ish I remember," I whispered as she slumped into my arms. "And now you would leave me."

"You are not alone." She touched my face gently, like she had when I was a child. "You stopped Merlin, you saved the falak, and you will free the stones. Send their power out into the world, Zam. That is where they belong. Where the ground heaves and pools bubble, that is where the power of the earth is strongest, and you will free the stones."

Her hand slipped from my face and her body changed in my hands, the weight of her lessening until there was nothing there, just a wisp of the material she'd been wearing and nothing more.

I reached back for the flail and dragged it to me, laying it on the pile of stones in front of me. All of them, I'd brought them all to her and now I had them back.

A stick poked at me and I looked up into the very, very old face of Flora. I knew her by her green eyes and that alone. "What are you going to do with them now?"

"What should have always been done," I said. "I'm going to set them free."

. . .

WE STAYED WITH KIARA'S PRIDE FOR ONLY TWO DAYS.
She assured me we were part of the pride, and I knew
it was the truth, but we didn't belong. They protected
those who belonged to the desert, and I . . . Maks,
Lila, and I were there to protect pretty much everything else.

The first morning came a smell like rotting flesh
through my window. Rotting flesh and . . . "Steve?" I
rolled over Maks and climbed up to the window
ledge. Balder snorted and shook his head as I hopped
into his stall. There, circling the courtyard was a
lumbering, rotting to the bone in places, Steve.

I grimaced. "Even in death, he couldn't fucking do
as he was told."

"Useless piece of shit." Lila shook her head.

Maks climbed through to Balder's stall and stood
with me. "I can take it from him—"

We both turned as a snarl ripped through the air
and Kiara raced across the courtyard in her lion
form. She slammed into his legs and sent him flying.

"Ohhh, shit," Maks said and then burst out
laughing.

Because Kiara sent dead-Steve head first into the
poop pile. His bare legs and what was left of his bare
ass stuck out like he'd been planted there, kicking
feebly, unable to right himself on his own.

Kiara grabbed his foot and yanked him out. He

wobbled and pushed to his feet, doing a slow turn. Now, all of this was funny, but the amount of shit in his mouth and stuffed up his nose and in his eyes . . .

Lila sighed. "A rose by any other name . . . or in this case, Steve is still Steve and his mouth is still full of shit."

Kiara grabbed him by his other leg and swung him around, smashing his head into the ground. Again he got up. Unable to die now because of Maks's magic.

I stared at Steve, and while I wouldn't say I was moved to pity, I was moved to some sort of compassion. A gentle touch on Maks's arm and he removed his hold on Steve's body. The asshole of all assholes fell to the ground in a crumpled heap. Kiara stood over him a moment, then grabbed his foot and flung him back into the shit pile.

At least there, he'd do some good for the world. And Kiara got her moment to get in one last blow. I hoped it helped her heal and move on with Bryce.

A day later, we were ready to go.

Saying goodbye to Bryce was the hardest part of leaving. I was sure we'd be back. I just didn't know when, or if he'd be here when I came home.

"Kitten," Bryce said as he pulled me into a hug.

"Fuck, not you too," I muttered.

"Shem spread the word." He didn't let me go. This was no one-armed classic hug of a brother to his little sister. No, this was a hug that said it all. He knew I was going for what could be a long time. Maybe we would never see each other again. Maybe one of us would die for real before we got a chance to say these words.

"Kiara is good for you," I whispered. "And you're going to have beautiful cubs. Name a girl after me. Please."

He snorted and didn't let go. "What about you?"

"No cubs for me, I think." I sighed. "I don't think it's in the cards for my life. Which means you need to have extra."

"Be careful. We just got our family back, I . . . I don't want to—" And then he choked up and the side of my face got wet from tears that weren't my own. And he hugged me tighter, and I clung to him as if I were that little girl in the dark again, crying after a nightmare.

"I'll be safe."

"Promise," he whispered.

"Promise."

And then like the brother he was, he shoved me away. "Go on then. Get the hell out of here."

I wiped my eyes and lifted my hand, but he had his back to me. I bit my lower lip as he leaned against the wall and his shoulders shook.

Crying for me, grieving me going. My big brother had finally shown me that he loved me, and I was leaving him behind.

I spun and ran, found Balder by scent more than

anything and leapt on his back with my eyes closed and my own tears streaming. He bolted off without waiting for a signal.

Maks leaned over and took my hand as we galloped away, and I squeezed it hard. The falak—we named her Faith—coiled around my neck and Lila perched on the front of the saddle.

"We'll be back," Lila said. "You know that."

"Feels like I'll never see them again," I whispered.

That is the curse you hold, Zam; the curse to love deeply.

THE RIDE TO THE ORACLE'S HAUNT WAS RIDICULOUSLY quiet. Easy even. Not one fight. No serpents or gorcs. Nothing.

Not one thing.

My sleep was filled with nightmares. Maks and Lila were no better and we often ended up piled together, clinging to each other for comfort.

The haunt bubbled with its superheated pits of toxicity and I paused beside the first one. "Marsum."

Yes, I know. This is really goodbye.

I bit my lower lip. "I'm sorry."

You saved my son and the Jinn. This is a price I willingly pay for my people. Just as I know you would for yours.

"Do you want to say anything to him?" I offered

SHANNON MAYER

the flail to Maks. He shook his head. And Marsum said just one thing.

Tell him I'm proud of him, of both of you. And maybe even that little dragon.

I nodded and lowered the flail into the pit beside me. The spiked flail shivered and convulsed as it tried to drink down the liquid and couldn't.

I let the handle go. "Goodbye."

See you on the flip side.

Maks grabbed me and I buried my face against his chest. This shouldn't be so hard. There shouldn't be so many goodbyes after we'd won the battle. After we'd won the war.

The flail sunk beneath the fluid and we stepped back to give it room. Super charged, superheated, it shot into the air in a spew of fluid that cut through the sky, carrying the flail up with it.

A boom like thunder rattled the air and the flail shattered. Colors—far more than had been in the stones—shot in every direction as the power of the jewels was scattered throughout the world, where they were meant to be.

One down, one to go.

We rode to the Oracle's Haunt. "Are you sure?" I asked the falak as she shimmied off me and made her way, her tiny legs pulling and her tail dragging, toward the stone that led into the Oracle's Haunt.

She turned and waved at us as the rock shimmered and she slid through. Gone. And for the moment, safe. No one would look for her alongside the Oracle. They would come for the Oracle, and not even see the tiny dragon in the shadows.

"Thank you," I said, holding my hand up, palm out in a simple wave.

Balder snorted and bobbed his head. "Yeah, let's get out of here."

We rode through the blasted lands quickly, heading south, finding our way to the Blackened Market.

We paused on the edge of it and I stared at the ruins of a place that held so much corruption and pain for those who would look to us for help.

"You ready to find the hatchlings?" I said to Lila. "'Cause I'd bet money the second we step in that direction all this quiet we've been enjoying will be over."

Lila swooped over our heads. "Then bring on the noise. We've got babies to save!"

Maks moved Batman close enough that our legs bumped and he leaned over and kissed me. "Only if you promise that at some point, you're truly going to show me evidence of this amazing Indiana Jones. Human who can do what no supernatural can."

I laughed and kissed him back. "That's an easy promise to make."

"Race you," he yelled as he booted Batman forward. Balder flicked an ear at me and I looked over my shoulder at the desert I called home, the desert that I'd loved and protected even when at points it had tried to kill me.

"I'll be back," I whispered. "We'll all be back. Try not to get into trouble while we're gone."

Balder snorted and I leaned forward. "We had to give them a fighting chance against a unicorn, you know."

He reared up and plunged forward, galloping flat out within just a few strides. The wind whipped around us, drying the last of the tears on my cheeks.

We'd be back. I felt it right through to the center of my heart and soul.

Just as soon as we were done with the adventures that waited for us out there in the big wide world without walls.

AFTERWORD

So I guess you can tell that Zam, Maks, Lila and the horses (aka one horse, one unicorn) are off on some more adventures! The truth is, I'm sure they will have hundreds more adventures . . .and one of them you can read for FREE!

Yup, that's right! Sign up for my newsletter, and January 1st, 2020, I will have a FREE read for you "Den of Thieves" will be the continuation from this last moment with the group.

Newsletter Sign Up

If you're already signed up, then you'll be good to go! Be sure to open the newsletters as they show up (even if you don't read them) the reason is, that newsletter provider programs WILL think you aren't interested, and will start sticking them in SPAM of all places ;)

Windburn

Ash

Rootbound

Destroyer

The Nix Series

(Complete)

Fury of a Phoenix

Blood of a Phoenix

Rise of a Phoenix

The Desert Cursed Series

(Complete)

Witch's Reign

Dragon's Ground

Jinn's Dominion

Oracle's Haunt

Wyvern's Lair

Emperor's Throne

Fine even MORE at

www.shannonmayer.com

CPSIA information can be obtained
at www.ICGtesting.com
Printed in the USA
BVHW041143040322
630682BV00013B/159

9 781987 933598